BEFORE YOU KNEW MY NAME

When she arrived in New York on her 18th birthday carrying nothing but $600 cash and a stolen camera, Alice was looking for a fresh start. Now, just one month later, she is the city's latest Jane Doe, an unidentified murder victim. Ruby Jones is also trying to start over; she travelled halfway around the world only to find herself lonelier than ever. Until she finds Alice Lee's body by the Hudson River. From this first, devastating encounter, the two women form an unbreakable bond. Alice is sure that Ruby is the key to solving the mystery of her life — and death. And Ruby — struggling to forget what she saw that morning — finds herself unable to let Alice go. Not until she is given the ending she deserves.

JACQUELINE BUBLITZ

BEFORE YOU KNEW MY NAME

Complete and Unabridged

AURORA
Leicester

First published in 2021 by
Little, Brown Book Group
and Allen & Unwin Australia

First Aurora Edition
published 2021
by arrangement with
Little, Brown Book Group
and Allen & Unwin Australia

A catalogue record for this book is available
from the British Library.

ISBN 978–1–78782–709–7

Published by
Ulverscroft Limited
Anstey, Leicestershire

Printed and bound in Great Britain by
TJ Books Ltd., Padstow, Cornwall

This book is printed on acid-free paper

For my Dad, on the other side

The desire to go home that is a desire to be whole, to know where you are, to be the point of intersection of all the lines drawn through all the stars, to be the constellation-maker and the center of the world, that center called love. To awaken from sleep, to rest from awakening, to tame the animal, to let the soul go wild, to shelter in darkness and blaze with light, to cease to speak and be perfectly understood.

Rebecca Solnit

If I can make it there, I'll make it anywhere.

Theme from *New York, New York*

You will already have an idea of me.

There are enough of us dead girls out there. From a distance, so many of our stories look the same. That's bound to happen when someone on the outside tells the story, speaks as if they knew us. They pick over our remains, craft characters from our ashes, and this is what the living get left with. Someone else's impression of who we used to be.

If I tell you my story. If I let you know what happened to me. Maybe you'll see who I was. Who I *am*. Maybe you'll like the truth of me better, and maybe you'll wish this for every dead girl from now on. The chance to speak for herself, to be known for more than her ending.

Wouldn't that be something. After everything we've lost.

1

The first thing I understand about the city I will die in: it beats like a heart. My feet have barely hit the pavement, the bus that delivered me here has only just hissed away from the curb, when I feel the pulse of New York, the hammering. There are people everywhere, rushing to its rhythm, and I stand open-mouthed in the middle of the widest street I've ever seen, smelling, tasting the real world for the very first time. Though I am named for a girl who fell down a rabbit hole, I feel in this moment as if I have climbed up out of the darkness and left the distortion of my old life behind me. If you were to look back, you'd see all the four-way stop signs and the star-spangled flags of small-town America waving us goodbye. You'd catch a glimpse of untended roads littered with potholes, and the windowless convenience stores set down on otherwise empty lots. You'd see rusted ice freezers next to sliding glass doors, and the nine-dollar bottles of liquor on dusty shelves. If you looked hard enough, you might even find my name traced in that filmy coating, there between the expired packets of potato chips and the fading jars of salsa.

Alice Lee.

I am here. She was there. And then she ran away to New York City, leaving all that dust behind her.

The second thing I understand: I cannot fall back down that rabbit hole. Not even if Mr Jackson shows up at the bottom, his delicate fingers beckoning. I need to prove I can make it on my own, that I can survive just fine without him. I will not be like my mother, who forgave any man who said sorry. I have learned her own failed lesson, see. That when a man discovers where to hurt you, the way he touches you changes. He won't be able to stop himself from pressing hard against that spot, no matter how many times it makes you cry.

I will never let a man make me cry. Not ever again.

Reaching inside my travel bag, I swing it to the front of my hip bone. I run my fingers over the black vulcanite of the old Leica buried at the bottom of the canvas, feel for the grooves of the detachable lens as I walk. I don't know why I need this proof, when I have been feeling the weight of the camera, the bump and knock against my thigh, the whole journey here. It is not as if it could have suddenly disappeared from deep inside my bag, cocooned by my sweaters and socks and underwear. But I need to reassure myself the Leica is safe and intact, all the same. Because this is what I have left. This is what I brought with me, and it is a small triumph to know that Mr Jackson will soon realise what I have taken from him. If he does not miss me, he will at least miss how he used to look at me through that lens.

Everyone's lost something, Alice.

Isn't that what he told me, just the other day?

★　★　★

For three glorious weeks in the late summer of 1995, my mother appeared on a billboard in Times Square. In the months before I was born, if you were to stand out front of the old Roy Rogers restaurant, you could look across the street and see her beautiful face decorating the side of a tall, wide building, right there between ads for the Donahue talk show and a movie called *Showgirls*, coming soon. I know these details from my mother's stories of that summer. How she ran away to New York after one too many beatings from her father, as if there was a magical number for the endurance of such things, and he finally exceeded it in her eighteenth year. And how, her lip still bleeding, she stole money from my grandfather's wallet to buy a bus ticket from Bayfield County, Wisconsin, to New York City, the most faraway place she could think of. Her first night in the city, trying not to fall asleep in a back booth of some dingy 8th Avenue diner, she met a semi-famous photographer. Before the night was over, he had shifted her into his apartment, cleaned her up, and when she looked nice and pretty, he said he was in love with her. He wasn't, of course, or he was for a time, but he loved his rich wife in the Hamptons more than he loved my mother, so he eventually left her. She was already pregnant when he snapped the picture of her smiling face that would end up reigning over Times Square those three sultry weeks.

'You were there with me, Alice Lee,' she would remind me. 'Everyone looking up at us, as if we belonged there.'

I never knew if my mother told my father what he was really seeing when he took that picture. If he ever knew his unborn child was also there in the frame. The finer details of how I came to be were smudged, blurred out, by the time the story made its way to me.

These are the things I think of. The two of us on a billboard, high above Times Square. My presence unnoticed back then, just as it is tonight, as I wander past streets lined with busy restaurants and glittering signs, a crossword puzzle of names running down the sides of the fanciest buildings I've ever seen. Who do you have to be, what do you have to do, to get your name up there?

Just a few weeks from now, when people can't stop talking about me, this city will give me a whole new name. My real name will be a question no one can answer, so they will call me Jane Doe. A dead girl who —

But we are only at the beginning of things tonight. My name is Alice Lee, and I have just stepped off an overheated cross-country bus, only just started to make my way up an avenue called 7th in the city of New York. I am alert, alive, present, as I breathe in the peculiar smell of cardboard and piss and metal that is my first hour in this city. There is an order to how things happen, a trail of breadcrumbs I need you to follow. Right now, I want you to get lost with me, as I turn the map on my second-hand phone this way and that, following the blue dot that is me, right here, pulsing. In this moment, the lines and circles make no sense to me at all.

Here we are, on an island. Surrounded by water, and somehow this makes it easier to breathe. Delivered to a busy bus terminal with two bags and six hundred dollars in cash, and an unfamiliar address stored in my phone. I am eighteen, just turned, and there are a million things I cannot do, but I can do this. You can't exactly call it running away. Though to be sure, like my mother, I waited to collect that extra year. Years are funny like that. The way a certain accumulation gives you permission for all kinds of things. Eighteen years old, and you are suddenly able to consent. Does that happen at midnight, or one minute past the hour, or is there some other calculation that makes you ready? Able to *consent*. Does that mean I did not consent before? It certainly seems that way to Mr Jackson.

Fingers travelling all over metal and lens. I cannot think of him without touching what used to belong to him.

I used to belong to him.

Now I belong only to myself. I am no longer a minor, a ward of the state. With the addition of just one day, there's no more threat over my head, no more list of strangers with the power to control my life. I'm eighteen years old and suddenly nobody can touch me. I'm so light with this realisation that, were it not for the weight of my bags, I might actually skip. Manhattan's wide, heaving streets seem made for skipping this first, beautiful night, as horns honk and engines hiss, and passers-by talk too loud on their cell phones.

I shimmy around these noises, careful to avoid all the concrete cracks, and the large, metal-framed holes that seem to puncture the sidewalk at increasing intervals. Cellar doors, I realise, but only after I see some of those rusty traps open up, men in aprons climbing onto the street from hidden staircases, crates of flowers, bags of fruit in their arms. I have no idea where they bring these gifts from. What gardens have they been tending to underneath my feet? Perhaps there is a whole other city living, thriving, beneath me. The thought makes me speed up, shift my body closer to the curb, away from those holes and these men. I have only just hoisted myself up into this new world; I do not want anything or anyone to pull me back down.

As I travel further north, I move my head left to

7

right, up and down, acknowledging every unfamiliar thing, greeting each green and white street sign, each gift store Lady Liberty statue, some as big as a child. Halal and kosher signs blink their welcome, and the cross-signal man clicks at me. It's my heartbeat that's as loud as the city now, taking it all in, and I have the sudden impulse to click my own fingers, hail a cab like they do in the movies. But the traffic is moving south on this street, cars weaving left and right as they pass me, claiming and conceding inches from one another at best, and no one looks to be getting anywhere faster than me.

Feet aching, muscles stiff from the long bus ride, I consider calling Noah, asking him for the shortest route to his apartment. But we haven't spoken to each other yet. Not really. Text messages hastily sent and quickly answered don't count, and I don't even know his last name. Thinking about it, I should probably be a little wary. A man opening up his home to a stranger like this. *Room available,* the advert said. *Own bed, shared bathroom.* As if it might be normal to share the bed, too. *$300 P/W — all included.* I don't know what *all included* means. I hope it means breakfasts, or a cup of coffee at least. I've booked the room for one week to start, and that'll be half of the money in my pocket gone. I don't let myself think about what might happen after those seven days are up, except to remind myself that a week is long enough to find another way. If something is wrong with this Noah surname-unknown guy, I'll simply find that other way, and fast.

It's not like I haven't had to do this kind of thing before. Only this time, if I have to start over, I'll be starting over in New York City.

Despite my sore feet, I feel a slow fizz of excitement, as if this city is carbonating my blood. I have come back to the place I was conceived. All those years of moving around the Midwest, of not knowing the kids in my class, or the name of my mother's latest boyfriend, or where she was when she didn't come home at night — they were merely lessons, preparation. For this. For standing on my own two feet, unnoticed, in the best possible way. Within twenty-four hours of arriving here all those years ago, my mother had come to rely on the sympathies of strangers. I won't do that with this Noah whoever, even if he turns out to be the nicest person in New York. I won't do that with anyone here. I have earned my independence, and I won't squander my future on something so hard won. I have 79.1 years promised to me, that's the life expectancy they gave to girls born in 1996, like me. 79.1 years — I learnt that in second or third grade, in some school, in some town I can't quite remember, but I've never forgotten the number, or how it felt to count out the years I had already used up, subtract them from the life span of a girl, and see what I had left. Here, tonight, on my eighteenth birthday, I have more than sixty years ahead of me. I'm going to make a whole world of those years, starting now.

Later, when we get to that next part, it won't take long for a man with fingers at my neck to prove me wrong. He will mock my sincerity, laugh at the idea of a girl like me making her own world. He will be so sure of his own right to my body, he will leave nothing but the memory of that girl behind.

We will keep coming back to this part. No matter how hard I try, the streets and sounds of Manhattan will fade, the men with their fruits and their flowers will disappear, and we will end up down there on the rocks. It's inevitable, no matter how much I try to distract you. Because this hopeful, heaving night is just one part of my story. The other story is this: there is the body of a dead girl waiting, down on the banks of the Hudson River.

The man who did this has left her there, gone home. And soon there will be a lonely woman who looks down, across, at the dead girl. I can see this lonely woman coming, or see her already there, and she's sadder than I have ever been, because her sorrow is still simmering. It hasn't boiled over and scalded her life, which makes her feel that nothing important, nothing meaningful, has ever happened to her.

I am about to happen to her.

2

Ruby Jones has no idea how old she is. Or rather, she knows her age solely in relation to calendars and dates. The number itself remains foreign, this tally of her years on the page, as if the age she has landed at is an irrefutable place, a landmark plotted on a map. In other words, Ruby Jones does not feel thirty-six years old. This age she notes down on forms, the number of candles on her cake, consistently confuses her. So much so, she has been known to experience a jolt of surprise upon discovering this famous woman or that, someone whose life she has observed from afar, is in fact much younger than she is. She could swear these women, with their multiple careers, with their multiple marriages and multiple babies, are her contemporaries. Maybe even older, with all that life crammed in.

The truth of it is this: Ruby is approximately three years past pretty. Though camera filters are designed to hide the facts of the matter these days, it is a reality she sees in the mirror every morning: the slackening jaw, the fold-down corners of her mouth, the stomach rounded and hips fleshed. She has not had the opportunity to age with someone, has only herself to wake up to each morning, and this is what she sees. A woman well past pretty, still sexy, maybe even beautiful at times, but there is little youth to be found in her features now. She can no longer look young without artifice, and this she cannot deny.

How to be thirty-six, then? How to understand in

her bones what this means, when it is nothing like they told her it would be. *They.* Her mother. Women's magazines. The authors who wrote her favourite books growing up. People who should have known better. All Ruby knows for sure is that she is suddenly older than she understands herself to be. Which is how it comes to pass that, in the middle of a makeshift dance floor in Apollo Bay, three hours' drive from Melbourne (and half a world away from where she wants to be), eighties songs shrieking from cheap speakers in the corner, Ruby Jones makes the decision to throw those thirty-six years she has accumulated up in the air. To close her eyes and see where they scatter.

She won't fully understand the gesture as it happens, misremembered lyrics bellowed in her ear, friends stumbling into each other, pulling her into their circle. She is drunk, they are drunk. Sally, the bride, will end up throwing up on the beach as midnight approaches, and Ruby will hold back her hair, soothe her, and tell her what a magical day it was.

'I wish you had someone who loves you, too,' Sally will mumble when she's done, mascara tracking down her face. 'You're such a great girl. Our precious Ruby.'

This sentence. This wedding. This late-summer night of clinking glasses and shoeless dancing and misty rain. It has all become too much for 'precious' Ruby (or too little, she will decide, when she is thinking more clearly). Her friends in their expensive outfits, drinking their fancy wine, pills popped surreptitiously between the speeches and the band. Sally, drunk-crying, wearing a dress she dieted herself into all summer, marrying the great guy she met on Tinder barely a year ago. The 'right swipe', they called it in their vows, and for the life of her, Ruby couldn't remember if left or right was the way to say yes.

Later, at the beach house she and her friends have rented for the weekend, Ruby takes a pillow and blanket and quietly pads out to the downstairs balcony. It is 3 a.m. and everyone else has passed out in their shared beds, couples curled into each other or snoring obliviously against each other's backs. Ruby is, as usual, the only single person in the group. Though she doesn't exactly consider herself single, not privately at least. There should be a better word to describe the state she has found herself in.

Alone.

That would do it, she thinks, folding herself down onto a damp, wicker sofa. Someone has removed the spongy seat cushions, Ruby can see them stacked under the lip of the second-floor balcony above her, but she does not have the energy to drag the cushions over. It has started to rain in earnest now, and she is glad for the discomfort, for the wet on her face and the unyielding sofa base, pressing into her hip. Back in her room, the world had started to spin. Now, she can see the black of the ocean, hear the inky water of the bay slapping against the sand. The sound seems as if it is coming from inside her, it's as if she is the one cresting and falling, and it takes a moment for Ruby to realise she is crying, out here on this balcony, alone with the rain and the waves and the starless sky. Soon she is crying as hard as the weather, the accumulations of the past few years rising up out of her. This is not where she intended to be.

Life, she understands in this moment, has stopped happening to her. She has stood in the middle of too many summers and winters, too many dance floors and other people's parties, and simply woken up the next day older than before. For so long, nothing has changed. She has been on pause, while the man she loves goes about making his life. Offering the tiniest of spaces for her to fit into, asking her to make herself small, so he can keep her right here. Alone.

Alone, here.

She doesn't want to be here any more.

The plan is not entirely clear as dawn approaches, waves and rain and tears saturating everything around her. Ruby won't even really understand, some days later, as she scrapes together her life savings, books her one-way ticket from Melbourne's Tullamarine airport to JFK, just what she's doing, or why. She only knows that she cannot stay *here* any longer. That she needs, desperately, for something, anything to happen to shake her out of her current state, and New York seems as right a place as any for reinvention.

In this way, our worlds are spinning closer every second.

★ ★ ★

I have an image of her on the plane, coming closer. The way she keeps reaching back towards Australia, folding time in on itself, so that Ruby is both 35,000 feet above her old life and stuck smack in the middle of it. I see her memories playing like an old mixtape, a best-of compilation she has heard many times, but up there in the air even the smallest moments seem tinged with tragedy. The way he looked at her when . . . the first time they . . . the last time she . . . and now she's pushing her forefinger hard against the small airplane window, blinking back tears. She watches her nail turn white, tiny, perfect icicles forming on the other side of the thick glass. Around her, people have already reclined their seats and started to snore, but I know that Ruby is wide awake for the entire flight, just like I am wide awake that whole bus journey from Wisconsin, this whole same day we make our way to New York City.

And just like me, Ruby Jones cannot help but spend the journey returning over and over to the lover she left behind. The proof of him. For me it is a stolen camera. For her it is the last message he sent, right before she boarded the plane.

I missed you. Past tense.

I missed you.

As if there are already years, not hours, between them.

★ ★ ★

We arrive within minutes of each other.

'Where to? WHERE to, lady?'

The cab driver at the bustling JFK taxi rank speaks louder this second time, half-shouts at Ruby, and she blinks away the vastness of his question, the heart-stopping open space of it. He just wants an address. She has an address — she can give him an address, if her sleep-deprived mind will just remember the details.

'I . . . uh . . .'

Ruby reads a street name and building number from her phone, offers it more like a question. The driver huffs his acknowledgement and pulls out into the snaking line of traffic exiting the airport. It's getting dark, there is a grey tinge to the air, something glassy over her eyes. She tries to shake off the lethargy of more than thirty hours of travel, tries to find some small, preserved part of herself that is excited to be here. She felt it, briefly, when she landed at LAX. A little arms-out-wide moment at all the freedom ahead of her. But that was hours ago, hours of transit and bad coffee, before another flight jolted her three hours ahead, so that she's missed the sun twice over, and has no idea what time it's really meant to be.

As Ruby looks out the cab window at her new surroundings blurring by, she thinks maybe that first view of New York's famous skyline will cheer her up. An iconic bridge she will recognise, or one of those familiar buildings, lit like a Christmas tree. For now, it's grey plastic bags floating like bloated birds in the trees, and a freeway knocking up against the sloping yards of thin, slate houses; if she can just keep her eyes open, just hold on, she knows these houses and church billboards and chain-link fences will soon give way to shimmering water, to neon lights, and those famous metal buildings, narrow as fingers, beckoning. And with this last thought, Ruby acknowledges she is delirious. Seeing bloated birds and beckoning fingers — she must be dreaming more than awake right now.

(I am stepping over cracks, shimmying around people, waving at my street signs and statues, as she presses her forehead against the glass of her passenger-side window, watching for those beckoning fingers. At what point in this journey do our paths begin to cross?)

Struggling to keep her eyes open, Ruby wills the driver to go faster. She wonders if he knows what an important role he is playing in her life right now, delivering her to a new world, a beginning of things, like this. As the driver talks to someone on his mobile phone, his voice so low as to be indecipherable, she acknowledges this man could not care less about her, or the way her heart has seemingly moved up into her throat. It is clearly nothing new for him, this transporting of another lost, hopeful soul to whatever awaits them in New York City.

She watches his hands slide across the steering wheel, each turn like a clock counting down and understands it is of no consequence to a stranger that she has come here with no plan, no calendar of events. He just wants to get her to her destination, drop her off and get back to whoever he's talking to, maybe show up at someone's door himself. Ruby is a task to complete, irrelevant to him and to New York, that neon glow outside her window, getting brighter. She suddenly feels like laughing.

I could, she muses, *change my name, make up a life. That's how anonymous I am right now.*

And then.

'Here.'

'Wha . . . ?

The car stops suddenly, and the cab driver half-turns towards Ruby.

'You say, here.'

He points to a five-story apartment building on his right. Scaffolding one floor high runs alongside the façade, and a series of wrought-iron fire escapes snake up to the roof, giving off the impression of a building under perpetual construction. Ruby sees that the numbers above the wide front door match those she read out to the driver back at JFK.

Scrambling for her wallet, Ruby over-tips for the ride, and the driver finally looks at her now, shakes his head slightly, before he pops the trunk and hoists her

17

suitcases onto the street.

As Ruby watches him speed away, she fights the urge to wave him back to the curb and ask to be returned to the airport. Instead, as the yellow cab disappears from sight, she struggles her suitcases up the concrete steps that lead to her new home, before using her elbow to hit a buzzer that says press here. She hears the echo of her arrival on the other side, as she waits, trembling, for the door in front of her to open.

★ ★ ★

Mine opens with a knock.

As Ruby Jones was delivered to her new front door, I was following the blue dot of my phone all the way to the edge of Central Park, then veering around it, just like the map told me to. Keeping the Hudson River on my left, stores soon turned into apartments, and bags of household rubbish began to appear on the curb. Rows of thin, leafless trees started to grow up out of the pavement, shin-high fences made of iron turning each one into tiny, walled-off gardens, and it was clear, strange as everything seemed to me, that I had reached the streets where people lived. The frantic pace of Midtown seemed a world away up here on the Upper West Side, the night sky pressing down on my shoulders, the residential streets all but empty. I wasn't worried though, you could still feel the presence of people on nearby streets, sense all the living going on around me. Other than a small, involuntary jump when a man smoking in a doorway whistled at me, I felt oddly calm as I approached Noah's apartment building.

Still. My heart is in my throat when I knock, as if the gesture is pulling all my courage up out of me. I am sweating slightly after being buzzed in from the street, a set of narrow stairs climbed, the Leica pressing against me. Rows of doors remain closed to me, and then the one I have been looking for is right there in front of me.

Own bed, shared bathroom. $300 P/W — all included . . .

Yes, I'll be paying cash . . .

No, I'm not allergic to dogs . . .

Here is the full address, if you're taking the train the closest stop is 96th and Broadway . . .

I'll be coming by bus, I should arrive by 9 . . .

As you will.

As you will. A strange sign off, I thought at the time. But I appreciated this Noah's efficiency throughout the process. Deal done inside a few text messages, hardly any questions asked. No unnecessary niceties or chit-chat. I don't even know what his voice sounds like, I realise now, as my knock echoes on the wood between us. The door to Noah's apartment creaks open and I see one blue eye first, then the peak of a dark blue cap. A polished black shoe. And then something cold and wet brushes against my hand. Before I have time to pull back, a large brown dog pushes through the half-open door and lunges at me.

'Franklin!'

19

Noah appears in flashes between paws and chocolate fur, pulling at the dog's collar, and the three of us stumble through the door together, a laugh bubbling up out of me from a source I never knew existed. It has an immediate effect, like cool water on a hot day. Any tension I felt slackens, like the strap of my bag as I let it fall to the floor. For a second, Noah and the dog disappear, and it's just me, standing in the most beautiful room I have ever seen. The polished wood under my feet gleams, and tall, wide windows above thick-cushioned seats give way to walls of books and couches big enough to lie flat on. I can see small, brightly coloured toys, bones and rubber chickens and tennis balls, all scattered across the floor and — my mouth drops open — a shiny black piano sat on the other side of the room. Above the piano is a huge, glittering chandelier, something I have never, ever seen in real life. Each piece of dangling crystal is so delicate, so perfectly formed, that I think immediately of raindrops. Or tears.

A strange thought comes to me, lands on my shoulder like a feather. How much sorrow has this room seen?

And now I am aware of Noah holding the collar of the dog, both of them watching me. With my eyes and mouth wide open like a fish in the sand, I know that I have just given myself away. I might as well have pulled out the six hundred dollars cash I have in my purse and admitted this is all I have in the world. I am not, and this must be perfectly obvious, even to the big old dog, someone who is accustomed to nice things. I turn to look, *really* look, at the man who lives here, the owner of the piano and the chandelier and the books and the dog. He is staring just as hard back at me, a half-smile pulling up the left corner of his mouth. I see now that he is *old*. Like grandfather old, maybe sixty-five or seventy, and shorter than me, just. He's wearing one of those fancy polo sweaters, the ones where you can see a neat shirt collar poking out from underneath, and it looks like he has no hair left under his Yankees cap. Tufts of eyebrow, pale blue eyes. That half smile of his, and long, fine fingers, reaching for mine. 'Hello,' he says, 'Alice Lee. It's very nice to meet you. Franklin' — Noah gestures to the big, brown dog now straining towards me — 'obviously concurs.'

Later, when I look back at all the beginnings that turned me, inch by inch, towards the river, I will see this was the gentlest of them. Shaking the soft, warm hand of an old man, and then a tour of his apartment, with a large brown dog leading the way. Fresh towels on the dresser in the bedroom and a closet of empty hangers, 'Should you wish to hang up your things.' The offer of a late-night coffee —

Yes, please' — and the shaking of heads — 'No, don't worry about that now' — when I offer to pay upfront for my week long stay.

'Plenty of time for that, Alice.'

Noah says this over his shoulder as he leaves to make me that coffee, and I sit down hard on the edge of my new bed, Franklin at my feet. Seven nights. Half my money gone. Yet that same laugh bubbles up out of me again. The one that feels like cool water on a hot day.

'You're going to be all right, Alice Lee,' I say out loud to the towels and the hangers and the chocolate-coloured dog. And it's nice, in this moment, to believe it.

21

★ ★ ★

Ruby Jones is not all right.

For a start, her body and the clocks say different things. She has been in New York City a few hours, but she feels so disoriented, it could be days or mere minutes. When she opened the door to her studio apartment, she wanted nothing more than to crawl straight under the covers of the wide, low bed sat barely a stride from the door frame. But it was still early, so she put on a thick coat and ventured one block over to Broadway, hoping to stretch out her aching legs. Exhausted to have travelled so far, Ruby struggled to see the endless scaffolding and stores and sidewalk cracks, the people walking too fast, talking too loud, as anything other than props, extras, on a movie set. Caught somewhere between reality and delirium, she wandered up and down the street, aimless and cold, before buying a slice of cheese pizza for $1.27 and a $59 bottle of Grey Goose to wash it down. Taking this first New York supper back to her room, she was soon sat cross-legged in the middle of that low bed, licking grease from her fingers and drinking vodka straight from the bottle.

Catching sight of herself in the floor-length mirror opposite the bed, Ruby could not help but laugh a little, her hand pressed up against her mouth to catch the sound.

The woman in that mirror had hair almost as greasy as the pizza slice, ruddy red cheeks, lips that were starting to chap. What an ignoble start to her adventure, she acknowledged, pulling at the loose, purple-black skin concertinaed under her eyes, taking full stock of her tiredness, before returning the vodka bottle to her mouth.

This is so exciting Ruby! What an awesome thing to do! Omigod, you're so brave!

After she announced her plan to move to New York for six months, it seemed everyone spoke to her in exclamations. There was something about what she was doing — quitting her day job, giving away most of her furniture and clothes, compacting her life into two metallic blue suitcases — that seemed to inspire people, her news triggering far away looks and hushed confessions everywhere she went. *I always wanted to . . . I wish I could have . . . Maybe one day I'll . . .*

For a while there, Ruby was privy to a whole world of secret desires, shared without invite by both strangers and friends. Now, vodka at her lips, the room rocking slightly, she finds it odd to think of all these people living ahead of her, somewhere in the tomorrow of Melbourne. From her new time zone, she will perpetually live behind them, chasing hours long ticked over in Australia, even though people back home assume she is the one out in front. Taking a self-appointed sabbatical to live in New York City, just because she can. She might as well have told people she was heading to the moon.

'Am I brave or just crazy?' she asks the vodka bottle and the room and her hazy reflection, none of which offer a satisfactory answer before she capsizes into sleep.

And now it's 2 a.m. this next, first morning in New York, and she's wide awake. The bed sheets are soaked through with sweat, and when Ruby stands up to go to the bathroom, she feels like she is pitching forward, as if her body wants to be somewhere else. *Somewhere else.* When she is already as somewhere else as she's ever been. Here in this city of — what is it now? Eight million? Nine? No matter, given she knows exactly two people out of that number, a couple of former colleagues who have made it clear they would love to catch up, *Sometime soon, Ruby. When you've settled in.*

Well, she thinks. Here I am! All settled in. And not feeling very brave at all.

What would those friends and strangers back in Melbourne think of this admission?

Returning from the bathroom, still unsteady, Ruby sits down on the edge of her bed just as a siren starts up outside her window. It is a familiar sound in the dark, yet somehow different to the ambulance calls she is used to hearing back home. More melancholy, perhaps. Or — she moves to the window now, peers down onto the empty street — this New York siren seems resigned, somehow. Weary from overuse, as if the worst tragedies have already happened. It is another delirium-induced musing, this prescription of poetry to an ordinary thing, but something else, too. The beginnings of a new kind of loneliness, where Ruby will soon find herself talking to objects as if they are people, holding conversations with her hairbrush, and her vodka bottles, and the pillows on her bed, just to say anything at all. In these first, early hours, it is as if Ruby senses this impending isolation, the days ahead where she will barely speak to anyone unless she's reciting her breakfast order or saying thank you to strangers for holding the door.

Turning from the window this first lonely morning, closing the blinds against the piles of black rubbish bags and jungle-gym scaffolds and scattering of parked cars on the street below, Ruby concedes that sleep is no longer an option. Instead, she carefully unpacks her suitcases, hangs up her dresses and jackets, lays out her shoes. When this task is done, empty suitcases stored by the door, she compiles a list of things that might make this room, with its clean linen and private bathroom, feel more like home. A glass for her vodka. A candle. Dishes for the microwave in the corner, and a vase for fresh flowers. Little anchors, trinkets to remind her that she lives here now.

Here. Ten thousand miles from Melbourne.

Ten thousand miles from him.

We both had to leave, you see. And maybe Ruby is right with this next thought, pushing through the vodka and jetlag and grey light of early morning:

Maybe the people who appear brave are merely doing the thing they have to do. It's not a matter of courage then, to pack up and leave a life. Just a lack of any other option, and the sudden realisation you probably don't have anything left to lose.

I may be sleeping soundly this next, first morning, as she makes her lists and thinks her delirious thoughts. But make no mistake. Though we came from very different places, Ruby Jones and I might as well be the same person when it comes to how we landed here in New York City.

3

Let me tell you about my first seven days.

It's like I'm living inside one of those Sunday afternoon, old movie musicals you don't mean to keep watching, but it's all so bright, so joyous, you can't look away. Even when it rains, which it does a lot, there are no grey skies here, not to me. Sometimes, when I am wandering through Midtown, I stop in the middle of the street, just for a second, to look at the Chrysler Building, glittering skyward from her perch on Lexington Avenue. I think she is beautiful, the way an old-time beauty queen is beautiful, all silver sparkles and sash and crown. I always wave to her, subtly, though I don't think anyone notices, and then I get going across the street, so I don't get run over by a cross-town bus or a honking, yellow cab.

I know about cross-town now. I know about uptown and downtown, and the way Broadway rambles around New York like a river. I know about boroughs and blocks, and I know which side of the pavement to stick to. I'm not even afraid of those cellar doors any more, the ones that lead down to basements filled with flowers and fruits and every other imaginable thing. It's as if the girl who arrived a week ago has lived a year in this city, that's how much things make sense already, in a way those small towns from my childhood never did.

There are so many places I have yet to see, whole new maps I am making, but for now it is enough to wave at the Chrysler Building, and walk block after block, taking pictures of every new thing I encounter. I love looking at the city through a camera lens; it changes everything when you are the observer, instead of the observed. This must be something my father understood, and Mr Jackson, too. The calm control you feel when you wind, focus, *click*. Perhaps things would have been different for my mother — perhaps things would have been different for me — if she'd been on the other side of the camera, too. I do wish, when I let myself think about her, that I could show her what I've captured of this city she loved and left too soon.

I don't know if the pictures I've taken are any good, mind you. The old Leica is not like any camera I have used before, and I'm still learning how to hold it, how to move the focus lever with my thumb and keep the small body steady with my other hand. The viewfinder is tiny; at first, I couldn't see anything through the small window, but after a week, I think I'm getting the hang of it. It's like learning to see a whole different way. When you adjust the aperture, narrow the opening of the lens, background objects come into focus. Kind of like you're pulling the world into you, bringing it closer. Nothing seems so far away anymore.

I should thank Noah, mostly. I *do* thank Noah. Every night before I fall asleep. Because now that my first seven days are up, he's letting me stay on rent-free at his apartment — a brownstone, I know this term now, too — until I get a job and can pay my own way. That's how he put it when he made his offer over coffee and fresh bagels, partway through that first week. I told him right then and there I didn't want to be a charity case. But I had already fallen in love with my bedroom and the piano and the barrelled bay windows — 'What do you call these windows, any-way?' I asked him, peering down onto the street — and I knew I would miss the wet leather of Franklin's nose, the constant press of it against my hand. Besides, it was clear from the beginning that Noah would be easy to live with. He liked my questions about where to go and what to see in the city, and he didn't ask too many questions of his own, though I did share a little about my life with him over that breakfast.

'I don't want to rely on you,' I said. 'Not after what I've been through. But I would really, really like to stay here.'

This is our solution: we will keep a ledger on the refrigerator door, a tally of my days here. Noah makes a new mark every morning, a quick flick of black ink on a white sheet of paper, so we have a record of what I'll need to pay him back some day. As the days turn into weeks, those black marks will spread across and down the page, but I never do get around to adding them up. At the beginning of things, I just sort of see them as the sum of my survival.

If I can make it there . . .

You know how many songs there are about New York? When you live here, it's like the streets serenade you. Remember when I said I would not squander my independence? If you knew what came before. Not even the stuff I told Noah, but the stuff before, and before and before that. Well, you'd understand why it's a place, not a person, I have given my heart to this time around.

I mean, can you imagine? That a place can feel like a person? That a place can comfort you and sing to you and surprise you. A place where simply stepping up out of the subway onto the street can give you that fizzing under the skin sensation you get right before you kiss someone? When I told Noah about this, when I said it was almost as if I had fallen in love with New York, he smiled funny, and called me *Baby Joan*, and I still don't know what that means.

(Truthfully, he says lots of things I don't understand.)

The point for now is this: I am happy. Whenever my worried feelings creep back in, I just head outside, no matter the hour, and I roam the streets and avenues and river paths until I shake the worry off. And this! Noah bought me a pair of sneakers. I came home from a long walk on Day Five, and there they were in a box on the bed, the price scratched off, so only the .97¢ part of the sticker remained. Purple, thick-soled, smelling of rubber and dye, and so much newness. It was like sliding my feet into the future. Into all the possibility ahead of me. That's what I felt, and I may have cried a little, but I didn't tell Noah that, or say thank you out loud, because I can already tell he wouldn't like this kind of thing. I just wrote out an IOU from the Post-it pad in the kitchen, sticking the word *Sneakers* on the refrigerator door, next to our ledger of days.

It is strange to think that only a week ago, everything I had was counting down to nothing, from my depleting cash, to the single roll of black and white film in my Leica, to my thin-soled shoes. My life was about subtraction and holding on to whatever was left over. Now the calculation has changed, life has spun me around, filled me up, and I am dizzy with happiness. I'm living in a stranger's apartment, in a strange city, and both make me feel like I just might belong here. Noah with his ledger and his gift of new shoes, knowing without asking that all that walking around hurts

29

my feet. And New York itself, baptising me with its spring rain, washing us both clean. This new, old city of mine, where if you look left, right, up, the view changes before your eyes. Of all the patterns, I already prefer the perfect lines the avenues make. The narrowing of distance to something you can see, understand. When I ventured further south yesterday, one street wound into another, right under my feet, with no warning at all, so that just a little veer to the left, and I was lost for the first time. I missed the certainty of my uptown avenues, the arms-wide openness of Columbus and Amsterdam, so I caught the 1 train home.

Home.

When I'm out there exploring, I see so many workers whizzing past me in their white sneakers and power suits. The quick legs and stiff arms of people in a hurry. I do not like the way they never stop and look around. They never look left, right, up, to see the city from a different angle.

Watching these people go by each day, I vow that when I get to their age, I will never wear a restrictive pencil skirt with sneakers. I will not stride along too fast for my surroundings. I will learn to walk slowly and gracefully in pretty high heels, or maybe stay comfortable in my sneakers, roaming the avenues, avoiding pencil skirts altogether.

These first seven days, I still think this is something I will get to decide.

★ ★ ★

Just a few streets over from Noah's apartment, Ruby can barely get out of bed. It is as if the moment she stopped needing to be somewhere — work, brunch

30

with her friends, her twice-weekly PT sessions — the weight of her sadness piled down on her, made her limbs and eyelids heavy. While I am traipsing around Manhattan, peering through my lens at the world, she remains stuck in her room, staring at the concrete ceiling, hour after hour sliding past her. From this prone position, she has had plenty of time to ponder her plight. Is this a midlife crisis come early? Extreme fatigue? Situational depression? Or is this simply what it feels like to be absent of hope, hollowed out?

You have to get to the worst thing, eventually.

Someone once told her that, a friend reasoning their way out of a run of bad luck. At the time they meant it as self-comfort, assuming there had to be a limit to their trials. Things could only get so bad before life turned around again. But now, blankets pulled up to her chin, the sounds of the Upper West Side clanging outside her window, Ruby wonders if she heard the sentence wrong. Maybe her friend was really saying you can only outrun your sadness for so long. It will catch up to you. Eventually. Back in Melbourne she had been living in a kind of emotional stasis, avoiding feeling sorry for herself by never really letting the reality of her situation sink in.

Perhaps this was the worst thing. Pushing her feelings so far down they calcified, became an anchor. And now, with no place to be, no one to see, she has suddenly found herself unable to move.

And just what is that reality she's been avoiding, the one keeping her in bed this whole first week in New York City, as winter turns to spring outside her window? Only this: the man she loves is going to marry someone else.

She knew this when she met Ash. Thought nothing

of it. New co-worker at the ad agency, newly engaged, ho-hum, lots of people their age got married. It was only later, when Ruby knew the pressure of his hand on her hipbone, the weight of his lips on her shoulder, that this became the fact upon which her life turned. A wedding date was set, and her relationship to time changed. The future contained a marker, an end date, and somewhere along the way Ruby stopped making her own plans. She had an ever-decreasing amount of time to change Ash's mind, to help him undo his impending mistake, and if that meant living exclusively in the present, being available to him whenever he asked, it would be worth it when he did change his mind.

Except, he didn't.

A little over six months from now, he will be a married man. The colour scheme has been decided, the tableware ordered. RSVPs are coming in, and Emma, his fiancée, has had two of her four dress fittings (she cried at the first one).

'Did you — want to come?'

Ruby could never decide whether Ash's halting question was naïve or cruel. Delivered as it was with his chest against her naked back, his left hand resting against the curve of her stomach. Now, alone in a different bed, across an ocean, she understands it was both, and something begins to stir in Ruby Jones. A small heat, as if someone is blowing on a fire deep inside her, willing it to burn. And just like that, oxygen applied, the first explosion occurs. One big enough to propel her out of bed and into her running shoes. Fully upright for the first time in seven days — if you don't count the small circuit she has made of finding takeaway food and vodka to bring back to her room — she feels wobbly, uncertain. But as she ties her laces in double knots, Ruby feels anger coursing through her like fuel. Ash inviting her to his wedding — while she could still taste herself on his mouth — was a deliberate severing, a way to turn their connection to string. To reach for her body while pushing away her thoughts, her feelings, her *heart*, was cold and calculated. It hadn't shocked her at the time because, in truth, that is how it always was with him.

No wonder she's gotten used to pushing her feelings way down.

Outside it is pouring, but Ruby barely notices the heavy fall. She heads east towards Central Park, splashing through dark, oily puddles, wiping rivulets of rain from her eyes. When her muscles start to protest, she relishes the pain, pushes herself to go faster. If she's going to outrun anything, she reasons, it will be that terrible numbness keeping her in bed all these days. Better to feel the ache of tight quads, taste the metal of her heart at work, than to let another day pass her by. Entering the park, feet crunching wet gravel, she heads for the nearest reservoir, the memory of a map in her mind, a look of determination on her face.

Upon reaching the lake, Ruby inadvertently starts running the wrong way. Keeps to the left, runs clockwise as she would back home, and she is soon made aware of her mistake. Joggers coming towards her frown or sigh, a few shake their heads as they pass, and one or two make a show of having to step around her. She starts to say sorry and then changes her mind. Stubbornness prevents her from turning around, running the wrong-right way with the crowd, and something else, too. After years of making herself small, it is exhilarating to take up space for once, to

33

force people out of *her* way.

Ruby is still on that runner's high when she returns to her apartment building an hour later. Saturated through, she is so wet she has to stand on the street and twist the rain from her T-shirt before she can go inside. The guy at the front desk shoots her a rueful smile as she passes by him, but she grins and tells him she likes this kind of weather.

'It's so refreshing!'

And now the desk guy looks concerned, as if Ruby's sudden display of positivity has thrown him off (yes, he's noticed the takeaways and vodka, formed an opinion of this new lodger from her infrequent appearances these past few days, and privately concluded she'd be gone within a week).

'We've got umbrellas to borrow. If . . . if you want,' Ruby hears him say unsurely to her back as she steps into the small elevator at the end of the entrance hall, before the doors close between them.

When she steps under the shower a few minutes later, Ruby remembers the alarmed look on the young man's face and starts to laugh. To be found odd in New York feels like a triumph, the opposite of disappearing. There, under the hot shower water she closes her eyes and laughs so hard she cries, emotions mixing like wet paint, dripping from her skin. This will be the real beginning, she decides. A kind of baptism, from which she will emerge renewed. Getting out of the shower, towel wrapped tight around her tingling body, she pads to her small closet, finds her prettiest dress. Fingering the soft cotton of the skirt, she imagines herself flowing through the streets of New York in the summer, leaving a bright, happy trail of colours behind her. There is a whole world outside these brick walls, and she's finally ready to crash her way through it.

This is the thought she is turning over, smiling at, when her phone buzzes from the nightstand. Turning from the closet, Ruby reaches for the phone, checks the glowing screen.

Hi.

Images of pretty dresses, of warm summer days and bright colours disappear. The anchor tugs, and a second text message arrives.

I wish you were still here.

Ash.

Ruby sits down hard on the bed. Holds the phone away from her, brings it back to her chest. She sits a full five minutes like this before, heart hammering, fingers trembling, she begins to craft a reply.

★ ★ ★

You mustn't think she's the only one. I might be having a better time of it right now, but I too have moments where the past feels present, pulls me in. Here's the thing. You don't get off a plane or a bus and leave your old self behind. No amount of running or sudden realisation can rewire you like that. Not entirely, not the way those self-help books and daytime talk shows would have you think (I used to watch a lot of those with my best friend Tammy). The way I see it, damage gets packed in your suitcase, people stay on your skin. Some mornings I wake up with Mr Jackson right there behind my eyelids, as if he crept into my bed in the night. And sometimes — it happened yesterday — it is my mother who makes an appearance, the smell of powder and roses, that signature, skin-soft scent of hers inexplicably filling the room. I don't like it when this happens. Like Ruby, my heart hammers and my fingers tremble. But, unlike Ruby, I do not respond. I wait for the hammering to slow, the trembling to cease, and I stay facing forward. My mother can visit. Mr Jackson, too, if he wants. I just never let them stay too long.

★ ★ ★

In the beginning, I disappeared on purpose. Extricated myself from a life I didn't want, just like Ruby did. But unlike Ruby, I didn't tell anyone where I went. Not even my best friend. I let Tammy think I had stayed right where she left me; I wanted to slip out of my old life unseen. And if certain people stayed on my skin, if they came along in my suitcase uninvited, at least they wouldn't be able to cause any fresh wounds. That felt like a start, like I would have time to heal from all the ways they had hurt me.

I wanted to start over. I *wanted* to disappear.

But that's not the same as being forgotten. To be clear, I never, ever wanted that.

4

We are eating breakfast on Day Eight when Noah offers me a job. The next in a series of unexpected gifts. Over the last few days, he has continued to leave mostly small, always useful items in my room, so that I will come home from exploring the city to find a silver water bottle or sports socks on the end of my bed. Whenever I emerge, holding the latest trinket he has left for me, he merely waves at the refrigerator door, where my collection of IOUs is growing.

'I'm not a fan of delayed gratification,' he said yesterday, when I protested the purple, puffy jacket sat waiting for me on the dresser. Socks and water bottles were one thing, but the jacket felt extravagant, and I wasn't sure I should accept it. 'You'll pay me back sometime,' Noah said calmly, dismissing my concerns. 'Until then, with all that walking you do, there's no point in catching your death, Baby Joan.'

I read about crows, taffeta birds I used to call them when I was little, both afraid and fascinated by their crinkle of black feathers. Crows are known to randomly leave presents for people they like and trust; shiny, pretty things, and practical objects too. It's their way of communicating without words, and I've come to think of Noah's gifts in this way.

Even if I don't fully understand what I have done to earn his trust so soon, or why he has decided to take me under his human wing.

(*Death birds*, my mother used to call them. Harbingers circling, waiting. We never did agree on her superstitions.)

And now the biggest surprise of all. The offer of money and independence. A job! Noah says I can be his assistant, helping him with the dogs. Noah is a dog walker, see. Up here on the Upper West Side. He used to have some other job, some suit and tie affair downtown, and it must have been important because he owns this place — barrelled windows, piano, chandelier — but he definitely prefers dogs to people these days. Plenty of dogs around here need walking, too. It's not like they have their own yards to play in, and I've never seen one roaming the streets on its own, so it makes sense when Noah tells me he's been thinking about introducing a home-care service to his business. It will mean people from the neighbourhood have a place to leave their fancy purebreds and cute old mutts when they go out of town on business trips, or spend their weekends in the Hamptons, which is a place rich people seem to go to a lot, though Noah tells me he hasn't been there himself in years.

(Noah doesn't appear to have any friends. If his phone rings, it's only ever about a dog. And while there is a lot of expensive-looking art on the walls of his apartment, I haven't yet come across a single framed photograph. I didn't bring any with me either, so I suppose it's not so strange. Or if it is, we are only as strange as each other. No doubt there are people he sees behind his eyelids, too. People he consciously blinks away, but I figure it's none of my business who they might be. He is kind to dogs, and to me, and that's all I need to know about him for now.)

My mouth is full of bagel and cream cheese as Noah explains the terms of his proposition. Rent, he says, will be taken out of my salary from now on, and this will also cover food and amenities for the apartment. He refers back to scribbled notes on a yellow pad between us, combinations of words and equations in a scrawl I can't make out, and when he looks up, he tells me this should leave me with a hundred and fifty dollars per week, cash in hand.

'You'll be required to work four days, 8 a.m. to 3 p.m. A combination of dog walking and dog-sitting, depending on who comes in. Each dog will come with its own care routine, and you'll never have more than two, plus Franklin, to look after at any one time.'

He crosses something off in his notes and looks at me with his bright eyes, his hand extended. I see an image of black feathers, rustling.

'Are you in?'

Alarmingly, I once again want to cry, but I nod silently instead, tongue pushing against the roof of my mouth, because I once read you can't physically cry when you do this. Even so, my eyes pool with water as I shake Noah's hand. I know there could not possibly be any combination of numbers in his scribbled equations that would cover rent and food and bills, and still leave me with money in my pocket. I know too, that Noah doesn't really need to be in the business of more dogs, that he works not for money, but for contact with his four-legged friends, and a chance to be out in the world from time to time. I'm not always able to read people's motivations right, but I know without doubt that this new home-care business has been formed around me. And I sense, grasping at a future truth, this might be Noah's way of making sure I come back to him each day.

Thoughts swirling, I am overwhelmed at the door Noah has swung open. I do not know why he is helping me like this, why he shows me a kind of care he doesn't seem to afford many, if any, other people. Later, when we have grown more accustomed to talking about real things, I will ask him why he placed that ad for a room in his apartment, what motivated this self-confessed introvert to open up a door in his life, too. For now, it's enough to know that I am profoundly grateful for this place I have arrived at, and as we map out my first shifts at our new doggy daycare, I allow myself to believe I deserve what comes next. The beginning of a life where I take up space, where I belong.

In a world where some of that kindness of strangers I've so often heard about is finally directed at me.

★ ★ ★

Are you surprised at how little time it takes for my barriers to come down? I suppose, if things had turned out differently, you might think it a good thing. The way I readily embraced this fresh start, when girls like me so often fall back on their old ways. You might even admire my resilience, want to bump your fist against mine, congratulate me for all the positive changes I am making in my life. How about we stay inside that fantasy a little while longer, hey.

★ ★ ★

It is as if Ruby has a fever. It has something to do with sex. Or a lot to do with it. Ever since Ash reached out via text, her body has insisted on responding to the slightest provocation. Cool sheets touching her bare legs. Hot shower water running down her back. Even the way she bites into an apple or slides food from

40

fork to tongue somehow feels erotic. She dreams of sex, wakes up soaked in the sheets of it. Upon opening her eyes each morning, her collarbone aches, hot, as if this is where the electric cord of her desire is wired.

And that cord keeps leading her back to him.

Ruby is used to wanting Ash from afar, but this new fervour feels different. It isn't, she soon realises, entirely about her lover, though the memory of his mouth, his hands, instantly and consistently makes her stomach flip. She remembers her grandmother gossiping about a cousin known for her scandalous love affairs — 'Oh, that woman was always on heat' — and this curled-lip, old-fashioned saying perhaps comes closest to describing the state Ruby has inexplicably found herself in, after a week of feeling nothing at all.

(She has forgotten the small explosion, and the woman on the dance floor at Sally's wedding. It isn't always the right moments we remember.)

Trying to distract herself, Ruby makes lists of places to see, in this second week that somehow feels like her first. Highlighting place names in her journal, she visits the Met, takes the Staten Island Ferry, catches a train to Brooklyn, and walks back over the bridge in the rain. This incessant spring rain is now as much a part of the city to her as the garbage and the scaffolds, as the chain stores on every corner, and the cardboard MetroCard she has in her purse. She is making acquaintance with New York, buoyed by a savings account that affords vodka Martinis and French candles for her little studio, and the new Diane von Furstenberg dress she wore to a play at the Lincoln Center two nights ago. One of her favourite film actresses stood half-naked on the stage, so close Ruby could see the coffee stain of her nipples. New York!

This is the city of her social media posts, of her messages to her mother, and phone calls with her older sister, Cassie, at home with her family in Melbourne.

There is, however, another New York. The New York of staring at the ceiling in painful anticipation, of waiting for that early morning bell, the electronic ding of Ash's text messages, the scramble for her phone. She sleeps naked, ready, and he has been unfailing in his appreciation so far. Ash, it turns out, is as present in this city as the one she left behind. It's as if that first week's silence has made him try harder to reach her, and their conversations feel as urgent as they did when they first discovered each other, what seems like a lifetime ago.

I can't sleep, Ruby. You've got me in a wild state. I was thinking about you all day. Show me your —

'No,' she told Cassie last night. 'We haven't spoken since I got here.'

She hates the lie, knows how disappointed her sister would be if she knew Ruby was still communicating with Ash. But, as she tells herself each morning, this is just a small lie. One small lie, and three hundred square miles of everything else. Tomorrow, Coney Island. The American Ballet. Cabaret in the Village. Another rooftop bar and another over-priced cocktail. She's trying to do better. But she never promised to be perfect.

Perfect is something Ruby Jones thinks about a lot.

She assumes Ash's fiancée is perfect. Ruby will not be the kind of woman who disparages the soon-to-be wife. She will not be a cliché, no more of a cliché than

42

she has already become, at least. Which means she often swings too far the other way, idealises a woman she has never met, never spoken to. Imagines clean teeth and tidy nails. Clear lip gloss and light foundation. Capri pants and a purposeful watch. A ring finger heavy with a single diamond, and long, shiny hair. A double degree earned easily, and a year spent volunteering overseas. One book read at a time, and a signature dish she brings to parties. Requested by the hosts of course, because everyone loves Emma's — and here, Ruby's list of imagined credentials falters. It is one thing to create a version of Ash's fiancée in her head, form the outline of a person based on the little she knows from social media and overheard conversations. It becomes painful to insert that creation into a whole world, a real world this woman shares with Ash, filled with friends, dinner parties, weekends, plans. When she considers this, Ruby understands, her bones aching, that she is just a scrawl across the page, while Ash's fiancée is a series of fully formed sentences and punctuations; she makes up whole paragraphs of his life.

Ruby would be foolish to dwell on everything she is missing out on.

Better to focus on what she herself brings to Ash. The things she brings out in him.

'I'm not like this with anyone else,' he once told her, and Ruby believes this, at least, to be true.

(Are we ever the same person with someone else? And if we're not, what happens when one of you leaves, where does that version of you go? This is something I have thought about a lot since my mother left me.)

Perhaps it is the weather, Ruby thinks, causing her fever. The way the constant rain evokes memories of long afternoons spent in bed, reminds her of entwined limbs and slow kisses and drowsing in someone's arms. Exploring the city on her own these past few days has clearly exacerbated her longing, drawn out her desire for connection. It can't help that most of her memories of long afternoons spent in bed are imagined, not real; since Ash, there has been no one else, and he was seldom available to her for longer than an hour or two, at best. Ruby's heart twangs at this truth, a guitar string plucked, and it occurs to her, all of a sudden, that what she really needs is to be touched. It has been days since she has experienced any form of human contact. Weeks, even. A person could go crazy from that kind of deprivation.

Two days ago, Ruby ran past a small massage parlour on Amsterdam, sandwiched between a computer repair company and a cheque-cashing store. DEEP TISSUE, 1 HR / $55, MID-WEEK SPECIAL the handwritten sign in the window said. It's worth a try, she thinks now, and before she has time to change her mind, she's back out in the rain, heading east. *I'm slowly coming to understand this place*, she thinks, crossing this street, then that, until she reaches her destination. A little bell sounds as she enters from the street, and a slight man in what looks like silk pyjamas nods from the front desk. She appears to be his only customer, and he is soon leading her to a small room out back, with just enough space for a bed and a cane basket for her clothes.

'Underwear on,' the man says, and then turns away so she can undress. When he cracks his knuckles, places his hands on her, the world flashes orange behind her closed eyes. It is not pleasurable, exactly, as this deceptively strong man pushes down, cracks bones, kneads into muscle, but it satisfies something in Ruby, brings her back to herself. She has a body, she is nerve and sinew and gristle, and she is in New York City, and she drinks too much vodka, and makes herself come better than even her best lover can, and she pays too much for dresses, and sometimes she doesn't get out of bed until noon. Her ponytail has bumps, and her teeth are crooked, and as the small man pushes his elbow into the crevice of her left shoulder blade, causing bright sparks beneath her eyelids, Ruby thinks she might have given 'perfect' a little too much weight. There is something about being a work in progress, after all.

When the massage is over, she feels light, spacious, as if the man back in that cramped room has somehow untied all her knots, pushed her out to sea. Is that all it takes, she wonders, slightly embarrassed at her own simplicity. Someone taking care of her for an hour, placing her at the centre of things. She might go back to this man every day, if that's the case. Just to see how much more he can undo.

Ruby is smiling, imagining herself completely unfettered, when her phone vibrates in her jacket pocket. Someone waking up on the other side of the world, she thinks. Probably Cassie, whose children generally have her up at ungodly hours. Taking the phone out of her pocket, shielding the screen with her palm, it takes three reads before she fully comprehends the message. Even then, sentences fully formed, she struggles to make sense of the arrangement.

Work is sending me to New York in July for a conference. Can you believe that shit? Start finding the best rooftops, babe.

45

Ash. Following her to New York. Two months before the wedding. Two months before he will marry his perfect girl.

The chain in Ruby's stomach twists. The rain suddenly feels like a slap.

To think she was this close to floating away.

5

At dinner one night, partway through our second
week, I ask Noah to tell me about the city. Now that
we're working together, we have taken to sharing meals
and stories, too. Where our first conversations were
like trading cards, each of us collecting basic information about the other, trying to make a set, now we
talk over cereal or sausages about science, and poli-
tics, and religion, and all the things that come into my
mind that I want to know more about. He says I must
have had a pretty poor education, and when I think
about all the different small-town schools I went to,
and where I ended up, I can't disagree. I don't mind
so much when Noah tells me the truth, which he does
quite often, now that we spend a lot of time together.
The idea that truth is hurtful puzzles me. Seems like
lying to a person does all the damage.

'I had to teach myself most things,' I told him the
other day. 'From library books and TV shows, mostly.
Or watching what other people do.'

'An autodidact, then,' he answered, and when he
explained what that word meant, I said there should
probably be a nicer-sounding word for something as
important as growing yourself up.

'Indeed,' he said with a smile, because he seems to
like truth from me, too.

When he asks me what it is exactly that I want to
know about New York, I shrug and say whatever it is
he thinks I should know. Things that might not be so
obvious when I look left, right, up.

Here are some interesting things he shares with me over take-out Chinese: there are 472 subway stations operating around the city, transporting five and a half million people from here to there each day. It *is* in fact important to stand back from the platform like the announcement says, because each year something like a hundred and fifty New Yorkers get struck by the 400-tonne trains whizzing by.

'How many don't make it?' I ask, and Noah says around a third of the people hit by trains are fatally injured, which makes me wonder about the ones who survive.

There are plenty of hospitals to help with that, he assures me. Ambulances are dispatched from city-run and private operators, hurtling towards traffic accidents and fires and all kinds of private disasters a thousand times a day. A person dies every nine minutes in New York City, but two babies are born in that same amount of time, so you never know if that ambulance is speeding towards life or death when you hear it pass by.

'I'm getting used to the sirens,' I say, and Noah nods.

'Best that you do, Baby Joan. Lest they become the only thing you hear.'

When he tells me there are more than six thousand places of worship across the city, we stop to consider all the leaps of faith people make, the deities they pray to. I am feeding the last of my egg roll to Franklin when Noah says that if you could hear all that praying, you'd be listening to eight hundred different languages at once, everything from Yiddish to Urdu to French Creole, and this makes me question how New Yorkers ever understand each other. 'That's the magic of living inside a three hundred square mile "melting pot"', Noah responds, before telling me at least half the city's population comes from some other country, or a different part of America.

'How many come from Wisconsin?' I ask, but Noah says he doesn't know anything about Wisconsin, except that the architect Frank Lloyd Wright was born there, and he himself has no desire to visit.

'I don't miss it,' I say quickly, just in case he thinks I might.

Eventually, with all this talk of ambulances and people and prayers, I ask Noah about the two holes in the ground. The ones downtown, where those giant buildings used to be. I was small when it happened, too small to understand, but yesterday I went to the memorial, and as I traced the names of all the people who died that day, felt the grooves of their existence under my fingertips, I knew something irretrievable had been lost in this place. I did not take a single photograph, although some people were taking selfies by the twin pools, posing at the edge of all those names.

'Nearly three thousand people died at Ground Zero on 9/11,' Noah tells me. 'And we've lost many, many more rescue and recovery workers since then. Turns out all the debris down there, all that dust and ash, was toxic. Enough to cause cancers that are still being diagnosed today.'

I shudder. Thinking of dust and ash and feeling, suddenly, as if I can taste the dead in my mouth. Noah stares at me and then smiles softly.

'You know something? When a star dies, the dust and gases left over can form a nebula. Which is truly one of the most beautiful things you'll ever see. But nebulae get even more interesting, because they also signify regions where bright, new stars are formed. Stellar nurseries, they call them. Stardust then, is both the end and the beginning of things. A galactic reminder that birth and death are not so very different.'

'I didn't know,' I tell him, truthfully, 'that stars could die.'

I suppose I thought some things are just always there. Thinking back now, it seems so obvious. That everything changes. When Noah shows me images of nebulae on his laptop, he is right that stardust is the most beautiful thing I've ever seen. But the thought of stellar nurseries and dying stars make my chest tight. It is a reminder that nothing is constant, when I so desperately want everything to stay exactly as it is right now. Eating dinner with Noah, waiting for two short, fat corgis to be dropped off tomorrow, and knowing where I will be, not just tomorrow, but the day after that.

This too. I am tired of beautiful things making me sad. I should like to love something without turning it over and discovering exposed wires, cheap parts on the other side. For the first time, I wish he wasn't so insistent on telling me the truth of things.

But I thought you wanted to know how things work, Baby Joan.

I can almost hear Noah say this in response to my sudden melancholy, and as we clear the table and prepare for bed, I force a smile for all he is teaching me, all that I am learning about the world. I don't tell him that I never want to look at nebulae or those holes in the ground ever again.

★ ★ ★

Something happens on Day Thirteen, the same day Ash tells Ruby he is coming to New York. I decide to take photographs of the Empire State Building, which I don't like nearly as much as the Chrysler Building, but they're going to project paintings onto the building's façade once it gets dark, an exhibition of some artist I don't know, but would like to, because you must be something when they let you use the Empire State Building as your very own art gallery. I catch the 1 train and most of the cars are half empty tonight, so I have my pick of where to sit. As we wind our way downtown, I read the subway adverts for life insurance policies and community colleges and try to catch the graffiti slogans whizzing by outside the window, all the obscure messages sprayed across the subway tunnel walls. Who writes these things all the way down here? How do they get over the sparking tracks to paint their thoughts across the broken, dirty concrete? As the train slows between stations, I look to my left and see a blood-red sentence dripping, fresh: Your days are numbered. I stare at the bleeding letters running down the wall and feel that tightness in my chest again, before the train hisses beneath me and we're jolted forward, away. Just a stupid message, left by someone making their art amongst the rats and the rubbish, but still, it makes me think of dying stars and holes in the ground, and suddenly I don't feel like taking pictures of a building anymore.

It is as if, here on this train, I have suddenly been reminded to not lose sight of the other me, the one who knows that life and people play all sorts of tricks on the unsuspecting. I am not someone who doesn't know about corners and turning, after all. I am not someone surprised by the way life can change in an instant, with no regard for how happy you might have been just seconds before, your hand twisting against the handle of the kitchen door.

When we get to 28th Street, I'm tempted to stay on the train. To just keep going. As people exit onto the station platform, I reluctantly follow their lead, like I'm some kind of fish, and there is no choice but to swim the same way. The crowd is thick, and I am careful not to adjust my stride or break the rhythm as I am picked up in this swell of people and propelled forward. We move up the stairs in formation — one, two, three, four, five — I look down to watch my now-smudged sneakers as they slap down on one step at a time. Then a turn onto a landing, before the next set of stairs. This is where the crowd usually disperses; there's room for us to spread out. I'm still watching my feet when I start getting knocked by people passing on my left. It's as if they're doing it on purpose, leaning into my path, one after the other, and I soon realise each person butting up against me is in fact shifting away from an obstacle on their own left. I look over, around them, and catch a glimpse of something on the ground.

It takes me a few seconds to comprehend that this obstacle people are moving around and away from is in fact a man, lying on the ground. He is flat on his back and his shirt is unbuttoned, exposing a smooth, dark chest that I catch in flashes between legs, shopping bags, coats. I soon see he is young, more a boy than a man, and I push back against the people rushing by, shift sideways through the crowd, until I'm standing right in front of him. Over him. His eyes are closed, his lips pressed together, and I can't tell if he is breathing. I want to lean down and put my hand to

52

this boy's mouth, feel for warm air, but I can't seem to make my arm move. People continue to move around us, some look over their shoulders once or twice, but nobody else stops. It's as if my body is listening to their unspoken warnings. *Danger! Stay away! This is not safe for you!* But up close, he looks like a sleeping child; if my arms won't move towards him, my feet won't let me walk away.

Soon it's just the two of us. A young man laid out on his back, and me, hovering over his body, unsure of what to do next. His feet are bare, dusky pink soles caked in mud. He must be freezing. I think this at the same time I reach down, remove my sneakers and then my socks. They are white, thick and new, and I'm thinking of Noah as I wrestle one of these socks, then the other, onto this young man's feet. I would give him my shoes next, if his feet were small enough. He doesn't stir as I touch him, but I can feel the warmth of his skin. I know what dead bodies feel like. Not like this. Emboldened, I kneel down and pull his shirt closed, fumble with a middle button to fasten the threadbare material across his chest. And then I lean back on my now-bare heels and start to cry. Is this all I can do? Give him my new socks, cover his chest?

This is someone's baby.

Someday soon — it's coming — I will think, *Doesn't he know I'm someone's baby? Doesn't he know that I was loved?* But right now, I'm fighting back tears for this child lying on a slab of concrete halfway underground, walked around, walked over, as if he's not even there. As another train arrives and I hear people swarm towards the stairs, I take a ten-dollar bill out of my purse and gently tuck it into the pocket of the boy's shirt. And then I turn, run up the subway stairs,

53

out onto the crowded street, as if I am being chased. It's dark, but you wouldn't know it from all the illumination up here. The brightness of the city hurts my eyes. I walk a block or two with a sneaker in each hand, the soles of my own bare feet picking up the dirt and grime of a city where no one gives me a second glance, no one asks if I am okay. People walked around the boy and now they walk around me, as if I am not really here.

I want to go home.

Where would that be? I feel like I have been living inside a dream these last two weeks, and now I'm waking up to the same cold, hard bed, to the same cold, hard wall pressed against my nose. I'm fourteen and my mother is dead on the kitchen floor, and I've still got my schoolbag in my hand when I call 911, her blood all over my fingers. I'm fifteen, shunted to another small town, to live in another small house, with my mother's cousin. I'm seventeen, and Mr Jackson has his camera pointed at my trembling, naked body, and I'm eighteen years old, alone on a bus from Milwaukee to New York City, putting twenty-seven hours between me and this man, this life.

Your days are numbered. What would the exact equation be to leave that life behind? What calculation of time and distance would enable me to safely move away from the edge of things, from the danger of being pulled back in? Noah shook my hand, bought me sneakers, tells me stories about New York, but would he miss me if I never came back to him tonight? Would he find another stray to fill up the lonely parts of his life, all the corners I have seeped into these past thirteen days?

Does Mr Jackson miss me? Did he ache to find

54

me gone? I miss him. That I should not feel this way doesn't make it any less true. I have been facing forward for days now, hiding from my old life, but the way everyone walked around that young boy tonight, the way he didn't seem to matter, this has wrenched me back. A yank at the core of me, turning me around, as if a rope is being pulled. I am at one end, and who — *what* is at the other?

If I leave again, would anyone miss me when I'm gone?

6

This story really starts in a small town, sixty-some miles west of Milwaukee. The first steps towards now, towards here, begin with the waving of a scrap of paper in my face.

'Go on, Alice. You know you want to call him. Or' — Tammy pulls a face — 'you're gonna have to work something else out quick. There's no room up at the cabin, and besides, Dad's . . . '

She doesn't have to finish the sentence. Tammy's father is drying out. Again. Only this time, he says he has God on his side. Something about a new church by the frozen lake, and being reborn for Jesus, which means he's ready to repair his relationship with his daughter too, if she'll come keep house with him. He wants her there before St Patrick's Day, thinks she'll help keep him steady, but he doesn't know her new boyfriend, Rye, lives one town over from that church, peddling everything from oxy to heroin out of his basement.

Tammy thinks one man will make up for the other.

She is my best friend, but I wouldn't go to the lake with her, even if I was invited. There is nothing good waiting for me in those cabins and churches, in the basements full of boys who will probably never leave the county, let alone the state, unless it's to go to jail. It's been nine months since Tammy and I graduated, a new year has turned over, and I am more certain than ever that small towns are not for me. I wasn't conceived in one, and I sure as hell don't want to die in one, either. What I need, then, is a job. The kind that pays well, or well enough, so that the distance between stuck and leaving is shortened, narrowed to an end point I can see.

If I was eighteen already, I could work clearing tables at Jimmy's bar; Tammy's cousin has always been nice to me, and the tips alone would buy me a ticket out of here. But my birthday is still four whole weeks away, which also means Gloria D, my guardian, still has signing rights to my bank account, and therefore to my freedom. A regular job just isn't going to cut it.

'I promised your mom I'd look after you until you're eighteen,' she used to say. But I think it's more about the government cheques that will stop when I age out of the system.

I stare at the piece of paper in Tammy's hand, the potential of it.

'I don't know, Tam . . . '

We're sharing her lumpy double bed, tucked up inside another cold, grey-sky morning. Lying so close to my best friend, I can smell the remnants of last night's Marlborough lights on her skin, mixed with years-old Chanel No. 5, a powdery scent so familiar I want to bury my face into her neck. Knowing she'll be gone by tomorrow makes me want to cry. But crying won't help my situation; feeling sorry for yourself gets you exactly nowhere.

Nowhere. I'm already in the middle of nowhere.

Worse — I'm trapped within it. In this town where the sky pushes down on you. Air all heavy and close to your nose, as if the pollution from other, nicer towns has been diverted here, set down right over our heads. I'm not sure what my mother was thinking when she came back to her home state. Why she couldn't just stay in New York City.

Tell me about where I was made.

I would ask her this all the time. I never tired of her stories about New York, loved learning that Manhattan was an island — 'Not all islands are tropical, Alice' — and knowing there was a place where you could catch trains at any hour, where restaurants never closed, and people from the movies walked right by you on the street. I thought it all sounded so romantic, even if I didn't really understand what romantic meant back then, just liked the sound of the word, the click of it in my mouth.

From what I know, a man brought us back to the Midwest. Some guy and some promise, both of which ended up broken. My mother stayed because it was a thousand times cheaper than anywhere else, and there were other men and other promises waiting, but mostly, in those early years, it was just her and me, making a home wherever we found ourselves. To be honest, each time we packed up and moved, I mostly felt relief. Knowing another man had gone, and we'd be back to the two of us again. It was always better when it was just the two of us.

'Why did she leave me *here*?'

'What?'

Tammy is up on her elbow now, facing me.

'Huh?'

'You mumbled something, Alice. What did you say?'

I had not meant to ask that essential, unanswerable question out loud. This would break all the rules. There are some things you only speak of when you've had enough cheap booze to pretend you don't know

58

what you're saying. When you've drunk so much alcohol you can no longer hide the fact you're split down the middle with grief, still fresh with it. As if it all happened yesterday, not years ago, when you were only fourteen years old. In these moments, while your best friend holds your hair back, and you throw up weed and last night's tin-can spirits, everything comes tumbling out. Words as violent as the bile burning your throat. How you wanted to die too, on that kitchen floor, how you wanted to climb right into the fire as they closed those dark, heavy curtains around her coffin.

I was fourteen years old when my mother shot herself in the head. She pulled the trigger a half hour before I arrived home from school. Ensuring she would be well dead by the time I got home. How do you ever find the right words to question that?

If the pain slips out when you are drunk, you never reference it the next morning, never talk about it when you're sober. Just the same way you never ask Tammy what she meant when she said she had uncles not monsters under her bed when she was growing up, and you know to pull her away when she attempts to stumble off with a pair of college footballers at those Friday night parties you gatecrash together. You take care of each other at night. And then you wave off that care in the morning. These are the rules you've got going, and this is how you both survive.

'Okay, weirdo. Whatever.'

Tammy shrugs away my long silence, then waves the strip of paper in my face again.

'Call him, Alice. Call Mr Jaaaaaaackson. You're not a student any more. He's not your teacher, and besides' — she reaches over and moves a wayward

59

strand of hair away from my eyes, her own eyes glinting — 'he's hot. So, so hot! And let's be honest. It'll be the easiest money you're ever going to make around here. Hell, I'd do it too, if I were half as pretty as you. But ain't nobody needs to see me like that.'

Tammy folds the piece of paper into my hand, closes my fingers around it with her own.

'Call him. Do it. What have you got to lose?'

She doesn't wait for me to respond.

'The way I see it, Alice Lee. The answer to that would be nothing the fuck at all.'

★　★　★

'You comfortable, Alice?'

'Uh-huh.'

I'm lying. My legs already ache, and a muscle in my left arm won't stop twitching. When he first moved my arms, when he asked me to hold still in this position, I wondered how hard it could be to stay like this. Reclined on a small couch in the pose he'd asked for, comfortable in my jean shorts and white singlet, it really did feel like the easiest money I'd ever make. Two hundred dollars to stay still and let a man draw me. Easy. It only took a minute for everything to start aching.

'This is just the practice round, Alice,' he'd said as he lifted my arms over my head. 'Just so I can get a feel for how to capture you best. Every single body is different, and I need to learn about yours. Okay?'

When he leant in so close, I could smell weed and Scotch, and see how his fingers were stained black at the tips. I stared at his short, dirty fingernails, as he bent one knee and gently pushed my legs a little

60

further apart. It made my stomach flip, the nearness of those fingers, and my nerves threatened to reveal themselves in a stupid, girlish giggle. I didn't want to do anything wrong. And not just because of the stack of twenty-dollar bills he'd put down on the table next to me. I wanted to please him.

Mr Jackson.

We all wanted to please Mr Jackson.

Once, in junior year, he'd come over to my desk, and I could smell that heady combination of weed and Scotch, even then. I was holding my breath as he stared at my sketch of a ballerina at the barre, the tension I had tried to capture in her muscles, when, without saying a word, he ran his fingers lightly between my dancer's charcoal legs. Just for a second, a gesture so quick no one else in class would have noticed. But I felt it. I felt it as if he had run those fingers between my own thighs. As he walked away, I had no idea whether the butterflies swarming in my stomach signalled pleasure — or a desire to run from the room.

In my final semester, he talked to the class about life drawing, how you couldn't really paint people unless you understood what was happening to their bodies, to skin and bone and curves. He said the best portrait artists always began with the naked form. He wanted to bring in a life model for us to draw but the school board wouldn't allow it, so we'd just have to take his word for it — or see for ourselves once we graduated. 'Maybe even try it from the other side,' Mr Jackson had teased the class, staring straight at me.

'It's Jamie, not Mr Jackson', he'd chided when he helped me take off my coat this afternoon. 'I'm not your teacher any more, hey.'

And I'd automatically said 'Sorry, Mr Jackson'. Which made him laugh, and lightly touch my cheek. He said he was glad I had called.

'It isn't easy in this town' — he'd waved his hand about, as if there was no need to finish the sentence.

He understood. I didn't need him to tell me that it's never easy around here.

The ad Tammy pressed into my hand said: LIFE MODELS WANTED. $200 CASH. POTENTIAL FOR FURTHER WORK. My hands shook when I called his number.

'Yes, I'm eighteen now. Yes, I've done this before. Yes, I'm still painting, and yes, it will be good to see you, too,' I said on the call.

All lies, except the last part, or maybe that was a lie, too. Thinking of two hundred dollars in cash, and the distance this could buy me.

Now, I am alone with Mr Jackson for the first time ever, watching him look from me to his sketch pad and back again, his tongue set between his teeth as he draws. He doesn't look like the other men around here. He is slight, and tanned, and he has stubble instead of the full beard everyone seems to grow these days. He's not wearing shoes, and his jeans, frayed at his ankles, are taut around his thighs. He used to wear slacks when he was teaching. In jeans he looks lean and coiled, and I realise I'm sketching him too, working out the curves and lines of his body.

Skin and bone and curve.

'That's a serious face you had just now,' he says, stepping out from behind his easel. 'Just when I think I have you, Alice, your expression changes.'

'Oh. Sorry. I guess I'm . . . concentrating. And, um. My arm kind of hurts.'

I let it drop and sit upright on the couch.

'It's harder than I thought.'

A slip. My second lie is revealed so easily, and he catches it immediately. Sees what he must have suspected. I have not done this before.

'You want something to help you relax? It's after' — he checks his watch — 'two o'clock.'

I nod, and Mr Jackson — *Jamie* — rolls a tight smoke, then sits down beside me. The couch is draped with a white sheet. Our thighs touch and he doesn't move away.

He holds out the joint and I take a deep drag, feeling a burn in my throat and nose. It's better quality than I'm used to, and the second hit makes me cough until I'm doubled over.

'God. You really are an amateur, Alice.'

Mr Jackson says this affectionately, laughs softly as he pats his hand against my back. With my head between my legs and his hand on my back, I'm afraid to sit up. The room is too small, it's spinning around me, coming too close. It might be his fingers or the smoke, or what I'm doing here. With my art teacher, who used to look at me in class, and now he's reaching around, sliding his hand over my belly, pushing me upright again.

'Can I take this off.'

Maybe it's a question. Some other day I'll wonder if it wasn't really a question at all. I'll wonder if I could have said no to the weed, and those stained fingers pressed against my skin, pulling the straps of my singlet down. I'll wonder why I didn't try out that word, see where resistance would take me. But for now, I simply close my eyes and nod. Missing the look on his face as he removes my singlet, and then my shorts.

63

Unaware of the gleam when he reaches for a camera sat next to that stack of twenty-dollar bills and fixes the lens on my body.

Does it matter that I never actually said yes? I knew what was being asked of me. *Life models wanted. $200 cash* — Mr Jackson was clear enough about what he wanted. I don't suppose I had any right to be surprised by the camera, or what it would lead to, eventually. It must have seemed, to him at least, like a natural progression.

He might even say I asked for it.

★ ★ ★

Back in Melbourne, Ruby is showing her sister the website of the long-stay studio apartment she has booked on the Upper West Side.

'It's small,' she says, taking a sip of the wine Cassie has poured for her, 'but it has everything I need.' Next, they look at maps of the neighbourhood. 'I'll run here,' Ruby says, tracing her finger around the blue of the Jacqueline Kennedy Onassis Reservoir in Central Park, 'and maybe here' — her finger travels to the western border of the map, to a thick green line that snakes alongside the Hudson River. 'Riverside Park. I read it's less crowded there. More . . . local.'

'Is it safe?' Cassie asks, and Ruby rolls her eyes.

'New York is one of the safest cities in the world these days.'

'Yes, but you're going there by yourself,' Cassie says. 'You have to be more careful when you're travelling on your own.'

'I'm *always* on my own,' Ruby responds, and now it's Cassie's turn to roll her eyes.

'Yes, well. We know why that is, don't we! Here's hoping you do more than run in New York then, little sis. Or' — Cassie tilts her wine glass at Ruby, narrows her eyes — 'here's hoping you run for long enough that you finally get away from that man, and the hold he seems to have on you.'

★ ★ ★

I moved in. I supposed you could call it that. The way I just never went home that first afternoon. That first night. We didn't *do* anything. Not really. And we still don't. Although, it has been one week since he slid my singlet off. Since his fingers pressed against my skin as he rolled my shorts from my hips. He'd said 'No underwear' during our first phone call, when he told me what time to come over to his house. 'And wear something soft. No lines, I don't want lines, Alice.' I had followed Mr Jackson's instructions carefully, dressing as if it were 90 degrees outside instead of 40, shivering under my thick winter coat. There wasn't much for him to peel away that very first afternoon, not much effort required to leave me completely exposed on his small, sheet-draped couch.

A week later, and my stomach still flips at the memory of it. Up until then, I had never been naked in front of a man. Never been looked at up close. Oh, I'd had sex before, if that's what you can call it. Fumbling fingers, and thrusts under sheets at various parties, but nothing like this. I'd never been seen until that moment, with Mr Jackson sliding to the floor, looking up at me. The way he said 'Like *this*' as he reached up and spread my legs. On his knees, with those fingers running up the insides of my thighs, pushing them further apart.

'I want to photograph you like this, Alice.'

The room tilted sideways. He used to watch me in class. I had that same stomach-pit feeling of sinking and floating, and I wanted him to keep touching me, wanted to cover myself, wanted to get up and run. I stayed perfectly still instead, pushed all the shaking deeper. This is what he had said was required of me, after all.

'I will need you to stay perfectly still.'

I said, 'Yes — of course. I have done this before.'

He now knows this to be untrue, although I haven't yet told him my real age. It's not a lie exactly to keep that from him, not like the lies I've told Gloria — when I went back to pick up some clothes, I told her I was going to the lake with Tammy — but more like an omission. Something better left out of the story because it doesn't serve any purpose. It's bad enough he knows I lied about my experience as a model, that he could see the way I flinched every time the camera clicked.

I still jump a little now, though I am getting used to our new routine. I thought, last night, wide awake on this couch, how quickly the strangest thing can come to feel normal, ordinary. That first afternoon, as he photographed my naked body, I sent myself somewhere else, somewhere above the lens, maybe even out of the room entirely. I trembled as he took one shot of me then another, sure he was coming too close, seeing too much. But I never once asked him to stop, never asked him to go back to his easel instead, and when Mr Jackson was done taking his pictures, he wrapped me up in a soft blanket and we talked all night about art and God — 'I believe they're the same thing,' he said — and we ate homemade nachos, and he never touched me, not in the way that leads to other things. I slept on the couch, wrapped in that blanket, and the next morning when I showered, he photographed me there, through a half-opened shower door, and later, back on the couch he wanted to do it again — 'The light is beautiful right now, Alice' — and this time I didn't send myself somewhere else. I stayed locked on the lens, that single eye opening and closing on my body. I felt powerful, staring straight back at it. Mr Jackson showed me some of the images later, and the pale exposed skin, the soft triangle of hair between my legs meant nothing to me. I couldn't stop looking at the way my eyes were blazing. The slight snarl of my lip.

He said I was mercurial and made up my bed on the couch once again.

And now we are a whole week into this new arrangement. Our conversations have ranged all over the house, and when he goes to school for the day, I am happy here on my own, looking through his library of books by men with names I only sometimes recognise. Nietzsche, Sartre, Jung. And someone called Kierkegaard, who says: *It begins, in fact, with nothing and therefore can always begin*, which I like the sound of, and almost understand.

When Mr Jackson comes home with groceries and beer, we cook dinner, drink a little, and then he photographs me a new and different way.

'It's not pornography,' he says one of these nights. He has asked me to put my hand between my legs — 'relaxed, like *this*' — and perhaps he has caught my hesitation this time, the confusion around where this might lead.

67

'Pornography has its own purpose, its own merit, Alice. Don't let the conservative claptrap of this town turn your head. But we're not doing that, anyway. This is about your body, about showing the world how you inhabit your strong, beautiful body. All the incredible things you can make it do.'

Later, he shows me some videos on his laptop, pornography of *merit*. Women and men coiled around each other, gasping, clinging, looking, for the most part, like they are in some kind of pain.

'Agony and pleasure. They can look like the same thing,' he tells me when I start to protest, and it is true I cannot see the difference, cannot understand whether I am afraid or expanding somehow as I watch these scenes unfold. I know I ask to watch more, and I know I am wet, saturated by what I am seeing on the screen. I feel conflicted by this pleasure, the way it both horrifies and excites me.

What Mr Jackson is showing me cannot be unseen, this much I do know. But, as he leaves me alone for yet another night, I cannot for the life of me figure out what he expects me to make of this new world, beckoning.

★ ★ ★

Later, I see what he was doing, why he made me wait. He needed to know I could be trusted. He needed to know he was safe. As if my safety did not come into it at all.

The night of Ruby's work farewell, she finds herself thinking much the same thing. Ash had stayed away from her all night, kept to the other side of the bar, so that she spent the whole evening looking for him, forgetting it was her own party, barely registering each 'I'll miss you' or 'Remember when . . .' that came her way. By 11 p.m., it was the knot in her stomach, not the cheap champagne, making her sick, and she excused herself, walked home in tears. How could Ash ignore her like that? On the one night no one would have questioned their closeness, when everyone at the agency seemed to be throwing their arms around her, confessing their affection. Even then, he kept his distance from her.

He showed up at her apartment twenty minutes later.

'I have half an hour,' he said, checking his watch. As if thirty minutes could make up for the whole night she had lost waiting for him. When he leaves that half hour later, booking an Uber from her phone instead of his own — 'Just to be on the safe side' — she wonders if he had planned it this way all along, and simply neglected to tell her. Had he considered letting the night be about her, about what made *her* feel safe, for once? Or was it only ever about him?

She knows the answer to that, of course. We both do. But at this point, we're still weeks away from understanding the real consequences of our connection to such careless men.

7

It happens during one of the last big snowfalls of the season. Mr Jackson arrives home late from school with little flurries on his shoulders and in his hair. We both stand in the open doorway and watch as snowflakes weave their way to the ground, streetlamps turning on one by one, their glow making it look like it's the stars that are falling. I'm not wearing a jacket and he puts his arms around me, pulls me in close. We're there for minutes or hours, I don't know which. I only know that I am shivering, and he too is shaking when he turns to face me.

'Alice?'

The kiss is gentle, a question. I try to answer against his mouth, but I am suddenly as slivered as the swirling, falling snow. I am in pieces as he pulls me inside, closes the door, his mouth still on mine as we stumble towards the couch.

We are about to fall when he breaks away and laughs, a sudden, awkward sound that bounces off the walls and puts a distance between us.

'Jesus. What a cliché I've become.'

I don't know if he's talking about the snow, or the kiss, or the fact he used to be my teacher, and I am a young woman, his muse. I cast my mind about, trying to find something clever to say, to show him I take responsibility for the kiss, for what it means, but I need more time to make sense of what I am feeling. All I know in this moment is that he should kiss me again, before something is lost. I don't have the words to say why.

'It's okay. I want this.'

This is all that comes out, a kind of plea. I do not want to stay on this precipice any longer.

He sways, glistens, and begins to undress me.

'Fuck.'

Hands on my breasts, then his mouth. One suck of each nipple, a brand new sensation felt deep in my belly. And then he is kneeling, his mouth moving from thigh to thigh, before his tongue pushes inside me. I don't move.

'Alice.'

Two fingers now, his tongue finding nerve. I see a match lit behind my eyes. Still, I don't move.

'Alice. You are so goddamn beautiful.'

Harder now. Deeper. His fingers spark, I feel like fire. It's okay. I want this.

'Alice.'

He keeps saying my name, only it sounds like someone else's name now. Some other girl he first saw when she was sixteen years old and he was closer to forty. After her mother had died, leaving her alone and sad, and before he looked at her the way he does now.

'Please, Mr Jackson,' I say over his head, because I know I am not going to take that two hundred dollars in twenty-dollar bills, the stack still sitting there on the table. And because I don't want to be alone and sad any more. I want him to help me forget my pain, dissolve it. And it does rise to the surface, scatter across my skin, as he enters me slowly, saying my name over and over, the sky now black outside, and me swirling, like snow.

He tells me I'm like the sky. That storm clouds pass across my face, and just as quickly it's clear skies, bright and shining. He says that's what he's trying to capture when he draws me, or takes those pictures, but he can't keep his hands away long enough now, and there is always another way for us to touch that gets in the way of the art. I'm getting quite good at it, too. I know where to place my hands, and my mouth. He's teaching me what to do, how to move my hips, what to say. I even let him film me sometimes, so that it's me with the glazed eyes, twisting and moaning like the women in those videos he showed me a lifetime ago.

'How many were there before me?' he asked, that first, next morning.

'Um. Three.'

I buried my face in his shoulder. Embarrassed. He had taught two of the boys at the high school.

'How old were you the first time, Alice?'

'Fifteen.'

Fifteen. My mother had committed suicide just months before and a boy wanted to say sorry. He was careful and clumsy, and it was over in a minute. 'Sorry,' he actually said, right at the end, and I was never sure for what, exactly. I felt nothing, did nothing. It wasn't terrible, it wasn't even bad. It was just nothing, because I couldn't feel anything at all back then.

Two and three were about trying to feel something, trying to feel anything at all. Wanting to be like the other girls in my class. Like Tammy, who told me what it was like to come — 'Like your body is a firework!' That's what I wanted, to feel like I was exploding, disintegrating, and that's not what it was like at all. With two and three, I felt heavy, stuck.

'They weren't . . . it wasn't . . . very good.'

But Mr Jackson wasn't listening. You can tell by someone's eyes when they're not listening, and his had taken on that familiar sheen.

'Fifteen? God, I'm a pervert for saying this, but that turns me on. See . . . '

And he placed my hand on him, moved it up and down.

'Did you do this?'

I shook my head, no.

'Did you do this?'

He pushed my head down.

'Did you do this?'

Sliding himself in and out of my mouth, watching me, smiling when I shook my head again. No.

'Alice.'

His invocation. My name as a kind of summoning. No, Mr Jackson, I did not do any of this. I would not have known how. In fact, I barely recognise the girl I've become.

It's as if he has dismantled my life and put me back together a whole different way.

* * *

The first time I come, it doesn't feel like fireworks. It feels like breaking into a run. That moment when muscles coil, and suddenly it's as if there is a hand at your back, propelling you forward. You go from heavy to light in an instant, you're sprinting, feet barely touching the ground. Everything rushes by and it's you right there at the centre, flying.

That's what it feels like.

And then you come crashing back to earth, heavy limbs and hard breath. Everything slows to its usual, unbearable pace, and the loss of that lightness is as painful as a punch. You were free, you were running. And now you are back here on the ground.

I never let Mr Jackson see how sad this loss makes me. How it makes me cry. Every single time.

★ ★ ★

It isn't always, only ever, bad. You should see them dancing with each other. The world held in their pressing palms. The way all the little bruises disappear. They fit together so well when they're dancing. You might even think it is love, when Ruby places her head on his shoulder, when Ash slides his hand to the small of her back.

They have their favourite songs, just like any other couple. Words they mouth to each other, melodies they like to wrap their bodies around.

It isn't always, only ever, bad. That's mostly why she had to leave him.

★ ★ ★

'So you're not going back to Gloria's, then?'

'Nope. She still thinks I'm at the lake with you,' I say, holding the phone out from my ear for a second, listening as Tammy takes a dramatic drag of her cigarette, the sound huffing down the line. I can just see her there on her father's porch, cocooned inside a thick blanket, trying in vain to stay warm, now that her dad has inexplicably banned smoking and drinking inside the cabin.

'You could quit smoking too,' I'd said, when she told me about these new house rules, but she'd laughed her throaty laugh and called me crazy.

'The fuck I'm supposed to do around here if I can't smoke or drink, Alice?'

We agreed she had a point.

Tammy knows I've been staying with Mr Jackson these past few weeks, has even suggested this was her idea all along, my 'Get the hell out of Dodge', as she called it. But, if I didn't know better, I'd say my sudden foray into rule-breaking has confused her, when this has generally been her domain. I know for sure she has never had any respect for Gloria, even if my mother's cousin kept me out of the system by taking me in.

'My mom chose her for a reason,' I've had to explain many times, usually after Gloria had pounded on my bedroom door, yelling at us to shut up, or I'd showed up at Tammy's house in the middle of the night yet again, because another man didn't want anyone seeing him come and go from Gloria's bed.

'My mom knew Gloria would let me be. It was never going to work with someone . . . parental.'

'She could have been *nicer* though, Alice.' This is what Tammy always said. 'It's not like your mom had just tragically died or anything, hey.'

Tammy, my champion, the first and only real friend I made after I moved in with Gloria.

'I like your jacket. And sorry about your mom,' Tam had said, sitting down beside me in the school cafeteria that first time we met. Letting me know, in two short sentences, that she wasn't going to make a fuss, and I've valued her economic version of friendship ever since. I also understand her well enough by now to know she's not concerned about me lying to Gloria. Just curious as to how I've managed to disappear.

(*It's easy*, I'll want to remind her later. If no one notices you're gone.)

'Enough about that bitch anyway,' Tammy says now, as if she's reading my mind. 'I want to know the juicy stuff. What's it like with Mr J? Is he as good as we thought he'd be?'

I've been drinking a beer during our late-afternoon call, and I swish it around in my mouth as I consider the question. I think suddenly — explicitly — of Mr Jackson's bourbon, how he poured it all over my nipples last night, and the slow way he lapped it up. Telling me nothing had ever tasted so good, and how, when he poured it lower down, the heat and rasp of his tongue set me spinning.

'Uh. Yeah. It's . . . good,' I manage to say, my face on fire.

'I fucking knew it!'

Even with our bad reception, I can hear Tammy clapping.

'Tell me more,' she starts to say, when I see a car pulling up in the drive. Mr Jackson has come home early today.

'Sorry, Tam. I gotta go,' I say quickly, my cheeks still flushed. 'I'll tell you every sordid detail soon, I promise.'

Tammy sighs down the phone. This is our first real conversation in weeks.

'Whatever, jailbait. Just be careful, okay — '

She doesn't get a chance to finish the sentence. Mr Jackson is already through the door, reaching for me. I hang up the call without saying goodbye, unaware we won't ever speak again.

Sometimes a person slips out of your life so easily, you wonder if they were ever really there to begin with.

★ ★ ★

Tammy called me jailbait. Tonight, filming himself slowly moving in and out of me, Mr Jackson said we were equals. That he had met his match, finally. When he was done, when his eyes fluttered backwards and he slumped against my warm body, I had a sense, for the first time, that he might be wrong. Because I felt, in that moment, the slick of him all over my skin, that I might be the powerful one. His needs could be met. He could be satisfied. But I could survive with a great, yawning hunger in my belly. I could make him happy, while my own bones were hollow with grief.

I heard my mother's voice then, remembered lying next to her in bed when I was maybe eight or nine years old. She had been crying and I'd come into her room, long enough after the front door had slammed shut for me to know it was safe. I crawled up next to her and wrapped my thin, child's arms around her, and she only let herself cry for another minute before she sniffed, wiped her tears on the sheet, and turned to face me. In the early morning light, her face was beautiful, the way some faces soften when sad, and she kissed my nose.

'Don't worry about me, Alice. I was just having a moment. He can go on to hell for all I care. Just another stupid man who thinks he has something over me. That I'll let him treat me bad because of' — she waved her hand around the room, and I knew she meant this bed, this house, this town belonged to him, and another move was coming.

She railed against the man some more, a guy whose name or circumstances I can no longer remember, and by the time the sun came up, she seemed cured of him, wiped clean of their connection. It was fascinating to watch, how quickly she could put herself back together again.

'That's because we're made of metal,' she said, when I asked her about it. 'These men think we're such delicate flowers. They have no idea how strong we are, Alice. How much we can take. They never doubt we need them more than they need us.'

'And it's best,' she said, some other day, 'to keep them thinking that way.'

★　★　★

'Tell me about your mother, Alice.'

Mr Jackson's head is pressing down on my stomach, he is lying sideways across my body. Though I feel his breath catch with the question, I cannot see the expression on his face as he waits for me to answer him.

Nobody asks me about my mother. Not any more. When it first happened, I had to talk about her. They made me talk about her, about finding her dead on the kitchen floor. Just to make sure I was okay. As if you could ever be all right after that. But then I moved in with Gloria and boxes were ticked and some other story came along much worse than mine. Soon enough, my story, *her* story, was no longer something anyone wanted to ask me about. Especially since I refused to share the kind of details people most

78

wanted to hear. I stopped talking about my mother once I realised no one could answer the only question that mattered.

Why did she do it? After all the times she had put herself back together, what made my mom kill herself that day?

I'm silent against the back of Mr Jackson's head. My fingers stop playing with his hair and hover somewhere unfinished between us.

He doesn't turn to face me.

'Tell me about her. Tell me what she was like, Alice. I would really like to know.'

'No, you wouldn't.'

I push him off me, draw my knees up to my bare chest. This is the first time I am the one to put distance between us, and now I wish for a wall.

'Alice.'

I'm so used to him saying my name. But this is different. There is something so adult in how he says it. Something that reminds me of the man he is to students who don't look like me. To them, he is an observant, exacting teacher. The kind of teacher who can turn a name into a command. I sense it, and if we were not naked here in his bed, I might have liked to give over to this safer version of Mr Jackson. I might have liked to open up the book of sketches I'm carrying within me, show him all the torn, damaged pages. But I can feel his skin against mine, the radiating heat of him, and I know these are not arms I can wrap around me. Not in the way of men who want to soothe. He does not get to change his role in my life now.

'I don't want to talk about her. About . . . it. I'm over being a charity case.'

'I don't think you're a charity case, Alice.'

'Sure, you do. Isn't that why I'm here?'

It comes out harsher than I'd intended, but there's truth in this accusation, too. He moves his arm away. Sits up and doesn't look at me. Just stares straight ahead for the longest time, as if measuring my comment word by word before he responds. When he does speak, his voice has an odd, flat sound to it, as if he is reciting lines from a script.

'When I was eleven years old, I watched my mother die of cancer. Correction. I watched her dying of cancer. Slowly. For three shitty years. Nobody ever asked me about it. I asked you because someone should have asked me. It would have helped if someone had asked me. I assumed you'd understand this.'

I stare at Mr Jackson's shoulder, the little muscle twitch that tells me how unprepared he must have been for my response. I want to climb right into what he is saying, I want to know everything, and tell him everything, I feel it all rushing forward in my mouth, but other parts of my body want to back away. To close the conversation down. My heart is jack hammering; I can feel the pulse in my fingers, and that familiar metal taste in my mouth. It is the taste of my mother's blood. Nobody knows I stuck my fingers in my mouth after they came to take her dead body away. 'I'm sorry. I don't like to talk about it. About her.' It is the only thing I can think of to say against that flinching shoulder, and the taste of blood on my tongue.

Mr Jackson is still staring ahead. He speaks as if we hardly know each other.

'That's fine then, Alice. Have it your way.'

'Okay.'

Okay.

It clearly isn't okay, so I turn his head, kiss him hard, instead of asking about that eleven-year-old boy, and what he saw. I am aware my silence is like a hand over his mouth, but I cannot give him what he needs from me tonight. There are ways to lose yourself; there are ways for the body to briefly forget what it knows. Mr Jackson was supposed to be this kind of forgetting, and I want to cling to this version of him for as long as I can.

Thinking back, he probably thinks I never did understand what it meant. To lose the person you loved the most.

★ ★ ★

When something so large has been said out loud, it sits and waits for you to address it, no matter how hard you work at ignoring it. I once read that a single cloud can weigh as much as a hundred elephants. It's not something you can see, this weight pressing down, but the heaviness is there, all the same. This is how it is with Mr Jackson and me. I sat for him yesterday, and for the first time I felt he was not seeing me, not really looking at me, as he shifted an arm or leg more carelessly than I've gotten used to. I think he might be angry with me, and I'm trying to apologise with my body, because once again I don't have the words to say how sorry I am. Last night, he was asleep before I came back from the bathroom, or at least he pretended to be, even when I ran a hand down his back, and rested my fingers on his hip bone.

I wanted to say, against his back — *Tell me. Tell me about your mother.* But my own mother danced too close to the surface, set my cheeks on fire. So I removed my hand and, for the first time, we slept back to back.

This morning, I followed him into the shower. I shivered so much, he pulled me into him, wrapped his arms tight around me, and we stood under the stream of hot water together. But he left as soon as we dried ourselves off, said 'Have a nice day,' and never told me where he was going. It's been hours since he left, and I've been sitting on the small couch, staring at his crates of books this whole time. I feel inundated with memories, swamped by them. The only thing to do is stay still. No noise, no light. If I concentrate hard enough, I can push the thoughts out, away. It's dusk now, I've made it through the daylight, the jarring bright of it, my flashbacks reduced to skimming stones, darting across the surface of my thoughts. My hand on the door, the yellow of the kitchen, the blood red on the floor, half of that beautiful face missing. No single image stays for long if I remain steady, if I don't move. I'm still there, staring at the wall, when Mr Jackson finally comes home. He immediately flicks on the lights, making me jump.

'Alice? Are you okay?'

I try to nod, but instead, the tears come. Fat, crumple-face tears that haven't been let out in this way since it happened.

'Where did you go?' It comes out as a wail. 'You didn't tell me. Where did you go and why did you leave me?'

And now I'm sobbing, the paralysis of the day giving over to the exhaustion of holding everything back. He stands there for a moment, watching me cry, then comes to sit down beside me. Arms go around me, and I fold into him.

'I'm sorry. I'm sorry. I'm *sorry*.'

I apologise over and over as I cling to him, nails digging into his shoulders, trying to crawl under his skin, wanting to get closer. The separation of this day has terrified me.

Mr Jackson holds me tight until the sobbing stops. When I'm finally spent, drained, I feel the rocking. The way he is gently moving me, soothing me, as if I am a child.

'I miss my mother so much.'

I immediately want to suck the words back in, but I push through the ache in my throat. It is a physical pain, knife-sharp, but the words keep coming. I do not want him to be angry at me.

'We looked after each other. It was always just — us. I don't even know who I am without her.'

Mr Jackson gently untangles himself from my arms.

'You want a drink for this?' he asks, and I nod.

'The whole bottle, maybe.'

I wait for him to come back from the kitchen with the bourbon — somehow, I knew it would be bourbon. He hands me the bottle, and I take a swig, grimacing as I swallow.

'Maybe not like that,' he laughs softly. 'Let's get you a glass, amateur.'

The familiarity of this pet name is calming. By the time Mr Jackson comes back from the kitchen with an ice-filled tumbler, I can breathe again.

'We had been doing really well. She had a good job, and we had been in the same place for two years. Two years was everything back then. And he . . . he was in jail, something stupid, I don't know. Petty something. I never really paid much attention to what he did. Unless it involved my mother.'

'He' — Mr Jackson interrupts me — 'Your father?'

83

'No. Hell no!' I shake my head vehemently. 'I don't know who my father is. Mike. My mother's last boyfriend.'

A memory. Mike is driving me to school and he's going too fast. There is no seat belt and I have nothing to hold onto, my fingers dig into the seat, tips white, and he laughs at my fear as we speed past the other cars on the road. When he slams on the brakes at a stop sign, he reaches out, puts his fat hand across my chest. 'Easy there, Alice,' he says, fingers grazing.

Another memory. He's kissing my mother in the kitchen, his hand under her T-shirt. She keeps pushing it away, giggling, and back it goes, and I'm standing in the doorway, watching this dance, feeling sick, because I know this means he'll be here tonight, and every night, until something bad happens again. They turn, see me watching, and he laughs that same laugh, the one that says he enjoys scaring me. I lock my door that night, push a chair against the frame. 'My mom had terrible taste in men,' I say, an understatement. 'And she was really, really beautiful, so there were a lot of men around.'

I pour another shot of bourbon, ghosts hovering.

'You're beautiful,' Mr Jackson says, and I want to be mad at him for leaving, I want to tell him I don't care what he thinks. But that's not how we do it, is it? When a man punishes us for our resistance, we scramble to make it right.

My mother, I think, might have warned me about him. Might have told me how all those terrible men said she was beautiful, too. Or perhaps she would have pushed me right into my teacher's arms, considered this her validation. I am beautiful, just like her. And just like her, I have something this man wants to capture, possess.

It occurs to me, briefly, as Mr Jackson places his hands on my tear-stained face, presses down, that he finds my total reliance on him the most beautiful thing of all.

Later, he shows me photographs of his own mother. Before she got sick. He looks like her, in the way that I look like my mother. A shadow version of the real thing, not quite as lovely. He tells me she was an artist too, and then he carefully takes something from a shoebox in his closet, wrapped in a red silk scarf and no larger than a brick. It is a Leica camera from the 1930s, beautifully preserved. His mother bought it from a second-hand store when she was a teenager, and when she got sick, she gave it to her son and asked him to take care of it.

'It's not worth a whole lot,' he explains. 'Maybe a thousand dollars. But I've moved around so much too, it's the only thing of hers I have left. Takes great photos, still. Back then, they built things to last.'

I ask him to show me how the camera works, confused by the unfamiliar dials and levers and discs. He loads a fresh roll of black and white film and gives me a brief lesson, never letting me touch the Leica itself, as he turns the camera this way and that. We are sitting side by side on the bed when he looks at me through the viewfinder, explains this camera model was one of the first to include a built-in rangefinder. How this feature changes the way you view objects through the glass.

'You start with two images, and this focusing lever helps you bring them closer together . . . see?'

He is holding the camera too close to my face, and I duck my head away from him, laughing as I hear the snap of the shutter.

'Silly girl,' he says, putting his mother's camera down and pulling me into his arms. 'You always were impossible to teach.'

★ ★ ★

Did I think we could just stay like this?

Did I think there was a place you could land, and everything else around you would fall away? That nothing and no one else would matter, because you were exactly where you wanted to be?

Did I think there was such a place, and such a time, and it would all stand still for me, because I was secure in that place, that time?

How else to explain my surprise when it all came to an end? How else to make sense of my utter confusion to find the earth shifting beneath me once again, spinning me away just as I began to get my balance. When this shift was what I had been taught to expect, my whole life before him.

He kicks me out on a Sunday morning, one month after he invited me in. It is the day before my eighteenth birthday, and the day my lie about my age catches up with me, surprising us both.

'It's my birthday tomorrow,' I tell Mr Jackson, into that place under his arm I fit so perfectly. I lick at the downy hairs of his pit. 'I just remembered.'

We've been living outside of time. I've stopped tracking days. A birthday feels odd to consider, evidence of life going on, when we have retreated so far from the everydayness of it.

'We'll do something special,' he says. 'Oh, to be nineteen again.'

'Mmmm.' I am drowsy, careless. Forgetting my first lie. 'I'm turning eighteen, silly. Don't add another year just yet.'

I don't register at first. The way his body tenses, the way he pulls away from me, his body beginning its retreat. 'Alice.'

'Mmmmmm?'

'*Alice!*'

He is gripping my shoulders now, his knuckles turning red. Something is charging under his skin.

'What? Ouch. That hurts, Mr — Jamie! Why are you looking at me like that?'

'Alice,' he says my name slowly. 'Alice, how old are you?'

'Huh?'

'How old are you!'

It is no longer a question, but a command. How could I have thought I had any power over this man.

'I . . . I'll be eighteen. Tomorrow.'

He looks at me for a second, and then he is up out of bed and across the room before I understand what is happening.

'Fuck. Fuck. *Fuuuuuck*. Jesus Christ, Alice. You're fucking seventeen?'

'Yes? Why — '

'I took pictures of you! I filmed you!'

He hurls these words across the room at me, looking like he's going to be sick, and I still don't fully comprehend what is going on, why my birthday has caused such a panicked reaction. Then slowly, up through the fog of my brain, I hear Tammy's voice the last time we spoke, the way she called me jailbait, and I cannot believe I never considered this. The girl so obsessed with the freedom that comes from turning eighteen should never have missed what she was not considered free of, all the days before.

'Jamie, I'm sorry. I thought you knew. And it doesn't matter. I mean, I said yes. It was my choice. It wasn't . . . you didn't . . . '

That strange, unrecognisable look has solidified, he is now staring at me as if he has never seen me before.

'Jesus Christ! I could go to jail for this.'

'No! I would never. It would never — '

'You have to go!'

He is pacing the room now, shouting.

'No, Jamie. Don't be silly. It's just one more day and we'll be fine. Just one more day and — '

'Shut up, just shut the fuck up. Get away from me, you stupid little cunt!'

These are the ugliest words he has ever said to me, worse than anything I could have imagined, and when he does not come to comfort me, I know that he means them. I say *Sorry!* over and over, but he has already left the room, I can hear him fumbling for his car keys in the hall.

'You need to be gone by the time I get back, Alice.'

Mr Jackson says this from the front door, and then I hear t open and slam shut behind him. His car revs, skids from the driveway. And I am, once again, on my own.

★   ★   ★

My chest is caving in.

He knows I have nowhere to go. He invited me in, with no real intention of letting me stay. Anger rises up in my throat each time I think of what he offered me, what he held back. This righteousness is a brief respite, before I throw up my sadness all over again.

88

I can't go back to Gloria's. She texted the other day to say she was out of town for the week. When I get home, we'll need to talk about your plans, she ended the message, and I knew what that meant: she was expecting me to leave after my birthday. *I'm going to stay up here with Tammy through the spring*, I had texted back, thinking I was creating space for Mr Jackson and me. *I'll let you know when I'm back in town.* Her Cool in response was enough for me to know that she wouldn't bother checking up on me. As for Tammy, we haven't spoken since she called me jailbait, outside of a few text messages we each take a little too long to respond to. I've been preoccupied with Mr Jackson, and she will no doubt have been busy monitoring her father's sobriety, and keeping her boyfriend Rye on the straight and narrow; I can see her drinking vodka from a can and rolling her messy smokes, as they huddle together by the water, inhaling harder stuff than whatever she could get hold of back home. I know she is as happy as she expects to be, which makes me happy for her.

I want more.

What I need then, if I want to get out of this town once and for all, is money. I can't believe I let Mr Jackson distract me from the only thing I knew for sure.

I make a decision that will change my life. Quickly, and with the clarity necessity brings. Going to where Mr Jackson hides the cash he makes from selling his art, I grab every last bill stuffed in that old film canister. Next, I throw my clothes into the duffel bags I brought over from Gloria's, just the clean stuff. I know I have left underwear and T-shirts in the bathroom, and I am glad. I want there to be evidence I was here. He will have to consciously discard this proof of me.

He'll have to know what he's doing as he scoops up my belongings, throws them in the trash. To consider his discomfort at this task is a small satisfaction, like an ice cube on a sting.

I have almost shut the door to his house behind me, locked myself out, when I turn back. There is something I want to take with me. A gap I want to create in his world. When I lift it from the box, the Leica is lighter than I expected it to be. Having never held it before, it feels even more precious in my hands.

It was his mother's camera. I know what this loss will mean to Mr Jackson, and my small satisfaction expands and bursts in my chest. There should be consequences when you hurt someone. I want him to know that I do not care for him, for his art, any more. He has shown me who he is, and now I will show him the real me, too.

I close my fist around the money. Press the Leica against my chest. A slut. A thief. A liar. Mr Jackson can cast me any way he likes from here. Because I know what I am. I am a survivor. I will turn eighteen years old tomorrow, and I am leaving on my own terms. Nothing — no one — can hold me back now.

Ruby Jones is telling herself this very thing as she weighs her suitcases at the airline counter in Melbourne, scans her passport, prepares to board her flight to New York City.

I'm ready, she thinks, for whatever comes next.

This optimism, despite everything that came before, is how I know she understands. That if you tell yourself a lie enough times over, you eventually come to believe it.

Eight

After that night with the boy on the ground, things feel different.

It isn't that I think the sky will fall. Or that I wouldn't know what to do if it did. You should understand that I'm still sure of myself at this point. But I was just starting to feel safe, starting to forget. Which is all that safety is, right? A forgetting of what you know. A refusal to remember bad things are only ever just around the corner.

Your days are numbered. Blood-red, leaking down tunnel walls. It felt like a warning, that subway graffiti. A reminder. Before New York, before Noah, I never truly believed I'd be safe.

Do you know how aware we have to be? Girls like me. The man ahead who slows down, who disappears into doorways. The man close behind who walks too fast, his encroachment felt on your skin, creeping. Vans with dark windows and streets with alleyways. A park at dusk, or empty lots, eerie, any old time of the day. The friend's father whose hand lingers, or the group of boys with beer on their breath. The door closing and the room spinning.

Do you know how aware we have to be?

Did that kid on the ground ever feel safe? Did he have a small life before something turned, twisted, and he became the kind of person others would step around? Did anyone hug him, love him, miss him when he was gone? There is darkness over my days now, a kind of cloud, and it isn't just the rain, or the fact that Mr Jackson has never tried to call me, or that no one at all seems to care that I'm gone. It's the record scratch of my new life. Baby Joan skips across flooded streets, takes photos of crowned buildings, collects facts about sirens and churches and stars. She walks other people's dogs and two days ago, when one of the dogs stopped to pee, she found herself out front of a photography school. Three blocks from Noah's apartment, with a sign on the door saying late spring classes were starting soon. She has flyers for the school on her bedside table, and she has Noah. And there, the scratch, the glitch. Once again, just like my mother, my life has grown up around a person, one person, who could get tired of me anytime, could ask me to leave. And then I would be alone again. Homeless, penniless and parentless, destined for street corners and coins thrown into coffee cups, and signs asking strangers for food. Can I — would I — survive another loss so soon?

I sit three days with these thoughts, my fears growing hot, until Noah is convinced I have a fever.

'You haven't been yourself,' he says at dinner, as if we have known each other for months instead of weeks. 'Do we need to take you to a doctor, Alice?'

The 'we' sounds out across the table, the simple promise of it. I feel a cool hand at my forehead. Perhaps he is not like the others. I need to know.

'Noah.' I look at my accidental benefactor sitting across from me, our mosaic of IOUs visible behind him. 'Why do you have people come stay with you?'

Franklin skulks at my feet, licks my bare ankle.

'I don't, usually,' Noah answers after a time. His smile is small, wry. 'Most times, Alice, people would show up at the door and I would turn them away. I even paid one or two to leave — for their troubles.'

'Oh!'

I see myself at the door that first night, bags and camera and hopefulness hanging off me, and watch as the door clicks shut in front of me. No blue eye, no bay windows or piano, or Franklin, knocking against my knees. Turning with my six hundred dollars in cash towards — what?

'I have so much, you see,' Noah continues, opening out his hands towards me, 'and I had a thought that someone else might need a little of it. However' — he brings his hands back together now, clasps them — 'the people who showed up were never quite what I had in mind.'

'But you made it so easy for me,' I push. 'No references needed, no credit card deposit like all the others asked for. You must have known someone like me would come along.'

'Indeed,' Noah sighs, his expression inscrutable. 'I suppose, Baby Joan . . . you were what I had in mind.'

Then, much more quietly, so I am not sure I hear him correctly.

'To be precise, you reminded me of a girl I once knew.'

Later, I will understand that when he opened the door to me, Noah thought, suddenly, of an open, eager face so oddly like his own. His one improbable, glorious attempt at immortality, many years ago. A girl gone to the other side of the world while still a child, address long since lost. For a time, before, the child used to visit with her mother. They would show up unannounced one day or another and she would clunk down on the piano, and he would give money to the woman for clothes, school, holidays. No room, no desire for a family back then, but he had reserved a pocket of himself for the girl, and when they went away so suddenly, the girl left an echo, an emptiness around what might have been. No life is without secrets, without doors closed. When I showed up at Noah's front door — young, dirty, hopeful — things inched open again.

Of course, he doesn't say this tonight. He merely makes to tip his cap at me, his smile widening to meet mine across the table.

I breathe.

'Not to mention the fact, Baby Joan, you clearly had nowhere else to go.'

★ ★ ★

Lucy Lutens wants us to throw a birthday party for her anxious Schnauzer, Donut. 'Nothing over the top, just cake and those tiny hats, and perhaps you could send me a few snaps of the festivities!' She has never missed his birthday before, but her cousin is getting married in Maine, and really, her own mother missed almost every birthday she ever had, and she turned out *just fine*, didn't she?

I am in the kitchen, listening through the wall to this woman's nervous chitter. I never meet with the clients — 'We don't want any unnecessary questions,' Noah said when I first started working — but I feel like I could match owner to dog all the same; it's as if the animal becomes a mirror of the person, picking up all their quirks and emotional ticks. Franklin for instance, is watchful. Attentive from a distance like Noah is, and then he will surprise me with a gesture that feels like affection. A wet nose against my ankle, or a nudge of his head against my leg. Just a brief touch, and then he's back to his side of the room. Lucy Lutens' dog is definitely not fine. Donut is skittery with other dogs, and resentful of me, as if it's my fault whenever Lucy leaves him. He sits at the door after she goes, little whining noises trembling out of his body, and when he has convinced himself she is never, ever coming back he puts his face against his paws and refuses to look at me for the rest of the day.

Noah says dogs produce the same kinds of emotions us humans do, but they think like a three — or four-year-old at best. 'Imagine yourself at your most vulnerable,' he once explained. 'When you feel more than you can ever make sense of feeling. That's a dog's reality, every day.'

It makes me think about what I was like at four years old. I don't remember being in my own skin, looking out at the world, but I do sometimes see myself at that age. I think you generally experience memories in this way, from the outside in, like your old life is a movie you once starred in. But sometimes something bad happens, something bad enough to make it feel like you're perpetually looking out from that bad thing, living inside it, instead of watching the movie version. Then, it gets hard to tell what's real and what's not. Noah said you can try to tap those kinds of memories out, shake them loose. 'But wouldn't that just leave you with a body full of holes?' I asked him, and he laughed at that, but not unkindly, and the next day he left a book about something called EFT on my pillow. Unfortunately, the book had a picture of a nebula on its cover, so I put the book in my closet, cover facing the floor, and never looked at it again.

Anyway, nothing so bad happened to me at four years old. Not that I know of, and I feel certain I would remember. Something better to think about: could you match the kid to the mom, the way I can match dog to owner? How did that small girl mirror her mother back then? Was I always looking for someone to love me, pay attention to me, see me? It is strange that I cannot really know this baby Alice. My clear memories — moving so often, starting at yet another school, the men always hovering — it's an older Alice who experienced those things, stored them up. Was little Alice waiting at locked doors, too? Pining like Donut does, for a woman who always, eventually, came back?

Sometimes I wish Noah didn't tell me all the things he tells me.

Only sometimes.

'I've never had a birthday party,' I confess when Lucy finally leaves, Donut collapsing into grief at the door. 'My mother liked to pretend birthdays never happened.'

If this surprises Noah, he doesn't show it. I think I would be surprised if someone told me they'd never had a birthday party. I might even be a bit sad about it. But he merely shrugs.

'Would you like to have one?'

'A birthday *paaaaarty*?'

'Yes, Alice. A birthday *paaaaarty*. Would you like to have one? Not experiencing something doesn't necessarily equate to a desire for that experience.'

I have come to appreciate the way Noah makes things I've never even considered seem obvious. I guess that's why I never feel offended when he talks to me this way.

I think about his question for a minute, really think about it.

'I would,' I finally answer, as new visions, possibilities bubble to the surface. 'I would like to have a birthday party at the very top of the Chrysler Building. I would wear a silver dress, and I would serve Manhattans in fancy glasses, and there would be balloons filled with glitter everywhere. People would pop them over me as I walked past, so that I would be super shiny, all night long.'

'Specific,' he says, with that small smile of his, before turning back to the day and the dogs. Leaving my birthday fantasy to glimmer, and then fade. But not before I've preserved the idea of it, like a memory of something that actually happened.

It is a measure of Noah's growing affection that he resists the urge to tell me how the insides of the Chrysler Building spire are in fact nothing more than a mass of concrete and electrical wires, an ugly series of crawl spaces that look nothing like its glittering façade. Nor does he mention the fact that, technically, I have no friends in New York City. No one to invite to my party. So that any balloons tied to the maze of rough cement inside the spire would remain intact, untouched, as I walked underneath them. Glitter floating inside, and me on the outside, looking up, looking in.

A nice but preposterous idea. Girls like me don't get fancy birthday parties. I turned eighteen years old on an interstate bus. The click of numbers on a clock, and I was born this many years ago. Never knowing what my mother thought as we were wrenched apart for the very first time.

Not knowing, either, what she thought when we were separated for the last time.

* ★ ★

A memory of my mother and me. She is in the bath-tub, a towel twisted around her head like a turban. She's laughing as she flicks soapy water at me, puts her hands out for me to join her. I slip into the warm water, lean back as she begins to wash my hair, her long fingers kneading my scalp. Balls of light, tiny planets, dance in front of my eyes as she moves her hands against my small head, and I feel the flesh of her, the fullness of my mother, against my back. 'You're my baby,' she whispers, and this is what I remember, even if I am never sure it happened that way. Even if this was only ever a movie. Starring someone else entirely.

★ ★ ★

Of course he does.

He throws me a birthday party at the top of the Chrysler Building.

I come back from playing with Franklin in River-side Park just as the sun starts to settle on the Hudson River. It is the end of my third week in the city, and the living room is filled with floating silver and white balloons. Propped against the window is a person-high cardboard print showing an aerial view of Mid-town Manhattan on a rainy, yellow-gold night. I am handed a reddish-brown drink in a sparkling glass, a dark cherry bobbing across the surface. It tastes like an idea I have yet to understand, a promise of adult-hood, rolled around in my mouth.

'To your first Manhattan,' Noah says, and we clink glasses, and though I am not showered with glitter, I gleam all the same.

'Happy Birthday, Alice.'

How strange to think I will never hear those words again.

★   ★   ★

We are drunk. Or I am. Three Manhattans in a row, poured from a crystal decanter, sat on top of the piano. I have saved every cherry, and now I bite into one, dark red juice trickling from the side of my mouth. It tastes sweet and bitter on my tongue and I understand this is a different drunk to anything I have experienced before. I am languid — I think that's the right word. Heavy. But not stuck. Clutched in my left hand is a cheque, made out to that little photography school around the corner.

'Enrolment fees,' Noah explained when I opened the envelope he gave me, the thin piece of paper falling into my ap. 'I can't have you hanging around the house for ever, Baby Joan.'

The cheque feels like a key to a brand-new door. I see myself in the summer, walking up the front steps of the school, see myself entering the building each day, ready for class. I imagine myself growing more and more familiar with this world as the days pass, and if I squint just so, I can even see that future me eating lunch with her friends, using the darkroom to complete her latest assignment, showing newer students how to find classroom B.

'Noah . . . ' I want to tell him about this older me. I want to express how strange and wonderful the idea of a future is. I want to thank him for making it possible, making her possible. I want him to know that, before, offers only ever came with strings. Conditions.

I was always counting down to the end of something, to when it would be taken away. And I want to tell him that I still don't understand why he would do all of this for me. A girl he met just weeks ago.

'Noah. Who were you before?'

Aren't all the answers found in the past?

'Before you?' he clarifies, putting his own Manhattan down.

'Well yes, before me. But I don't mean that exactly. I mean what was your life when you were young. When you were eighteen, like me.'

Noah tells me he was born across the river. Hoboken, a name that sounds to me like a candy bar, something soft, with a hard crunch in the middle.

'Baby Joan, you may have just perfectly described my adolescence', he says, smiling into the past, seeing his life in reverse, so that his mouth changes on the journey, falters at the corners until I can no longer tell if he is amused or sad.

'I wanted to escape. Much like you did. Only I had a smaller journey to make. I spent my whole youth looking across the river; Manhattan was my north star. I lived, until I arrived here, always wanting to be somewhere else.'

'Tell me about New York back then,' I say, because I want him to keep talking, and I have learnt he often shares pieces of himself inside other truths. Somewhere in the Manhattan of his youth, I will find the man he is now, and why he has chosen to help me.

'Back then, New York was still an idea. The best idea this country ever had. Now, it's more like a crass reality show. The streets have been cleaned up, the tourists come and come and come, there are half-empty apartment buildings right there in Midtown, whole blocks of concrete owned by people who will never live here, keeping their multi-million dollar condos just in case they visit sometime. In the seventies, you didn't visit New York. You lived here. You escaped whatever life your parents had made for you, and you landed in a place asking only that you live in it, make of it for yourself.'

I could listen to Noah talk like this for a year.

'I lived in the Village. Dirty beds, dirty bars, while my parents tried to wash things clean back home. It was dangerous and thrilling and a whole world in and of itself, a city perpetually in motion, and always outdoing itself. I watched those towers go up, they were monstrosities really, but I never minded them, because they reminded me of two giant fingers giving the up to everyone. I lived like that myself at the time, sure of myself and a little crass. I had a lot of friends, and then I didn't, because the eighties came, and people around me started to die. Lovers, friends, the boy genius who lived in the next apartment. They died, and the city lived, and it changed, because surviving changes everything.'

(This, I know.)

'The city kept moving. I kept moving. New York is made for second chances, Alice. I eventually met someone who knew someone who knew someone, and they introduced me to money. I made a lot of it. Sent it back across the river to my parents. Bought this place cheap from a man who recognised me from my life before. Even when I didn't recognise myself.'

'And the girl I remind you of?' I ask into the silence that follows, feeling we are coming closer to the story now. This night, the Manhattans, have loosened something.

'Ah, yes. Part of my life on the straight and narrow. A remnant if you will. My daughter would be' — he counts on his fingers, a whole life in his calcula- tion — 'in her mid-thirties, now. Hard to imagine. Half of this life of mine lived over again. I hurt her mother very much, the way you can really hurt some- one, which is to not love them the way you said you would. So, she left. Took the kid overseas, and my apology for the complication of my orientation was to let them go, no strings, no ties, no questions asked.'

Noah opens the door and I am standing there with my bags. A little girl turns to see her father one last time. Leaving, and never imagining she won't ever return to the house with the piano, and the chande- lier, will never again see the man who always talks to her as if he is reading her a story. You can't know how far some goodbyes will take you.

'Do you regret that?' I ask. 'How big your sorry turned out to be?'

Noah tells me he has many, many regrets. That any- one who says otherwise has not lived long enough, or they've simply lived too long to remember the truth of things. And yes, he regrets not knowing his child, not getting to see her grow up. More so now, for get- ting to know me.

'I don't know my father,' I say, wanting to stitch back together the small hole I have opened. 'He's somewhere here in New York. At least I think he is. I know nothing about him, except that he was a pho- tographer, too.'

'Is that why you came here? To find your father?' Noah asks, and I sense he is mapping out another daughter's journey home. 'No,' I answer honestly, though I wish, for his sake, I knew how to lie to him. 'I don't really think about him. Not in that way. He probably never even knew about me, to be honest. My mom could be like that. I just sort of learnt to deal with his absence, you know, until I didn't notice it anymore. There was no point wishing for what I couldn't have.'

Later, the simple absurdity of this sentence will reveal itself. I will come to understand that wishing for what you can't have is a desire strong enough to compel the dead.

'We're a pair,' I say suddenly, on this night when I still have so much to learn, the tang of the Manhattans now an echo in my mouth. 'Daughterless father, fatherless daughter. If life were a movie, you would suddenly need a kidney, and we would find out — *Ah!* — that you're actually my dad. Wouldn't that be something, Noah. Me showing up on your doorstep, and it turns out it wasn't an accident. That all along, I was meant to find you.'

I crush another soaked cherry against my teeth, grin red at him.

'Lord help me,' Noah says in mock horror, 'should I find myself responsible for a feral child like you!'

In the next room, on the refrigerator door, the IOUs flutter. Post-it notes documenting my debts. Sneakers. Jacket. Subway fare. And some notes I have added while Noah is not paying attention. There are actually quite a few of these other IOUs collected there now, little messages I've left for him, and I don't know if he ever looks, but the ones I've snuck into the pile say: *Friendship. Loyalty. Safety.* Things like that.

Things I can pay him back sometime.

Because I still think I'm going to make it. On this

night of my very first birthday party. I still think there will be a summer and school and people to eat lunch with, me sitting there at the centre of things, laughing, telling stories, making plans. New friendships will grow up around me, a wild garden of them, and when I call Tammy to tell her all about it, it won't matter that we let so many weeks go by without talking. She'll be so happy to hear what I've been doing, where I am, that she'll forgive me for not telling her sooner. 'You did it, Alice,' she'll say. 'You made a life for yourself!' But I'll know who really made that life happen, the person I owe it all to. Tonight, at my party, I never doubt there will be enough time to pay Noah back for everything he's done for me.

Because even when I'm in my mid-thirties, as old as the daughter he said goodbye to, I'll still have so many years left. I won't even be close to those 79.1 years promised to me. I'll be a famous photographer by then, they'll hang my pictures in galleries around the city, put them on the covers of magazines. And I'll look after Noah, the way he looked after me. I'll be the one to keep *him* safe this time. We have so much ahead of us to be thankful for.

To imagine it any other way would break my heart in two.

★　★　★

I suppose I let my guard down. At the end. When the sky actually did fall. The crack, and the flash of light, and the wet like rain. Air heavy like a boot on my chest. Dirt, and metal and being pushed down, down into the earth. It surprised me. The shock of how little you can mean to another person. How an entire world can be discarded so quickly. I was right to think I would never be safe, that I needed to be wary.

But it still surprised me. At the end.

9

Tomorrow, I will be dead. On this day before I die, where do you want to start? What would you like to look at first? I get up, I have sleep in my eye. I make a pot of coffee, the water hisses over onto the element, spits at me. I can't get the water temperature right in the shower. Sometimes I think the faucets are switched from day to day, just to confuse me. I eat a banana, the texture struggling in my mouth. I step around dog toys, kick them into the corner of the living room, and open the window to the day. The street is its usual mix of bloated rubbish bags and metal frames. You could swing down them, if they didn't always seem on the verge of collapse. The sky is blue, later it will rain again. There is dog hair creeping across my big toe. The day is light, bright, ordinary.

I get up. I have sleep in my eye. Make coffee, water hissing. Temperature wrong. Banana slick on my tongue, and the squeak of a rubber bone. Rubbish bags and metal and blue, blue sky. Rain coming. Dog hair itching my toe. The day is light, bright, extraordinary.

The morning passes. Neither slow nor fast. It just passes. I have had near on a month of these mornings and I am used to them now, accustomed. I make a cheese sandwich, leave the plate and knife in the sink next to my coffee mug. I should do more to help out with keeping the place clean, I think. I must not forget to show how grateful I am. I press down on another Post-it note and write the word *Help*, before a large bang outside startles me. My 'p' wobbles, shoots off the yellow paper as I drop my pen. I had intended to write: *Help more around the apartment* but the pen has rolled under the table now, and I cannot be bothered bending down to find it. *Help* will do, I think, smiling, as I post my final fluttering debt on the refrigerator door. This last light, bright morning of my life.

★ ★ ★

On this last, bright morning of my life, Ruby Jones looks out the window. Wrinkles her nose at the black garbage bags lining the street, piled one on top of the other. She imagines the smell of the rotting vegetables and soiled nappies, though the only scent in her room is the vague, musky remnant of her designer candle. She can see a lane of sky made between her building and the apartment opposite. Blue. No rain, but it is coming this afternoon, they say. The promise too, of a warm summer ahead, once they get past this temperamental spring. Meteorological broadcasts from a future, already laid out.

(They are right, by the way.)

She too has an unthinking routine on this last morning. Downstairs for coffee, back up to her room for a shower. Shoes on for a run, some stretches, and down to Riverside Park for a change of scenery, terrain shifting under her feet from street, to canopied path, to the pier. Listening to loud music through her headphones, trying to outrun the beat of her thoughts.

Ash hasn't mentioned coming to visit.

Not since he told her he might come to New York, and she waited hours before replying — *I would love that!* — and soon enough they were talking about

107

other things, and she couldn't, wouldn't ask him about his plans, until a week had passed, and then another. Until her first month in New York was nearly over. A whole month, and still, Ash remained the lump in her throat, the ache in her bones. That was not supposed to happen.

There are things Ruby has tried to do, remedies she's sought. Like downloading a dating app and engaging in tentative conversations with a few of the men who responded to her profile. One man, a Financial Manager living in Chelsea, seemed pleasant enough, until he sent explicit pictures of himself in the middle of an afternoon, asking *Can you handle this?* as if they hadn't just been talking about getting tickets to a baseball game. Ruby blocked him immediately, before shutting down her new profile completely, her cheeks hot with embarrassment, and not a little alarm. She had been this close to asking him to meet her for a drink. The unwanted pictures felt aggressive, sinister even. Would this Financial Manager have been the same way in person? New to online dating, Ruby had no idea whether this kind of behaviour was the norm these days. Perhaps she was supposed to laugh it off or admire the guy's misdirected confidence. It didn't make her feel like laughing, though. The whole episode made her feel queasy, and then sad. Ruby had been looking for a reprieve from Ash, a chance to replace the almost of their relationship with something present, real. Instead, she found herself longing for him more than ever, for an intimacy already mapped out.

That was not supposed to happen.

Scratching the navigation of strangers and dating off her list, Ruby kept on running. She started a daily journal. Wary of the words that tumbled out, embarrassed to see her heartache spread naked across its pages each morning, she discarded the journal five days later. She took herself to a talk on self-actualisation at 92Y, and another on guided meditation at ABC Carpet & Home, and she spent afternoons reading or people-watching from the damp wooden benches of the High Line. No longer a tourist exactly, Ruby spent the last days of my life trying on a different New York, and a different version of herself. Nothing worked, of course; anything she tried felt like a misstep, like she was still running the wrong way. Loneliness is disorienting like that; with Ash as her only lodestar, Ruby continued to feel utterly lost.

(She still has no idea where she is headed, the story that awaits her. But she's so close now. We're almost there.)

This morning, this very last morning, she is trying — and failing — not to think about her failures, or about Ash. She thuds past boats bobbing on the water as she follows the Hudson River south, before turning and heading up and out of Riverside Park. She relishes the burn of her calves as she takes the concrete steps to the upper levels, two at a time. Ruby has come to appreciate this park, with its statues and boats and wide ribbon of water. There is space here to stretch out, no need to check your speed against the person in front of you; she decides this will be where she exercises from now on.

(There's Noah, walking the dogs along the upper levels as she runs. He loves this park, too.)

Back in her room, flush from her run, Ruby grabs her phone and sends an impulsive SOS. Types out the sentence that has been swimming in her head for days.

Am I going to lose you, Ash?

His response comes back almost immediately.

Not at all. It's just getting harder to respond these days. So busy. See you soon!

Then five minutes later:

Maybe.

Something bristles in Ruby. Perhaps it's the post-run endorphins, her perception of pain reduced. A passive dismissal that might normally hurt her turns her top lip to a snarl instead. Despite her best efforts at distraction, she hasn't been able to stop herself dreaming about Ash coming to visit in the summer, imagining the dark bars she would take him to, the jazz clubs, the train ride to Rockaway for a day on the beach. The simplest of somethings they could experience together. She has let her mind wander to arms linked, necks kissed, and yes, the nights in bed. Hands over lips, gasps silent against these thin walls. Fingers tracing the bedhead, scratching, the way she would come against his mouth. Perhaps they'd never even make it to the bars and the clubs and the beach. *Maybe.*

How stupid can she be? Taking one message and spinning up a biography in this way. She rereads all of his old texts now. Paces her small room like a lioness, frustration growing. *It's getting harder to respond.* No! How pathetic can she be? Feeding on every *maybe* and *not at all*, feasting on scraps. He is not too busy to respond. He has no doubt made himself available to other people today, turning this way and that to give them whatever they need of him. Never what she needs of him, ever. In this sudden blistering rage at her lover, Ruby wants to kick something. She hates him in this moment, as a large raindrop splatters against her window. Slap against glass, slap against reality. Blue skies can disappear so fast.

Perhaps, just a little, Ash hates her, too. Despises her for leading him down a path he cannot find his way back from. Cannot make up for. He forgets all this in her arms, of course, or when he is alone in another wide, clean hotel bed after a conference and he's had one too many wines. In these moments, she is all he can think of. His mistress, the one whose body he has traversed and drowned in and drunk from over and over. Sometimes, the ache for her is no different from thirst or hunger. A primal need for her skin and scent. Other times, like now, when she reveals her neediness, when she sends her flare across the ocean, he wishes she would leave him be, thinks of life before her — and after her, too, if he could just say the words. Why doesn't she understand? Why does she keep coming back for more? She cannot lose him, not when he was never hers to begin with. She's the one who offered herself up. Agreed to their terms. This is not his fault. What is he supposed to do? Break off an engagement to the best woman he's ever known, give up the glorious future ahead of him? If he's honest, that was never going to happen.

If he's honest.

What use is it trying to get into his head, Ruby fumes. As thunder rumbles in the distance, she feels certain Ash has not been honest a single day of his life.

I have left some things out. The days after my birthday party, I begin to relax. Trust. I take more photographs. Spend time with Franklin at his favourite dog run in Riverside Park. Leave a message for the photography school, dog-sit, and write out more IOUs. Soon it will be a full month since I left Wisconsin. I have had two birthdays, and I have plans. I try to call Tammy, something I know I should have done much sooner, but she doesn't answer her phone. I make one other call, heart in my mouth. The school replies to my message and requests a submission, a portfolio of my work that should include, the form says: *A self-portrait, designed to show us the artist you intend to be.* I have taken photographs all over this city, and I have four exposures left. I have plans.

And then, one early morning, it ends. There was an I, and it was me. I was at the centre, looking out. Until someone decided to enter the space I had created for myself, take it over.

You think if you hold on tight enough when things try to pull you away, you can still make it. But then someone else takes up all the room, blocks the view, and suddenly you're pushed right out of your skin.

It's their turn now.

There was an I, and now there is a he, a him, a *his*.

The tip of his cigarette. Vivid red extinguished. The ash falls. Little pieces of burnt snow, drifting. A flutter lands on my shoulder. I go to flick it away. His hand comes down on mine and I —

I don't feel like telling you anything else right now.

10

In the hours before I die, Ruby Jones has slept on her anger and wakes up coated in it. Outside it is raining heavily, but she barely notices the weather. It is 5.55 a.m., early for her, but she is already up, pacing back and forth across the small path made between her desk and the bed. *God, this studio is too small!* Filled up with unnecessary things. She straightens the TV remote, pats down the corners of the bed, shifts her hairbrush to the bedside drawer. Does a 360-degree turn, then removes the hairbrush, turns the remote sideways again.

This is how people go crazy, she thinks. *I need to get out of this room.*

As she puts on her running shoes, Ruby hears a boom of thunder. Or it could be the hard slam of a car door. She strains against the sound and then shrugs. No matter, she's not afraid of a storm. A little rain never hurt anybody.

The street is empty as she exits her building and heads west towards Riverside Park, rain spiking across her face. At the first intersection, already saturated, she considers turning back, then remembers the pacing, the locked-in feeling she's had since yesterday.

'Fuck it!' she shouts out, and waits to cross with the signal, though there are no cars on this part of the road.

There is no one to startle on the street either, no dog walker with their twist of leashes, no nanny carefully guiding a wobbly-legged toddler. As Ruby reaches

Riverside Drive, she finally encounters cars, a row of them stop-starting, gushing by, each one sending up a spray of water as they pass. It is proof, at least, of other people. Even if she is the only one out here running in the rain.

Ruby considers staying on Riverside, but the pavement is narrow, and when car after car sends a muddy shower her way, she pivots and heads into the park. It's darker than she anticipated, the sky looks as if it is closing in around the trees, but she keeps going, sure there will be other runners and cyclists down on the waterfront trail. As she cuts through the upper levels of the park, Ruby searches for the stairs to take her down to the water, but the thick clusters of trees on either side of her don't look like she remembered them to be. Perhaps she has entered at a different spot today. Riverside Park is still new to her, and the weather may have turned her around, somehow. She knows from her maps that the park stretches for blocks, street above, river below, so it's not like she could get lost. She just needs to keep heading south, she tells herself, until she finds a landmark she recognises, something to orient her. Still, she feels a brief flicker of panic.

Thunder claps loudly over her head and Ruby startles, rolls her ankle. Her yelp of pain echoes off the trees as lightning jags across the sky, and she considers giving up, heading home. She is stopped, wiping her eyes and flexing her ankle, when two northbound runners come flying past her. They nod, give her the thumbs up, and she immediately feels foolish for letting her mind run away on her. This is New York, you are never the only one, anywhere!

Feeling less skittery now, Ruby puts her head down

against the rain and charges at it, mud splattering as her feet hit the ground. She finally comes to a set of stairs, steps cut into a sloping, wet bank, so that she has to descend gingerly, careful not to slip on the well-worn stone. There is a short tunnel at the bottom of the stairs, graffiti and old urine staining the damp concrete walls. Emerging from the tunnel onto the waterfront path, she lets out her breath — *Made it!* — and is surprised to discover that, left or right, the path remains empty of people. As lightning shoots above her head, Ruby feels a corresponding flash of alarm, her sense of relief diminishing. There were supposed to be people down here, there are always people down here. How had she not noticed the severity of this storm when she set out?

She stops and leans on a railing at the water's edge, wills herself to calm down. She's not going to last long in New York if she lets a little storm scare her. This is just rain, and some thunder and lightning, and a dumb Australian going for a run when everyone else was smart enough to stay home. Maybe they woke to an emergency message on their phones: *Flash flooding ahead. Stay away from waterways,* then rolled over and went back to sleep. No matter, she's not going to get swept into the murky waters of the Hudson today. *Antipodean jogger drowns* is hardly the way she's going out.

She might freeze to death, however, as ice-cold raindrops run down her neck and soak through her jacket. Pushing away from the rail, Ruby heads towards a pier she can see just ahead. She thinks she remembers stairs just past where all the little boats are docked, a steep set that will take her straight back up to the street, allowing her to avoid the dark thicket of trees

115

she ran through earlier. Calmer now, Ruby gets into a rhythm, watches as her feet slap against the wet path, one stride then the next. To her right, the river makes the same slapping sound against the rocks. Out on the water, boats rise and fall with the wind and waves, and across the river, the lights of New Jersey are filtered through thick, dark clouds. It would be beautiful, she thinks, if she weren't soaked through to the skin. A rare opportunity to have this view to herself.

She is approaching the marina when her foot cracks down on something round and black. She must have come down on whatever it was with her full weight, because bits of plastic scatter across the path. Some random object, meeting its end under her foot, dis-carded — or lost — and now shattered. She hopes it wasn't important, whatever it was, and says a silent sorry to the god of lost things. Running thoughts, she calls this kind of musing. Nonsense passing through her mind, cleaning it out. Already, she is less angry. More herself. Or perhaps, mercifully, less.

It's after passing another cluster of boats and a flooded ramp — rain falling, river rising — that Ruby notices her access to the upper level of the park is now completely blocked off by a tall chain-link fence to her left, running parallel to the water. She's obviously come further south this morning than she realised, to a part of the park under construction, and now her planned exit is somewhere behind that fence. She is going to have to turn back after all.

Fuck.

Another clap of thunder, a flash of lightning even closer this time. Lights pulse across the river and the yellowed windows of the buildings on the oppo-site bank go dark, like candles blown out. The rain is now coming down in one solid sheet, and it's so cold Ruby can see her breath, ghosts floating before her with every exhale. She has little visibility beyond these apparitions, and she stops to get her bearings, wipes the rain from her face. She can just about see a burnt, black structure out there in the water, behind an uneven row of thick wood posts, partially submerged. This part of the running trail is suspended over the river; just ahead, the track winds back from the shoreline before pushing outward again, creating a small u-shaped beach of moss-slimed rocks and rubbish below her. High above, cars swoosh by on the sodden, concrete freeway, but down here: no one.

Reaching for the railing directly in front of her, Ruby bends, takes a few deep breaths. It is when she straightens up and prepares to kick off that she sees it. Across the tumble of wet stone and weeds, no more than six or seven metres from where she is standing, there is something purple laid out on the rocks, right where the water slaps up against them. As Ruby squints through the rain she sees something else flow out from the purple, yellow reeds, rising and falling with the river.

There is bright orange too, glints of it, and as Ruby blinks through the rain and tries to focus, she understands she is looking across the rocks at fingernails, and a hand, and the yellow is hair, and she knows she is looking at a young girl's body before she feels it, before her heart punches hard in her chest, and her legs threaten to give way underneath her.

'Hey.'

Ruby doesn't know if it's a whisper or a shout.

'*Hey!*'

It's more like a cry this time, something hoarse and

desperate. Face down at the water's edge, the girl does not turn over.

Ruby is not close enough to see whether the girl is breathing. As her heart starts to sound in her ears, she makes to climb over the railing, but her foot slips on the wet, her shin cracking down on hard metal. Electric blues and greens flash behind her eyes as she stumbles back, almost falls over. Still, the girl doesn't move. Trying to ignore the pulsing pain in her leg, panic rising until she can taste it, Ruby pulls her phone from her vest pocket. Her hands are shaking so much, she hits the wrong numbers on her pass code three times over before the screen unlocks.

911. That's the number you call, right? She needs someone to tell her what to do.

'Hello? Yes. I think. Help. I can see someone by the water . . . there's a girl, and she's not moving. I think . . . I think she's not okay. I don't know what to do. Hello? Yes. *Please* — I think she's hurt. I don't know if I should go to her. Should I go to her? Please. Tell me what to do.

'She's not moving. She's not responding. She's not turning over. Please! I'm not close enough to see if she's breathing. Tell me what I need to do.'

Please.

★ ★ ★

She's not close enough. To see that I'm not breathing.

Standing across from my body. All that murky water in my mouth, in my lungs. Stripped below the waist, blood matting my hair. Left on the rocks to flail like a fish, until I stopped moving, eventually. Pulled away, mercifully, as he plunged in. And now a stranger is looking at my dead body. Now we're both scrambling to understand what it is we're seeing. What it is that's been done to me.

I now know that you can cry, scream, howl like the wounded animal you are. And they do not stop. It does not move them. They keep going until there is nothing left, until you are broken apart, obliterated.

Almost like you were never really there at all.

Ruby Jones is my only witness. I understand this suddenly, explicitly, and I grasp at this singular certainty, feel my way along it, until I find myself standing next to her, there on the waterfront path. She couldn't get to me, but somehow, some way, I make my way to her. I am in awe as I reach out to Ruby, but my fingertips turn to rain, drip down her cheek, and a second truth claps itself out above us:

She can only see the husk of me, left down on the rocks.

Turns out you have to learn how to see a dead girl. To recognise her. For now, I can do nothing but wait, terrified, beside this shivering stranger. Knowing she won't be able to feel my presence, find me for a second time, until she is ready to see what everyone else has missed.

★ ★ ★

Ruby is wrapped in something silver. Two kindly police officers keep calling her *Ma'am* as they take turns with their questions, pressing gently against her confusion. She is trying to cooperate, trying to swim up through her cold, saturated brain, but her eyes keep going to their belts, to the thick, black weapons heavy like rocks. Thinking how easy it might be for

119

someone to reach over and pull one free, grasp a gun or baton and —

She closes her eyes and metal comes down against her skull, smashes through skin and bone, breaks her into a thousand little pieces. She sees blood. Exploding. But it's just the sirens flashing, and the yellow of a girl's hair, and the slow, steady stream of uniforms making their way down to the river. She was moved away from the water once the forensics team arrived, but Ruby can still see the rush of activity down there, watch, as they make a crime scene of the body.

She feels like she's going to be sick.

The officers are staring at her; Ruby's hand has gone to her mouth. There is metal on her tongue, and it tastes like a gun, the cool, hard sensation of a barrel pushed against her face. Like a fist.

She doubles over and throws up on the gravel.

'Ma'am. Are you okay, ma'am? Can we get you some water, ma'am?'

And the questions stop as someone pats Ruby's shoulder, the female police officer perhaps, though Ruby cannot be sure, because rain and tears have blurred everything now.

'Did you notice anything just before you saw her? Did you see anyone strange in the area? Did anything seem out of place?'

That's what they kept asking her when they first came down to the river. And she's said *no, yes, um* to all variations of these questions, leaving a useless trail of words between her and these people trying to help, because she saw nothing. There was nothing. There was just the rain closing in, and the river churning, and the place she stopped to breathe, before turning for home.

'What's going to happen to her?'

Her one question for them. Left unanswered as she shivers in her silver wrap and another siren keens its way towards the river.

★ ★ ★

Later, Ruby sits on the tiled floor of her shower, water hitting her shoulders, spraying over her skin. She watches as this water pools at her knees. Tries to think of anything but this morning. If she closes her eyes, she's immediately back there, and the water trickling over her body turns red, covers her in thick, congealed blood. They think she didn't see; they think she had been moved far enough away from the water, but when my body was turned over, there was bright red at my right temple, or where my temple should have been. Ruby wasn't supposed to see my face, but those nice police officers were still asking her questions as the others got to work, the ones who lifted the caution tape with their gloved hands, darting under and around it, as if they did this all the time.

She knows she wasn't supposed to see that my face had been smashed in.

(What she doesn't know. In that moment, I looked just like my mother. That pretty, destroyed face of hers when I found her on the kitchen floor. *I'm sorry*, I want to say, the first of many times, for all the things Ruby will have to deal with now. I know what it's like for the horror to follow you home.)

Ruby was taken back to her apartment in a squad car; she sat in the back and apologised for dripping rainwater onto the seat, and tried not to cry when Smith, the female officer, assured her she'd done a great job today. 'Truly, you did everything right, Ruby,' Officer Jennings agreed over his shoulder. Ruby had been so relieved to see their flashing lights approach, to hear the sirens as they got closer. She doesn't know how long she was alone by the river before they arrived. Five minutes, maybe a little more. She spent that time sitting, standing, crouching, her phone pressed to her ear, a stranger's voice on the end of the line telling her to stay calm, reminding her that help was on its way. Ruby paced in the smallest circles throughout the call, trying not to look across the water. Careful not to touch or move anything around her.

'Keep as still as you can,' they said on the phone. And she knew what they meant by that.

Someone was there before you, Ruby. Please don't disturb anything they left behind.

They left behind a girl in a purple T-shirt. Face down on the rocks. And it was clear someone hurt the girl, someone did this to her. And maybe, it occurs to Ruby, that someone was still there in the park, watching as she waited for the police to arrive. Maybe that someone heard her stumble as she tried to explain where she was, where the body was in relation to her. When she couldn't give street names or directions, could only look around and describe her surroundings, trying, desperately, to give the police the help they needed to find her.

'There's an overpass. I passed the boats. There are wooden posts sticking out of the water. There's a road above us. I can't see any signs. I was trying to find a way out!'

Maybe this someone was watching Ruby the whole time, or maybe they were already long gone, and the girl had been dead for hours. Nobody said. How did the girl get down to the water's edge, anyway? Ruby had hurt herself trying to climb over the railing, she saw the investigators scrambling too, slipping on the wet rocks, struggling to find their footing as they approached the body. Was the girl already down by the water when she was killed, or did someone drag her off the walkway and throw her over the railing? How strong would you have to be to do that?

Why would anybody do that?

(We both ask this question over and over.)

The shower has been running so long that the water has gone cold, and Ruby makes herself think of Ash, heads for the only loop in her mind that feels familiar, her one reliable distraction. Remembering when she last saw him in person, she tries to focus on something alive and breathing and real. She has to think of Ash, or the heaving, bone-shaking sobs will start again, the ones that felled her when she first stood under this shower in her muddy running clothes, the water so hot it stung all over. Ruby's hands were trembling so badly she couldn't get them to cooperate, couldn't make her fingers unclasp her bra, or lift her saturated top over her head. As she struggled to undress, the hot, hot water needled at her newly exposed skin, and the sobbing came up out of her as a howl. Something animal and angry, something rage-filled, until it all emptied out, and Ruby was left sitting naked on the shower tiles, hyperventilating. It was as if she couldn't remember how to breathe. She kept seeing the body, kept feeling the terror of waiting out there alone, with that yellow hair swirling in the water, sky thundering above her. And then, just as suddenly as the crying hit, Ruby clicked over into a kind of numbness, found an empty space behind her eyes she had never known was there, a place where she could stare, unblinking, letting the water cool over her. Just so she could tremble in a different way.

Better to think about Ash, about the mess her life is in, because she can control that, she can live inside a comprehensible drama. She can be *that* woman. The mistress. The woman with no self-respect. She does not know how to be this other person. How to be someone who discovered a body. She does not know how to be someone who stood across from that body, waiting for the police to arrive, counting to ten over and over, answering the questions the 911 operator asked, and all the while staring at the girl on the rocks, wishing she would just lift her head, say Hey! back at her, even as Ruby knew, looking at those exposed legs, the twist of the girl, that it was too late. That there was no point climbing down onto the rocks, because the girl was already dead.

I found a dead girl today.

This is the text Ruby sends Ash when she finally gets out of the shower. She types out the words, and then switches her phone to silent, feeling that strange emptiness settle behind her eyes again, before getting into bed, still wrapped in her towel. She stares at the ceiling, listening to the rain outside, not even flinching when thunder shakes through the walls.

She gets up off the bed around three in the afternoon. She hasn't eaten. She can't eat. She needs a drink, she realises, whiskey specifically. The craving for that amber liquid, for the warmth of it, is her only sure thing, as if someone had fed her this as medicine, long ago. She pulls on tights, boots, a thick sweater.

All black. She feels safer, somehow, wrapped in dark winter clothing, the kind that swamps her frame, hides her. She's glad it's still raining outside, cannot imagine sunshine or blue skies. The world has shifted in just a few hours. The way it always shifts in just a few hours. It's not years or decades — that's simply how we tally the axis-shifts, how we adjust and recover from them. We think in years — *How was this year, what's your New Year's resolution, I'm so glad to see this year gone* — but it's really the hours that change us.

Ruby was a different person when she got up just a few hours ago.

It is possible, she considers, the girl was still alive back then.

(She thinks of me as *the* girl. The first of the many new names I will be given. 'I'm Alice,' I whisper, but the sound comes out as a rush of rain.)

Taking an umbrella from the front desk, Ruby heads back out into the wet. She makes it down the mostly empty streets quickly, heads towards the dirt-wood floors and fairy lights of a small bar she has walked by many times these past few weeks. Thinking, this will be a place where she will be left alone to drink, but she won't be alone. She never again wants to be as alone as she was this morning.

The sole bartender is distracted by a TV screen on the wall when she walks in; a basketball replay has his full attention. When he sets down her whiskey, the glass is almost full to the rim. He returns to the game before Ruby can say thank you, and she turns away, relieved he didn't want to make small talk. Slinking away with her drink, she sees two couches at the very back of the bar, ratty and low to the ground. Choosing the one in the darkest corner, Ruby tucks her feet up underneath her and is grateful for the first burn of whiskey in her throat, the small relief of it. Closing her eyes briefly, she wills for her mind to be as quiet as this corner, this place. Prays for the drink to calm her.

Flesh exposed, like bruised fruit. A hand splayed across the rocks.

She opens her eyes.

The older, serious guy who came later. O'Byrne, the homicide detective. He gave Ruby a card with his name on it, said they would bring her in for a formal interview tomorrow, but she should call immediately if she remembered anything. He said people can go into shock at first, and sometimes, when the shock wears off, they remember the important details better than they did at the start.

'You were in the park for a good ten minutes before you found her, yes? That's a real amount of time. You might have seen something, someone, and if you did, we want to know about it. You call me straight away, okay Ruby? If there's anything you remember better.'

The younger policeman, Officer Jennings, said Ruby did a great job calling 911 and directing the police to the body. He said she did a great job not being afraid. But Detective O'Byrne, he seemed disappointed in her, like she could have given him more.

I didn't see anything, Detective.

And now all I see is her.

The door to the bar jangles open and a couple stumble through the doorway backwards, shaking raindrops off their shared umbrella. They're young, laughing, and the boy kisses the girl full on the mouth before he heads to the bar. As the girl sits down on the couch next to Ruby's, she never takes her eyes off the boy. Even in her current state, it's easy for Ruby to see the new love shining off this girl. She's glowing with it, warming the room.

Ruby thinks: this young woman is so clearly in love with this young man today. In the same way it is raining today and she found a dead body today, and she is drinking whiskey in the afternoon. *Today*. Tuesday 15 April, four weeks after she arrived in New York City. Tomorrow, these things will only be true of yesterday. Tomorrow, it might be dry, blue-skied out there. Tomorrow, she cannot say *I found a dead girl today*. And tomorrow this young girl with her shining eyes, with her love-glow, may have loved a boy yesterday. She may have loved him with all the heat a body can generate, until some chance thing he said, some small action — or maybe a large one — took hold of her new love and crushed it, pierced through the cocoon she had created. It only takes a beat, a careless word, a thoughtless admission, for everything to change. So that, tomorrow, this young girl may find herself staring at the wall, wondering how everything is suddenly so different now, when at this very moment yesterday she was sharing an umbrella with a boy who kissed her in doorways, a boy who sheltered her and took such care. She will wonder at how quickly all that care can disappear.

He sits down with her today, this day, and this girl puts her leg over his thigh, easy, proprietary. They are ripe with beginnings and Ruby, already, has prescribed them an ending. *What's wrong with me*, she wonders. Why does she assume she knows anything at all about this young couple's tomorrows? Surely some people find contentment and get to hold on to

127

it. Surely, some people find their person, and stay with that person, and make babies and a life with that person. Not just some people, in fact, but *most* people.

Ruby is the odd one out, here.

Looking down, trying not to cry in this dingy bar, she sees her phone screen light up. Messages from Ash, three of them in a row. The first two messages must have come through when she was walking to the bar. Opening them now, Ruby sees a series of question marks, and then, timestamped a few minutes later, a misspelled sentence asking where she was.

His latest message, fresh in her hand, is all in caps.

JESUS RUBY WHATS GOING ON?

Her text to him when she got out of the shower:

I found a dead girl today.

Ash woke up to this.

Curled up on her couch at the back of the bar, ready for another whiskey, Ruby doesn't know how to respond. What would she say? She was mad at him, at herself, and she went for a run, and then everything changed, and now she doesn't know what she feels at all. Maybe if she could talk to him — but she knows she can't call, knows he won't answer at this time of day, even as her fingers hover over his name. Eventually, she puts her phone away. She can explain what happened some other time. It's not like he can come to her, shelter her. In the end, it doesn't really matter.

In the end.

In the end, you can't get back what you've lost. You can't bring back the dead. There is a girl who died today, and Ruby doesn't even know her name. She will need to wait for the police or the papers to tell her about this yellow-haired girl in her purple T-shirt, with her orange nails, and her bloody face. This girl, she thinks, would surely have something to say about all there is to lose — in the end.

Ruby's glass is empty. She heads back to the bar, walks past the nuzzling, love-soaked couple. Wanting, suddenly, to stop and tell them she's so very sorry. For everything that will surely come their way.

Eleven

'Tell me what happened.' Afterwards, Ruby can barely remember what she said in her official police interview. She knows Detective O'Byrne started by asking her questions about her career, why she came to New York, how often she went running. Understands he was trying hard to make her feel comfortable, mimicking the flow of a casual conversation, but the absurdity of it, sitting and talking to a homicide detective about her graphic design work back home — 'It's great, but it's not, um, my passion' — and how she is currently living off money once destined for a house deposit — 'My grandmother, uh, she left me $25,000 when she died' — or explaining that she tries to run every day: the madness of sharing such small details of her life made the words scramble on the way out, rearrange on her tongue, until she found she could not make sense of anything, could no longer tell what was important, and what to leave out.

She understood Detective O'Byrne would get to the river and the rocks eventually, that he was slowly guiding her there through the tangle of what came before, but she also knew she had nothing of value to offer him, no startling insight, no recovered memory pushing through to validate the way he looked at her so intently. Twenty-four hours after finding the body, Ruby had to admit she knew even less than she did when it happened.

When the interview was over, the detective thanked her for coming to the station, crinkled his dark eyes a little, kept his large fingers soft when he reached out to shake her hand. But Ruby was sure she had disappointed him yet again and had to look away. Walking home, she had the strangest feeling that she wasn't quite there on the street any more, was not entirely inhabiting her own body. It was like being drunk, but something more, too. A feeling that everyone around her was also drunk, and not in a pleasant end of the night way. Someone behind her coughed and it sounded like a slap. A man smiled at her and it quickly morphed into a leer. Buying fruit at Whole Foods, another man asked if she was having a nice day, and Ruby was certain he was goading her. Turning onto her street, for a brief, disorientating moment, she thought she saw the Financial Manager, the one who sent those explicit, unsolicited pictures of himself. Even the front desk guy at her apartment building seemed altered; she could feel his narrowed eyes stay on her as she waited for the lobby's elevator doors to open. For a second, she found herself panicking that he knew which floor she lived on, maybe even had a key to her door. How had she not considered this before?

Ruby's heart was still hammering when she walked into her studio. She double-checked the door and windows were securely locked, and then she lay down on her bed, hand to her chest, trying to calm herself. The guy at the front desk was clearly harmless. The Whole Foods man was just making conversation, and there was no way that creep from the dating app would know where she lived. They never even exchanged full names. She knows that, reasonably, but the strange feeling of being both in and outside of her body persists, even here in the safety of her room, so that she feels acutely aware of her heart in her chest and

131

separated from her own limbs at the same time. It does not help that whenever she closes her eyes, she can see flashes of red at a young girl's temple, the twist of bare legs, yellow hair floating. She had tried her best with Detective O'Byrne —

'I turned left here, no wait, I came down the stairs from the right, there' — but all she could really remember about yesterday morning was what he already knew: there was a dead girl in Riverside Park, and she found her, and it was obvious that something very, very bad had happened to the girl before Ruby came along.

She now knows that I was strangled to death; the latest headlines scream it. When she first encountered this awful detail, she immediately put her hand to her own throat, applied pressure to the cartilage she could feel straining under her skin. How depraved would a person have to be to take a life in this way, she wondered, her eyes filling with tears. To use their bare hands, to look up close at the pain they were causing. To imagine it, even a little, was horrific.

He's out there somewhere, she thinks. The man who did this. Right now, he could be down the street, or at Whole Foods, or there in her building. He could be any man she's met in New York City. The thought is terrifying, and she resists it as hard as she can, wriggles her fingers and toes, cycles her legs in the air, trying to focus on her body, her breathing, anything that feels like it's hers alone. She has an instinct that something got rearranged when she was down by the river, that there was a *before* Ruby, and now there is an *after* Ruby, a woman who no longer feels at home in her own body, as if the violation of someone else has somehow seeped into her own skin.

But nothing actually happened to me, Ruby reminds herself. *All I did was find the girl. I was never in any danger.*

And yet. What if that young girl thought she was safe, too? Right before that very, very bad thing happened to her — did she have any idea of what was coming?

It is impossible for Ruby not to imagine this.

And now, finally, slowly, I begin to take shape in Ruby's mind. A person begins to form beyond the blood and bruises, the broken things. A real person, a young girl who had a whole life, and she must have been so scared in those last, awful moments. This thought makes Ruby sit bolt upright. She has been wondering about the kind of man who could do such awful things, but this suddenly feels like the wrong question. Who on earth was the girl he did those awful things to?

Who *is* she?

From her new home base of fear and confusion, twenty-some hours after she discovered my body down on the rocks, Ruby Jones sets out to find me again.

'Thank you,' I whisper, as she reaches for her laptop, begins to search online for anything and everything she can find out about the case. Because, even if she doesn't fully understand this yet, Ruby has deliberately chosen not to forget me. When forgetting would no doubt be the easier path for her to take.

She has so much to learn. About herself. About dead girls. It is most definitely not going to be easy. But in this moment, what matters most is this: Ruby has decided to hold on to me just as tightly as I find myself clinging to her.

Unlikely she was prostituting.

Does not appear to have been sleeping rough.

Clothing suggests she was lower to middle class.

Crime scene tape flaps above the rocks. Police dogs have been brought in, grid searches have been completed and repeated. The heavy rain has made things harder, stirred up the ground, surfaced the muck of other mornings and washed away footprints and any other impressions he — the perpetrator — might have made on the only morning that matters. The most they have to work with right now, then, is my body. The impressions I have left behind, and those things *he* has pressed onto me.

There is evidence of a struggle.

My case file fills up with notes like this, a padding of words around the bare bones of the crime. Physical evidence packaged and labelled at the scene is examined. Samples come back from the lab, and databases are searched. The first forty-eight hours are critical, they say. But as time ticks down, there is no revelatory discovery, no match, no name. Led by Detective O'Byrne, a dozen men and women have turned me into their question, but the answer eludes each and every one of them.

'She is not giving up her secrets easily,' they say to each other. As if there are better ways for a dead girl to behave. Detective O'Byrne is different. He doesn't give up on me so easily. In these earliest days, he thinks about it like this: I am simply a song he can't quite remember. A melody he used to know, but for now he can only hear a fragment, a note hanging in the air as it repeats, over and over. The name of the song is tantalisingly close, but he can't quite get there. Can't get to that place, far enough inside his own head, where other people, other *men*, sing out. I see him trying hard, see the times he places his thick fingers at both temples and pushes down, elbows against desk, eyes squeezed shut.

The note hangs between us. He *knows* that he knows.

Someone took a photograph of him like this once. Printed it out, labelled it 'The Thinker'. It's still pinned on a precinct wall, some cluttered wall, amongst dozens of other snapshots documenting people and places and murders long solved. No matter that the real Thinker has his hand at his mouth. The photographer recognised the intent, the turning in on oneself, the folding of thoughts over and over until they've been reduced to something small and true. The truth wants to be told; Detective O'Byrne knows this most of all. He will get to that place, soon enough, he is sure of it. He will find the man who did this because signatures, calling cards, are always left on the bodies of murdered girls. This is why he keeps coming back to the list of potential weapons. Thumbs his way down the possibilities. Displaced fragments. Round in shape. Something brought down with extreme force against the right temple. Fresh haemorrhage. This came first, she was still alive. Before hands went to neck, before the crushing, the strangulation that killed her. Was that initial strike an accident? A moment of white-hot rage? Both of these things, intertwined? Thumb on words, pressing against the possibilities. Then fingers back to temple. A tap, mimicking the blow of a — what?

Figure out the weapon and you figure out the man.

135

For Detective O'Byrne, failure is not an option. It's nothing personal, he thinks. Just his job. He would obsess over any case this complex, *has* to make it his priority. That's what he's paid to do, and what he does well.

It's nothing personal. He is not making it personal when he puts his head in his large hands and aches over the already indisputable details of this case. Those grim facts written out across a young woman's body that he knows for sure to be true.

★ ★ ★

There is evidence of a struggle.

Something you should know. I did not want to die. I don't know if it makes any difference, but when the time came, I fought really hard to stay in my body. I tried my best, but I just couldn't hold on. I did *not* want to die. And now I am — Well. Ruby and Detective O'Byrne are not only ones looking for answers. Turns out they don't teach you how to be out of the world any more than they teach you how to be in it.

12

U Ok?

Ruby has been staring at her phone screen for twenty minutes. It is the first message she has received from Ash in three days. Three days. It's been three whole days since she found Jane's body. *Jane*. That's what the media call the girl — me — now. Jane Doe, an unidentified white female found murdered in Riverside Park. Blonde. Thought to be aged between 15 and 24 years old. 5'5 tall, 125 pounds. A scatter of freckles across her nose. No identifying marks, no tattoos, and no major dental work done. She looks like no one and everyone, and they have named her Jane.

The girl is now Jane.

Police say they are investigating every single tip phoned in. They hold press conferences, their faces like stone. Standing at podiums, they warn women to be careful, to avoid *situations*. News stories lead with VICIOUS ATTACK and BRUTAL SLAYING; the growing consensus is that this was a random attack, which puts my murder on the tip of all the tongues up here where it happened, though the whole city is spooked. Who is she, people ask? And how could this have happened? Nobody young and pretty gets murdered in New York City these days. Correction: nobody young and pretty gets *raped* and murdered in New York City these days. Quotes from 'police sources' on the exact nature of the assault dominate the story in the tabloid papers. It makes Ruby feel sick to her stomach.

(Others delight in it. They crawl right into the muck.)

Is Ruby okay, then? No. Like I said, she has not chosen the easy path here. She could have let me go already, turned me over to the people whose job it is to think about me. Instead, her need to know who I am has come on like a fever; after her interview with Detective O'Byrne, she has stayed holed up inside her room, moving between the bed and the bathroom, as if taking a third or fourth shower might cool her down. It never does, so she crawls back under the sheets, half wet, stares at the ceiling, until she switches on her laptop again, goes back to her search for fresh headlines and threads of new information about the investigation. The city honks and buzzes outside her window, beyond her closed blinds there are millions of people going about their days and their nights, doing the things they always do, good or bad, or both, but Ruby wants to shut all that living out. Now that she feels closer to the dead.

Cassie says she should come home. Says she was right to question Ruby's safety and the wisdom of her traveling alone.

Away from her laptop, there is only one safe place Ruby can think of.

The precinct is on a regular, residential street decorated with thin-trunked trees. Spears of metal make the first-floor windows of the street's ornate row houses look like little jail cells, but for the most part, the location feels innocuous, homely, and Ruby would not have guessed there was a police station nestled in the neighbourhood. When she'd walked here for her formal interview, she'd followed the blue dot on her phone and was confused when she arrived, thinking:

this is a street where people should be making dinner and playing with children, not investigating robberies and assaults and all the hidden, broken things. But then again, so much happens behind closed doors. Perhaps, she reasoned, it made sense for the police to slot themselves in amongst all that domesticity, amongst the kitchens and lounge rooms and curtains being closed around everyday life.

Best to keep the police close to home, maybe.

Seventy-two hours after my murder, on a grey-skied morning, Ruby finds herself returning to the precinct. She walks past the building a dozen times, but she never goes up to the entrance, cannot bring herself to do more than hover across the street. It is enough for her to stare at the front doors, to know there are people like Detective O'Byrne and Officer Jennings, that kind policeman, working away inside. Solving crimes, helping people, keeping them safe. Just a few days ago, she thought, *This is how people go crazy*. Now she understands she had no idea back then. What it means to need answers no one can give you.

Her body was found by a jogger. Such a famous line. Two anonymous women connected by just seven words. Just how close had they come to each other that morning? Close enough to change roles, play each other's parts?

The victim is estimated to be in her mid-thirties. She is 5'7, 155 pounds. She has brown hair, and brown eyes. She has a tattoo of a heart on her right wrist.

Was Ruby's life decided in the time it took to put on her running shoes? Had she arrived in the park just a few minutes earlier, might she have been the one in danger?

(How close do we *all* come?)

139

As she stands across from the precinct, Ruby thinks about Detective O'Byrne. By now, she has seen him many times on the news, read every single article about him she could find. It was no surprise to discover he is famous in his field, a respected, much decorated investigator known for solving many of the area's high-profile cases. The grim stuff, the murders of women and children, cases Ruby skipped over at first, but often returns to in the dark, pressing her tongue against the exposed nerve of violence when she cannot sleep. She wonders how much more Detective O'Byrne knows about this particular murder than what has been shared with the public so far. A girl was assaulted, strangled. A seemingly random attack. The perpetrator's DNA was found under the victim's fingernails (and other places Ruby doesn't like to think about). This is all common knowledge now. But what new secrets has the girl's body offered up to the medical examiners and photographers and crime scene investigators? Three days on, obviously not enough to give away her identity. Posters with a detailed sketch at their centre have now gone up around Riverside: *Do you know this woman?*

(A forensic artist has approximated my face, painted a small smile at my lips, coloured right up to the edges of me. It could almost . . . but the artist has softened my expression, widened my eyes. I look like a girl who knows nothing of the world. Who is going to recognise that?)

There must be more that he knows, Ruby thinks of O'Byrne, today. She can almost see him shifting all of the different pieces from hand to hand, rubbing the truth between his fingertips until it sparks. An odd image, and when she looks down, Ruby sees that she herself is pressing thumb to forefinger, a new and nervous twitch.

'Does he know who you are, Jane?'

Ruby doesn't mean to say this sentence out loud, but the words slip from her mouth, just as Officer Jennings quietly comes up beside her. She jumps, their faces mirroring surprise and recognition. He thinks Ruby looks nicer in the light, sexy even, then scolds himself for such an inappropriate thought. Smith sent him outside, said the Australian woman from the Riverside case had been standing out front of the building all morning, and he should probably go see if she was okay.

'Ah . . . Ruby?'

She nods and ducks her head at the same time, embarrassed. Jennings is looking at her with concern, and she remembers his softness down by the river. The way he breathed out slowly when she pointed to the body. Officer Smith had wrapped the blanket around her, squeezed her shoulders, but it was Jennings who looked like he wanted to cry.

'Hi, Officer Jennings,' Ruby says finally, willing the flush in her cheeks to settle. 'I . . . ah, I was just walking past. And I was wondering if there have been any breakthroughs. Or, you know, leads. In the case.'

While she is talking, Jennings keeps glancing back at the precinct doors, his discomfort clear. He should have made Smith do this part. His partner is far better with the traumatised ones, she somehow knows what to say, how to find the balance between professional distance and small comfort. He clears his throat, wishing he'd paid more attention to how Smith does it.

Mistaking this unease for censure, Ruby's blush deepens.

'Sorry. I didn't mean to be a bother. I shouldn't even be here, and I know I have no right to ask questions. It's lust . . . I can't seem to stop thinking about her. I'm going a bit crazy, I think.'

At this somewhat alarming admission, Jennings blinks through his nervousness, remembers something from his training, and takes a step closer.

'It's okay, Ruby. Did you want to come inside and talk? Maybe you remembered something? Detective O'Byrne is further uptown today, but I could . . . '

He trails off as Ruby shakes her head, tears pooling, then spilling down her cheeks.

At the sight of her tears, Jennings reaches over and awkwardly pats Ruby's arm, then coughs. His own cheeks are burning now. Will he ever get used to the crying?

(Think, Jennings, think.)

'Um. Ruby, I can get you some phone numbers. There are people — experts in this kind of thing — who can help you. It's pretty normal to feel upset after what you went through. Witnessing a crime can be traumatic, and lots of people say talking about it helps. So, you don't, you know, get stuck.'

Mortified that she's crying again, wanting nothing more than to get away from this awkward conversation as quickly as possible, Ruby nods at Jennings' suggestion, wipes away her tears with the back of her hand. Giving himself a mental tick for getting it right this time, the young officer practically runs across the street, back to the emotional safety of the station. Returning a few minutes later, he hands Ruby three or four glossy pamphlets, and feels even better when she rewards him with a half-smile.

The booklets he has picked for her all have covers showing a diverse cast of characters talking on the phone or walking together, holding hands. Everyone has a smile on their face, despite the words jumping off the paper. *Trauma. Victims. Violence. Grief.* Is this supposed to be her world, her people, now?

Ruby doesn't feel like smiling.

Still, the young officer is clearly pleased with himself, and Ruby can only thank him for trying.

'I'll have a read over these for sure. To make sure I don't' — she waves her hand about — 'get stuck. I appreciate this, Officer Jennings. Really. Thank you.'

'Don't mention it, Ruby. You've been through a lot. It's good to deal, right? And come by if you want to talk some more, okay. You're welcome any time.'

(An odd closing. More to do with her smile than anything else. They both recognise this, and Jennings has the sense to start backing away.)

'*Officer Jennings!*'

He has already crossed the street when Ruby yelps out his name, startling them both.

He stops.

Ruby takes a deep breath.

'Where is she? Can you tell me where Jane is?'

'Where Jane is?' Jennings repeats her question, confused.

'Yes. I mean, the girl. Jane Doe. Where do you take' — Ruby swallows — 'the bodies you find?'

'Ah, right. I get you.' Jennings wonders why he has suddenly started to perspire. 'She'll be down on 1st Avenue, reckon.'

'First Avenue?'

'Yeah. At the morgue down there. That's where she would be. They'll be hoping to ID her. If no one comes

143

forward to . . . ah . . . claim her, they'll keep her down there for a while, most likely.'

'And then?'

Ruby needs to know what happens if nobody claims the body.

Jennings rubs the back of his neck, feels a trickle of sweat under his fingertips. He hates thinking about this part. Never gets used to it. The idea of all those cadavers lined up, emptied of organs, lips sewn shut. That ugly ending doesn't feel right for a girl as lovely as the one they found by the river. He feels a sudden desire to protect Ruby from what he knows. It's the least he can do for her.

'You know what, hon? Odds are we'll find out who she is real soon. It nearly always happens that way, so don't you worry about it.'

Jennings gives what he hopes is a reassuring smile, and then he is gone, the doors of the precinct closing behind his back, and Ruby is left standing on the street, smiling faces staring up at her from the brochures in her hand. She unfolds the top one, but the print blurs, because she is crying again, fat drops onto the page.

U Ok?

Ash couldn't even be bothered typing out a full sentence. What room did that leave her to answer? How could she fit in all the things that make her not okay?

She thinks again of the line she has read in so many newspaper reports: *Her body was found by a jogger.*

Why did they never say what happened to the jogger after that?

★ ★ ★

144

Someone organises a candlelight vigil in Riverside Park. News of the intended gathering is shared locally, and on Saturday night, four days after the murder, around three hundred people make their way down to the muddy fields near the pier. The mourners are mostly from the neighbourhood, but some women come from across town, from their own dark places, called forth to memorialise one of their ilk, one who didn't, couldn't, make it home. The crowd is punctuated by these survivors, their pain red-tipped, fierce, as the faithful from different denominations hold forth, one grasp at comfort after another offered into the night. Candles quiver, wave, and when the talking stops, someone steps forward and softly sings 'Hallelujah' into the silent congregation, her head bowed down.

From a distance, three hundred candles held high is a beautiful thing to see. A glow of stars drawn down into people's hands. Faces are soft, warm, as people lean one lit candle into the wick of another, connecting each new flame, until the field flickers. Until the crowd appears to breathe light, a visible inhale-exhale of grief and prayer.

There is no name to be spoken, but I am recognised by each of the women present, clasped around their lifted hands, heavy on their hearts. I am their fears, and their lucky escapes, their anger, and their wariness. I am their caution and their yesterdays, the shadow version of themselves all those nights they have spent looking over shoulders, or twining keys between fingers. A man speaks to the crowd, entreats his gender to do better; people clap, cheer, but it is the silence of the women that binds up the candlelight, sends it skyward, a flare in search of every lost sister. So that when the man's passion is spent, it is the quiet rage of women that lingers, can be seen, glittering, from above. Long after all the little fires have been extinguished, and the mourners have moved on.

Ruby does not attend the vigil. She sits alone in her room, just a few city blocks from the park. She has lit her own candle here, a single flame weaving, pulsing in the dark. Cross-legged on the bed, drinking lukewarm vodka, she stares at this candle and feels nothing. Sorrow, she is earning, can be as quiet as a whisper when it wants to be. Whether it all roils inside her, whether the pain spills out like a swollen river breaching its banks, or the waters go still and she floats upon the surface, numbed — it is all the same feeling in the end. One of utter helplessness. Knowing so little is in your control, knowing you cannot claw your way back to the ignorance of safety. Sometimes, these past few days, she has raged against this loss. Tonight, she grieves. She is alone in a lonely city, and nearly as deep as her sorrow for an unnamed dead girl is this wretched thought: should anything happen to her in New York, she herself might end up unclaimed at one of the city's morgues. Because no one will have noticed she is gone.

★ ★ ★

The morning after the vigil, Ruby wakes with a vodka-thick head. Remembers blowing out the candle, can recall getting out of bed to lay down on the cool of the bathroom tiles after the room started to spin. A dim recollection too, of waking, shivering on the floor, a coarse towel wrapped about her shoulders. *Self-care of the drunken kind*, she thinks with a sigh, the towel now tangled under the bed-covers. She was not in a deep enough sleep to dream, but time has passed, it is now six thirty in the morning. She has managed to shut down the night, at least.

Padding to the bathroom, her head aching, Ruby's stomach suddenly lurches. A memory from last night dislodges, makes its way to the surface. After the candle, before the tiles. She was righteous, angry again. Ruby sees herself with her phone in her hand, bringing up Ash's name. The punching of keys, a furious list of sins building, text after text.

You don't . . . You never . . . I hate . . .

Picking up her phone now, she has to force herself to look at the screen.

Nothing.

She checks for his name.

Nothing.

Still, that memory persists. The feeling she's said something she shouldn't have. Never, ever does she let Ash know how much his distance pains her. She has never let him see her anguish, has remained stubbornly proud of this, clinging to impassivity as her only control. Did she let go of all that last night?

Vodka and dead girls have a way of loosening that grip, I want to tell her.

> Ash. I was really wasted last night. I don't remember what I said to you.

Ruby sends this message after composing and deleting a dozen others; the text immediately shows as delivered. An hour of conspicuous silence follows, where Ruby checks her phone compulsively, as if a reply might slip through unnoticed while she blinks. It is late evening in Melbourne. But definitely not late enough for her text to go unread — Ash would still be expecting work-related messages at this hour, he would have his phone within reach. Panic grows as time ticks on. What did she say in her texts last night? How bad did it get? Bad enough for her to delete the evidence after? The photos and words they've sent back and forth since she got to New York have all been deleted from her phone, too. Later, she will mourn this loss, but for now she feels sick. Has she said something she knew she wouldn't want to see the next day?

Ruby holds a pillow tight against her chest, tries to quiet her mind. And for the first time considers whether telling the truth might really be so bad.

It must be. How else to explain her nausea, her hollow limbs and heavy chest. This does not feel like liberation. She sends another message.

I'm feeling really awful about . . . everything.

Delivered within milliseconds. No response. Ruby lifts the pillow up to her face now, screams into the smooth fabric. A strange, muffled sound, more like the memory of screaming than the real thing. It is too early, she knows, or perhaps too late, for the half-empty vodka bottle next to the bed. But there is no denying her fingers are already twisting towards the smooth, clear glass.

Is this really who she has become? It would be easy enough to say yes. To reach for the bottle, shut down the daylight, too. Those people on Officer Jennings' brochures wouldn't blame her for that, surely. Despite their camera-ready smiles, they of all people would understand you can't survive every situation on your own. That sometimes you need help to get up off the floor.

But she isn't the one that needs help, is she?

Something she realises now. She went to the precinct because she wanted to be around people for whom Jane is the only thing that matters. To stay focused on that body, and to be closer to her too, the way she was just a few days ago. It doesn't feel right to have been there first and to just go about her life from then on, as if nothing had happened. She wants to be with Detective O'Byrne, sorting through evidence, looking for clues, finding the missing links.

This really is the only thing that matters.

I could help, she thinks, and then stops herself, feeling foolish. Maybe she has gone a little crazy, after all. Imagining a place for herself at the table like that. Imagining she could make a difference to the investigation.

Ruby hears Jennings now, the way he said it might be good to talk about what she experienced down at the river.

Messaging Ash is sure as hell not going to make things better, she knows. Cassie with her gentle scolding, and entreaties to come home, won't do either. But who does that leave, then? Like a whisper in another room, Ruby gets the feeling there is an important conversation going on without her that contains the answers she is looking for. She senses an invitation, waiting. If she can only figure out where those whispers are coming from.

Unsure what to do with this new concept, floating just out of reach, Ruby turns off her phone, puts it in a drawer, before lying back down on the bed. Eventually, she falls into a fitful, early-morning sleep, dreaming of a young woman with a spade as tall as she is, digging at the earth, singing as she works, and when she wakes from this dream it is near on midday. Ruby can hear workmen talking and laughing outside her window, hanging off their planks, swinging on their ropes. They are going about their business. The city keeps moving.

You need to keep moving, too.

These words come through more like a shout than a whisper, catapulting Ruby up and out of bed. She showers and dresses carelessly, ties her wet hair in a knot, and is out the door fast. It is chilly outside, but the April sun is a bright glare in a clear blue sky, and Ruby scolds herself for losing half the day already. Something shifted while she was sleeping. A click and unlock. She does not want to wake on the bathroom floor, or sleep while the sun is out on a Sunday. She does not want to cry on the street, and she does not want to send drunken, unanswered messages across the ocean.

What Ruby wants is to be useful. It might be foolish to think that Detective O'Byrne would have any use for her, but that doesn't mean she can't help in other ways. Even if it simply means remembering that every Jane Doe — *her* Jane Doe — is a real person, with a real name they deserve to get back.

What to do next, then? Who might want to talk with her about dead girls, who might want to climb down into the darkness with her?

The answer, when it comes, seems obvious. There must be other finders of the dead out there. She just needs to work out how to find *them*. Heading to the nearest coffee shop, carrying her idea carefully, as if it might break, Ruby settles on a high stool at the window and connects her laptop to the free wi-fi. An oversize latte is soon set down in front of her. The comfort of coffee, she thinks, before squeezing her eyes shut, willing inspiration to come.

'Finding a dead body' might be a good place to start.

She carefully types these words into the search bar on her laptop, holds her breath as the results appear. This feels like the beginning of something, that whisper from another room getting louder, but the first few search results are all about something called Death Clean-ups, an apparently burgeoning biohazard industry Ruby has never heard of. These grim advertorials for wiping crime scenes clean are followed by list after list of 'I found a dead body!' stories, blog posts decorated with words like *gruesome* and *horrifying* and *nightmare*. Ruby gives this content a cursory glance only; she is not looking for titillation.

Finally, three quarters down the page, a headline jumps out at her.

PTSD: When the body gets stuck in fight or flight mode.

So that you don't, you know, get stuck. Wasn't this the language Officer Jennings used outside the precinct? This isn't exactly what she had in mind, but she clicks on the link anyway, letting her breath out slowly as the article loads.

Her coffee is cold by the time she finishes reading. Here, laid out by a well-known doctor from Boston, is the clearest explanation for what trauma does to a person, to their mind and body. The flashbacks, the constant visions of the rain and the river, all the obsessive thoughts swirling around. The way she

151

keeps dreaming about dead girls. Not to mention her sudden paranoia, the idea that any man she encounters might be capable of murder. It's all explained by the doctor. This *hypervigilance*, he says, is a mark of Post-Traumatic Stress Disorder. And danger only has to be perceived, he asserts, for PTSD to be triggered. Encountering a dead body is actually right there on his list. A familiar song about the wonders of New York croons over the cafe's speakers as Ruby ponders this new information, wonders what to do with what feels, suddenly, like a key in her hand.

And then she remembers her earlier plan. To seek out other finders of the dead. Perhaps this is where they are hidden. Fingers typing fast this time, Ruby is astounded by the number of results that come up for her now, pages and pages of them. New York is apparently teeming with support groups for people in trauma. Feeling — oddly — like she is being guided, Ruby clicks on the link for a Manhattan meet-up offering support and friendship for people with PTSD, including those with 'non-traditional' causes.

Discovering a murder victim. Non-traditional? Ruby reads on.

The meet-up brief describes sessions that include individual sharing *(optional)* and group discussions: *We offer a place of non-judgement, where your safety is the priority. No formal diagnosis of PTSD is required to join. The group meets every two weeks, at a Midtown East location. Address to be shared upon RSVP.*

The registration form is short. Ruby fills it out and hits the send button before she has time to think better of it. Almost immediately, an email dings through with a generic welcome note from someone named Larry.

Congratulations! Know it takes courage to make the first step in your healing process. You should be proud of yourself . . .

Attached to the welcome email is a list of dates, locations and times for the group's spring sessions: the next meeting is set for Thursday, four days from now. Ruby barely even asks her big sister for advice, has never considered seeing a therapist. Is she really going to do this?

Over the speakers, a man is still crooning about New York; as he sings about brand new starts, the lyric sounds out across the cafe, lands right next to her, and the hairs on Ruby's arms bristle. There is suddenly no question. She will go to this meet-up. She will seek out people who understand. What is the worst that could happen? If she goes the wrong way, she'll find what she is looking for, eventually. Because you can find anything in New York, right?

Even a dead body, she thinks, alarmed to discover that, for once, this starkest of truths almost makes her laugh.

When I started showing up in her dreams it was an accident, by the way. There isn't exactly a difference between awake and asleep for me these days. She's the one who changes when her eyes are closed, she's the one who becomes more open. Remembering me standing next to her in Riverside Park, understanding that I followed her home — these are things she forgets in the daylight, and I didn't know there was a way I could remind her of them. Until it happened.

I try not to hold too tight when she does remember. I really am sorry for all the things she has to carry. That's why I pushed for her to seek help, back there

153

in the cafe. That's why I placed my fingers over hers, pressed down on the keys.

Well.

Truth is I can't touch anything, not really. But it makes me feel better to imagine. That it didn't all just disappear because someone else wanted it to. That I am still here. Even if no one can see me. Even if nobody knows my name.

Yet.

Small things have started happening, see. Important things. At first, they seemed like little accidents. But now, if I concentrate hard enough, it seems I can drop the beginnings of a thought into Ruby's head, cause her mind to ripple. It happened with that PTSD article. Just a small nudge, but she felt it, followed it. Noah told me all about trauma. Explained it almost as well as that Boston doctor. Back when we were talking about shaking memories loose, and I imagined a body full of holes. He told me there's a chance we inherit trauma, that bad memories can get passed down from one generation to another, and I thought about my mother at the time, all the things I never knew about her. But now I wonder if I've somehow passed my memories on to Ruby, accidentally pressed them into her bones. The way Noah made it sound —

But that's enough talking about Noah. My crow, my death bird. I don't want to think about him, don't need to, now that I've got Ruby. I should have paid more attention to the things he told me, yes. But that won't do me any good these days. Besides, when I do remember him clearly, I feel a pain as sharp, as awful, as anything I ever experienced when I was alive.

And what's the point of being dead if they can still hurt you from the other side.

It's as if they have forgotten me. The others.

Him.

The problem is, if I don't fully understand how I manage to push through sometimes, I understand even less about why. Most of the time, it's like I'm a silver fish, darting through a wave, a shadow too quick to catch. But there are times, when I see them up close — Noah shutting the door to my bedroom; Tammy checking her phone; Mr Jackson hiding a box of photographs in his closet, in the space where the Leica used to be — that the waves get too big, they toss me around, batter me against something hard and unyielding, and the water rushes in.

Is it them or me turned upside down when that happens?

All I know for sure is that Ruby is my only calm sea. When the others make me feel as if I'm dying all over again.

Or worse. As if I never existed at all.

★ ★ ★

We are getting closer, the quote says.

In the accompanying black and white picture, O'Byrne stares out, looking stern and assured. Looking like the kind of man who is used to being listened to.

Consider yourself warned, the quote goes on. You will be found. We are learning more about you every day. It is only a matter of time.

O'Byrne is bluffing, I want to say as Ruby reads this official statement over and over, her heart thumping.

He's trying to lure him out from wherever he is hiding. Trick him into coming forward. They don't really know anything about him at all.

I too have tried to get close to him. But the man who murdered me only has to think about what he did that morning for those wild waves to start up again, drag me under the roiling water. It feels like its own kind of warning, every time I come near. That while he is out there, going about his life like nothing has changed, he still has the power to destroy me. To take away what little I have left.

Is that how it happens, after they kill you? They keep on living their lives, keep getting up for work and eating breakfast and checking the weather and saying please and thank you and you're welcome, and they smile at their own reflection in mirrors and store windows as they walk down the street. Hiding in plain sight, if they bother to hide at all.

Thinking no one has the power to stop them. Not the girl then, or anyone now.

It's only a matter of time.

Before they find him? Or before he gets the chance to do it again?

13

'Six or seven people come along, most sessions.'

Larry from the welcome email is talking to Ruby over his shoulder as he sets out a series of colourful cushions on the floor of the community centre. He makes a circle of them, ten large pillows in total. He knows some members of the group will prefer to leave a space between themselves and the next person; then too, there is the small hope that more people will show up tonight. Find shelter at this meet-up, instead of wandering out there, confused and alone. Larry has been facilitating these support sessions for two years now. It is, as he has now told Ruby multiple times, his 'life's calling' — staying open to the many, many ways trauma can present itself, and finding ways to heal the damage that PTSD can cause. It's a job that never gets old for him. Not when you consider all the ways humans can hurt themselves, and each other, let alone the surprises an impartial planet can have in store. With his own life seemingly safe as a box, he is constantly amazed at what people are asked to endure.

Congratulations! Know it takes courage to make the first step in your healing process. You should be proud of yourself. We would love to have you attend our group session, where you will have a chance to talk about what is holding you back from living life fully. After twenty years in my own practice, I know that my life's calling is helping people heal from their trauma to become their best selves.

Best selves. Life's calling. To Ruby, that first email was so . . . American, and she is not at all surprised to discover Larry looks like a magazine ad from the 1950s, with his straight white teeth, and his sandy blonde hair touching the sides of bright green eyes. He looks like a clean slate, something fresh and open. Like all the dirt has been scrubbed away — or deliberately swept out of sight. That's the other side of America, after all. A country whose history is shiny on the outside, a glossy front, until you realise only one version of the story is being told.

(Ruby and I didn't study the same American history. But I think she is right about that part.)

These last few days, Ruby has almost talked herself out of coming to the meet-up many times over. But her nightmares have intensified since learning about PTSD, as if she has finally given her subconscious permission to have at it. She dreams of floods and gates that won't open, and yellow reeds wrapped at her throat. Sometimes — most times — she sees that bloodied face, eyes popped open, and wakes in a sweat, convinced she is back at the river.

(This isn't me, by the way. When she has this kind of nightmare, I don't stand a chance.)

There is something else, too. When Ruby got home from the coffee shop that Sunday afternoon, a message from Ash was waiting for her:

I'm in London. Jetlagged as fuck. I don't know what messages you're talking about, but all okay my end. Don't know about you though. You ever going to tell me what happened the other day?

He hadn't told her he was travelling for work. Crisis

158

constructed. Crisis averted. She called him then and there and told him about finding a dead body. Forgot she was angry with him. And now they're back on the merry-go-round.

(I don't stand a chance there, either.)

But she's here now — we're here now — following All-American Larry around the room as he finishes setting up, chatting over his shoulder about this and that, the weather, an Indian restaurant in her neighbourhood 'that you just have to try, Ruby. Oh, it's so good. I never was much for that vegetarian stuff, seemed like something was missing, you know? But they just might have me converted.' A laugh, a look up, and a quick sign of the cross, before he winks and gets back to loading fresh beans into an old coffee machine. He is excited to have a new person here tonight, feels like a man about to start a race as he wonders what this Australian woman's story might be. He doesn't have to do this, give up his free time to help people like her. The practice in Murray Hill, the patients he treats there — it takes more than enough out of him. But he made a commitment to give back to the community outside of those $350 per hour sessions, or rather, because of them. Sharing his good fortune and sound mind twice a month is his penance for making a living out of people's misery. It really is the least he can do. And besides, you never know where the night will take you. Trauma is unruly like that. All the messiness of real life, it's better than the best TV show. He never did make it as an actor. But listen, when life gives you lemons, you can always find someone to make you lemonade.

★ ★ ★

Ruby is busy worrying no one else is going to show up tonight, that she will end up the only attendee, when a young woman half-trips through the door, hair and bag and one shoe flying. After waving at Larry, who beams beatifically as if greeting a dear friend, the girl picks up her wayward shoe and shuffles over to the circle of pillows.

'Oops,' she says in Ruby's direction, offering a sheepish smile.

At Larry's insistence, Ruby is already seated cross-legged on the floor, and this slight, dark-haired person sits herself down directly across from her. Unable to think of something to say, Ruby starts pulling at a loose thread from the cushion she is sitting on, twisting it tight around her index finger, causing more and more cotton to unravel. Unlike Ruby, this new person appears to be completely relaxed. Despite the somewhat ungraceful entrance, she now sits perfectly upright on her orange cushion, smiling at each person entering the room — they are coming through the door thick and fast now — and she perhaps sneaks a look at Ruby once or twice, though Ruby, keeping her own eyes to the floor, cannot be sure.

Soon enough, the circle has filled up with people. Larry claps his hands, before sitting down on a spare cushion next to Ruby. With a flash of panic, she realises that instead of being the only one here tonight, she is the only new person in attendance. The only person who doesn't know the rules. As if on cue, after thanking everyone for returning to the circle, Larry asks Ruby to introduce herself as the group's newest member — 'And all the way from Aussie, too!' She sees eyebrows raise at this piece of information, and suddenly wants nothing more than to get up and run.

As the session plays out, nothing feels right. Not all those eyes on her. Not Larry's barely concealed glee at having a new story to bat around the circle, and definitely not the way she senses others in the group are impatient for her to finish introducing herself — details minimal as they are — so they can have their turn for the night, each person contributing a story seemingly worse than the one before, a Jenga tower of misery just waiting to topple.

At the base, on Ruby's right, is a middle-aged woman who, after a home invasion, has had triple locks drilled into every door in her apartment, including the closets. Next comes a man who found his three-year-old nephew drowned in a hotel pool three summers ago. On top of their stories comes the weight of an elderly gentleman who accidentally put a shopkeeper in hospital when he drove his Mercedes through a grocery store window. One traumatic event teetering on top of another, and though Ruby feels a heart-clench of sympathy for all the pain laid out in front of her tonight, by the time it gets to Tanker, an engineer in his late twenties who had a gun held to his head during a convenience store robbery that turned fatal for the owner, she has to admit she made a mistake in coming here. Her situation is so different, she almost feels foolish. It is as if Tanker and the other members of the group are still deep inside their disasters, struggling for the surface, while she sits outside of the experiences that led her here, watching from a distance. That's the best she can explain it without the therapy language they all seem so familiar with. The group members might suggest she is repressing her feelings, avoiding them, but really, after listening to the circle of stories tonight, what she wants to say is this:

I don't own my pain the way you do. I feel as if I have borrowed it from someone else.

It is unsurprising that she shakes her head — No — when it's time for her to speak.

From across the circle, the girl who fell through the door watches Ruby, her smile never shifting. Like Ruby, she declines to speak when it comes to her turn — 'I'm taking a break tonight, folks' — and her silence leaves Ruby feeling vaguely disappointed. This girl seems so different to the others, almost serene, despite her apparent clumsiness. From her tumble through the door to the curious calm of her smile, something about her makes Ruby feel a sudden pang at the thought of walking out of there alone tonight.

Had she known anything about the young woman smiling at her from across the circle, Ruby would have understood that Lennie Lau could see her isolation clearly, was immediately drawn to the painful beauty loneliness can wrap around a person. And she would have seen how Lennie was already hatching a plan to unravel that loneliness, to pull at it, like Ruby had pulled at the loose thread of her cushion tonight, only harder, so that with time and care, all that pain would come undone.

★ ★ ★

Lennie has already spilled her drink, and twice knocked her fork to the floor. She doesn't bother to ask for a replacement, just rubs the metal prongs against her ripped jeans and places the fork back on the table. She talks rapidly, gestures wildly, sending anything within elbow radius flying. The staff here smile benignly at her, bring her extra napkins, patting her on the shoulder as they pass. Ruby gets the feeling this girl is treated with affection wherever she goes.

They are at a small Italian restaurant on 3rd Avenue, a street over from the meet-up. Lennie had grabbed Ruby's elbow after the session ended, asked her if she'd like to go for dessert, and Ruby had looked around, thinking the invitation was meant for someone else. Strangely, wondrously, it seemed to be directed at her, as if this Lennie had somehow read her mind. The desire for good company felt like the memory of her favourite food, a longing she could taste. To be with interesting people again, to follow a conversation that wasn't just in her own head — Ruby hoped Lennie had not seen her eyes well up when she vigorously nodded yes to the invitation.

On the way to the restaurant, Lennie kept the conversation light and breezy, as if they had just walked out of a movie together, but once they sit down at their small table, she fixes her dark, intense eyes on Ruby, and the questions start.

'How long have you been here?'

'Where are you staying?'

'What made you choose New York?'

Finding her tongue fat from weeks of under use, Ruby can't quite form the words to answer this last question. She goes for what she hopes is a carefree shrug, a kind of *Who knows!* But her face flushes red, and she is grateful when the waitress interrupts her floundering to set down a glass of red wine. *Give me the whole bottle and perhaps I can explain it,* Ruby wants to say. Instead, she takes advantage of the break in conversation to switch the focus to Lennie.

'Were you born here?'

'Where do you live?'

'Are you studying, or working?'

Her answer to this last question makes Ruby's mouth pop open in surprise.

Lennie, a born and bred NewYorker, is an embalmer at a funeral home in Brooklyn. She specialises in reconstruction, which means she works with bodies that come to the mortuary visibly damaged. It's her job, she tells Ruby, to repair these bodies, to bring each dead person back to how they looked before it happened.

It. Whatever tragedy reached in and stopped the heart.

Ruby feels as if she can't breathe.

'I'm half make-up artist, half magician, I suppose,' Lennie continues, licking whipped cream from her fork, before waving it like a wand. 'If I do my job well, you never notice the tricks.'

Immediately, I can see the care Lennie takes with girls like me. So much of her work has an element of brutality to it; most people would recoil from the tasks she repeats on a daily basis. Puncturing organs, clearing intestines. Packing throats with cotton wool, stitching mouths closed. Inserting eye caps, draining blood, threading wire through jaws. These are just some of her so-called tricks. Dressing the deceased, doing hair and make-up — these gentler moments come after the hard work is done, at which point Lennie is as intimate with her bodies as any person could be. Taking her time, showing her respect, she offers her artistry as the smallest of consolations, and I see how this generosity of hers glows amber from her fingertips when she works, glistens like gold across anything she touches.

Lennie stumbled into this career a few years back,

after failing to get into med school.

'Funny, right? If you won't let me near the living, I can at least fix the dead!'

She had been working over the summer, helping at her cousin's beauty salon, when she started talking with a client who needed help for her super-dry, red-flaked hands.

'This woman was complaining about how her skin was so damaged from all the chemicals she works with, saying that everything seeps in, no matter how much she tries to protect herself. Turns out she was a mortician. Until then, I'd never met a mortician. I assumed they were all creepy old guys running the family business or something. But this woman, Leila, she was young, and beautiful, and running her own show. I had a gift for doing hair and make-up, and she told me there were other ways for me to use that gift. Ways to make a difference. I mean, at first it was just curiosity. Leila told me some crazy shit about her job, and at the time, I was in the mood for crazy. But then, well, it got important. The needs of the dead, and all that.'

Ruby nods, then shakes her head.

'I think I can understand that,' she says, though it comes out more like a question.

'You know how magicians take people who are whole and saw them in half, Ruby? Think of what I do as a reversal of that trick. I take broken people and put them back together again.'

Lennie does another wand-wave of her fork, sweeps it across the table — '*Ta-DAH!*' — making Ruby jump in her chair.

Lennie immediately sets her fork down.

'I'm so sorry, Ruby. I don't mean to be flippant

165

about this stuff. I've been doing this so long, I forget it's not everyone's idea of normal.'

Normal.

Ruby laughs at the word, but the sound comes out brittle, breaks when it hits the air between them. She wants to tell Lennie that *normal* feels like a foreign country these days. Wants to say she knows why the dead need magicians to put them back together again.

Tell her the truth, I am thinking, when something bristles on Ruby's skin, a gust of cool air in this warm room.

She shudders, and Lennie leans forward in concern.

'Someone just walked over my grave,' Ruby starts to explain, and then stops, shakes her head, as if to dislodge something.

Tell her the truth, she thinks.

'Turns out it's not so abnormal to me, Lennie. I found the girl. The girl who was murdered in Riverside Park.'

Now it is Lennie's mouth that pops open.

'Holy shit. From last week? The case that's all over the news?'

Ruby nods, and, with Lennie's coaxing, she begins to talk, letting out everything she has held in these past nine days. The running and the rain and the fear, and those tangled yellow reeds, and the moment she understood she was looking at a young woman's body. She speaks haltingly at first, but soon the words tumble out of her, a mouthful of rocks covered in dirt and sodden leaves and brown, brackish water, and Lennie, mercifully, does not flinch at the ugliness set down before her. It took her years, she assures Ruby, to get used to seeing the damage people can inflict upon each other.

'To have it thrust upon you like that. I cannot imagine.'

With Lennie's quiet understanding as a guide, Ruby continues telling her story. By the time she gets to her awkward meeting with Officer Jennings outside the precinct, she feels as if something has been extracted. Like a tongue curling against the hole where a tooth used to be, she casts about for what is left, and discovers, to her surprise, it is mostly sadness. She is grieving for the girl on the rocks as if she knew her, as if they were friends.

'It's so strange, Lennie. The way I can't stop thinking about her. I thought maybe I was just having trouble processing what happened — it's why I came to the meet-up tonight, like I might have PTSD or something. But it's not that, or not only that, at least. I feel . . . *connected* to this girl. Deep in my bones. Is that weird?'

'I don't think it's weird,' Lennie answers without pause, her dark eyes glistening. 'I've come to think that intensity, not time, is what connects us. And what could be more intense than being the one to find her? I'd say the weird part would be if you didn't feel anything at all.'

They have been talking so long, the lights in the restaurant have dimmed, and chairs have been lifted onto tables. Ruby knows they will have to leave soon, and this new, precious connection will be severed. There is something she wants to know first, something to hold onto when she goes home alone.

'Is that what happened to you, Lennie? Why you go to a PTSD meet-up, I mean? Because of all the things you've seen in your work?' Lennie considers the question, weighs the intent as if holding it in her hands.

'Ever notice how it's only ever women in those boxes?' she says, finally. 'The ones that get sawn in half. For a time, it got too much. I saw too many dead girls coming through the door.

'But Ruby' — Lennie reaches across the table, takes Ruby's hand, squeezes tight — 'I expect just one would be enough to break your heart.'

★ ★ ★

The invitation comes through just after 2 a.m. Ruby is awake, going over her night as if untangling a necklace, carefully picking at the chain of events, when the notification dings on her phone.

Dear Ruby,
    You are cordially invited to join Death Club at 11 a.m. this Sunday. We will convene at Nice Matin (see map — it's close to you!), where mimosas and in-depth discussions await. The founding members of the club look forward to seeing you there.

The short message finishes with an italicised quote:

'The boundaries which divide Life from Death are at best shadowy and vague. Who shall say where the one ends, and where the other begins?' ~ Edgar Allan Poe.

Though the phone number is unfamiliar, Ruby knows, without question, this is the work of Lennie Lau, the dark-haired magician from Brooklyn who puts women and girls back together again. She remembers how Lennie took her hand at the restaurant. What was it she had said? Something about too many dead girls coming through the door. To have met someone who understands this particular type of haunting, the way dead girls can follow you home — Ruby can hardly believe her luck.

And now her mind is racing ahead to Sunday, to this mysterious Death Club and what it might mean. Perhaps this is her chance to find what she's been looking for. She knows she shouldn't get her hopes up, not after the PTSD meet-up proved such an ill fit. But then again, look what came out of that. A new friend, and an invitation. There can be no harm in seeing where this takes her.

Besides, it isn't like she has anywhere else to be.

Me neither, I whisper. The sound of my voice prickles on Ruby's skin, and I know this is not entirely the truth of it. I know that dead girls are not supposed to haunt the living. That there is a somewhere else I should be. I sense it sometimes, almost like those whispers from another room that Ruby strains to hear. Far away, but also near — I think there is a place that offers disappearing. No more waves crashing, tossing me about. Just calm.

But I no longer want to disappear. Not when it seems so many people have forgotten me. Not when nobody knows my name.

Maybe Death Club is my chance too, Ruby.

My chance to be remembered. To have people know that I was here.

Here. In New York City.

To think Ruby and I both thought this was the adventure. We really had no idea.

14

Death Club was formed after Lennie fell, briefly, in love with a man. Josh was a tall, dark and handsome journalist doing a feature on the mortuary for a popular magazine, and he was especially interested in Lennie's reconstruction work. He followed her around on the job for the better part of a week, and there was something about the direct way he asked his questions that made Lennie's heart bounce out of rhythm. She found herself noticing his ever-dilated pupils and the white moons of his fingernails and the flat of his front teeth, and the specificity of these observations confounded her. Josh was definitely not her type — her last lover had been a petite hula-hooper she met at a burlesque show in the East Village — but there was definitely something buzzing between them. Or so Lennie thought, until she realised what she was really attracted to: Josh's intelligent curiosity, and his respect not just for his own work, but for her work, too. As they talked about their respective careers, discussing the way he told stories for a living, he suggested her job was to un-tell stories, wind her dead bodies back to an easier time, and perhaps that meant they were coming at the same thing, just from different locations. It was the most thoughtful description of her work Lennie had ever heard, and she knew she wanted to keep this man and his way with words in her life.

'I'd hate to think the most interesting thing about a person, what they're remembered for, is how they died,' she said at dinner after Josh's last day at the mortuary, which is when her new friend shared his secret with her. A few years back he'd nearly died himself, after a bike accident in Central Park left him with a broken neck and severe concussion. He'd spent weeks in hospital; for a while, it was touch and go as to whether he'd walk again. Though he'd since recovered physically — 'Clearly,' he said to Lennie that night, patting his legs — something about how he experienced himself in the world had fundamentally altered.

'Sometimes,' Josh admitted, 'I struggle with the fact that I survived. Have you ever heard of Cotard's Syndrome?' — Lennie shook her head, no — 'Well, it's quite the trip. There are people out there who think they are in fact dead. Living, breathing people who feel certain they have shuffled off this mortal coil, and they cannot be convinced otherwise, despite the . . . well, despite all evidence to the contrary. People with this delusion essentially think of themselves as walking corpses, the dead amongst the living, and no amount of reasoning can change their minds. It's a fascinating condition, but also terrifying. Because, since the accident, I've sometimes wondered if I'm not something of a walking corpse myself. Dead on the inside, you know?'

As Josh shared this startling confession in his matter-of-fact way, Lennie's quiet, bird-boned neighbour fluttered into her mind. She had known Sue for years now, ever since the older woman's Persian cat had claimed Lennie's couch as her own, one windows-open afternoon. They were almost friends, close enough to share a wine or two on warmer nights, but up until now, Sue had steadfastly refused any overture that

171

might formalise their relationship. Gallery openings, cheap Tuesdays at the local oyster bar, food festivals down on the water — Sue said no to every activity Lennie suggested, and then one night she said something more.

'I'm sorry but I don't live in the world like you do, Lennie. Not really. When my daughter died' — a car accident nearly twenty years ago, Lennie knew minimal details at the time — 'the best parts of me died, too. No one wants to spend time with a corpse, and rightly so. I've learnt to do things on my own, and now I prefer it that way.'

Sometimes, you just know what is needed.

'I have someone I want you to meet,' Lennie told Josh that night over dinner, and she told Sue the same thing, the very next day. Exactly what to do with this coupling came in the middle of the night, when she remembered a man at the mortuary who had just lost his daughter, a young woman Lennie worked her magic on, carefully erasing gunshot wounds and finger marks, so that an open casket might be possible.

'I don't understand what this means, where she's gone, and why I can't go, too,' this father had said to Lennie, sobbing into her shoulder. 'God doesn't answer me. And none of my friends will look me in the eye, let alone talk to me. Who am I supposed to talk to now?'

From this lament, the seeds of Death Club were planted.

We've each had our noses pressed up against death, Lennie wrote in her proposition. *It's this great big mystery, yet it clearly dictates how you — how we — live, at the same time. Maybe if we got to know it a little better, tried to understand it, we might find a way to break*

172

through the glass that separates life from death.

And who knows what we'll find on the other side.

The other side. The place where you make sense of things. Where a daughter can die, and a body can return from the brink, and another comes in on a gurney, and people continue to wake up and eat and sleep and dream and love and fight and cry and conspire, as if their turn will never come.

Lennie finished off her earnest invitation with the same Poe quote she would send Ruby many months later, and an entreaty: *Come explore the boundaries with me, please. It gets lonely out here on my own.*

Isolation makes everything less strange. You find yourself agreeing to things you might otherwise scoff at when you are someone who has regular plans on Tuesday and Thursday nights.

'I'm a misanthrope,' Josh said.

'I don't want to meet anyone new,' Sue complained.

But they agreed to that first meeting of Lennie's so-called Death Club, all the same. The first question, explored over tequila at a bar on Bedford, felt like the click of a padlock releasing: *Is death the end, or the beginning?*

That was nine months ago. By the time Ruby sits down with the trio at an outdoor table on a tepid spring day near Central Park, the founding members cannot remember life without Death Club's weekly, winding conversations. Neither philosophers nor debaters, these three very different people come with their questions and their musings, their common ground a place most other people avoid in polite, everyday conversation. Most meetings take the members far from where they started, and *every* meeting involves food and libations. In other words, the members of Death

173

Club generally arrive sober and go home drunk.

(Perhaps the only thing they've never managed to agree on is the name — 'Death Club? *Really*, Lennie?' — but their founder has steadfastly refused to change it, which is something I can appreciate.)

'Don't expect anybody else to understand,' Lennie advises Ruby with a smile, as she comes to the conclusion of Death Club's origin story. 'This is definitely not most people's cup of tea. Not when we live in a culture that likes to pretend the most obvious things aren't real if they're the slightest bit unpleasant. Most people avoid talking about death, they find it confronting — or scary. And if they think they've found a way to reconcile their fears, through religion, say, they'll go out of their way to shut down any questions that might threaten that safety. The only rule of Death Club, therefore, is that a difficult question is more important than a simple answer. Until one of us crosses over and comes back — for longer than Josh did, sorry — all we can do is keep asking our questions, no matter where that leads us.'

Ruby is following along eagerly, albeit anxiously. It hasn't helped that, since arriving at brunch, circumstantial evidence would suggest neither Sue nor Josh are particularly enthusiastic about her presence. While Lennie chatters away, Sue's lips remain pressed together, and Lennie's former crush barely looks up from his phone. Next to Lennie, they come off as clouds, drifting towards the sun, and it is only when a Bloody Mary is set down in front of Josh and he pounces on it, hands clasped around the tall glass as if in prayer, that Ruby realises he is in fact extremely hungover. Sue, on the other hand, is simply tired today. A lifelong insomniac, she was working online until 3 a.m. Meeting at this time, she says, feels like getting up in the middle of the night to eat dinner.

'My apologies,' she says to Ruby, when a series of small yawns overtake her. 'I am not used to being out at this time. Unlike my companion here' — she nods her head at Josh — 'who probably hasn't gone to bed yet.'

'Well not to his own bed, at least,' Lennie adds with a wink, causing Josh to stick his tongue out at her, mutter 'I wish', and, just like that, the table brightens, shares its first rays of genuine warmth.

How easy it is, Ruby will think later, back in her studio, to assume you are the cause of another person's discomfort or disdain, when the reality is, we all show up with our night befores, our midnight hours and too-early mornings. She had forgotten that making new friends is one of those confounding things, like picking up a second language or learning the piano, that seems to be much easier done when you're a kid. By the time people get to thirty-six — Ruby feels every inch her age for once — most people already have their friendships locked down. They have kids and partners and cousins and careers and mortgages that allow for kitchen renovations and a holiday in Fiji every two years. They have well-practised stories and roles to play, and any existential crisis they might experience is generally felt as a tremor, when Ruby's experiences are more like large earthquakes, rearranging everything.

People her age don't do the things she does.

(*Same*, I whisper, but she is too busy thinking about Death Club to catch the way my sigh makes the blinds in her room flutter.)

'I'm not entirely sure why I came to New York,' she

said at brunch, when the question came up again. But she might as well have said *Because I could*. Because her life was so empty of the usual trappings, so accidentally unconventional, it was easier to take a gap year at thirty-six than it was to stay put and be reminded of everything she didn't have. She wonders if anyone at the table had thought, *How could she leave a whole life so easily?* and they were too polite to say it. Then again, the existing members of Death Club did not seem to have many of the usual, grown-up ties to the living, either. Perhaps they understood, without needing to push.

'Divorced,' Sue answered when current relationship status came up.

'Divorced,' Josh nodded when Ruby turned to him (noticing, for the first time, the slate grey of his eyes, the glassy ocean of his stare).

'Anxious-Avoidant,' Lennie added, making them all laugh, so that Ruby's pause went unnoticed before she answered 'Terminally single', her hand reaching for her phone, which hadn't buzzed in twenty-four hours.

I'll get to know them all, Ruby thinks from her bed tonight, plucking at the strings of her strange afternoon, allowing herself to feel excited at the prospect of the next Death Club meeting. Her first *official* one, as Lennie pointed out over brunch, before rattling off a list of fancy places they might choose to meet at. Bemelmans Bar at The Carlyle, Oyster Bar at Grand Central. The recently reopened Tavern on the Green, or that hidden prohibition bar with the bathtub, which no one could remember the name of. Restaurants and bars Ruby had read about in top-ten guides, and seen little point in visiting on her own.

'Pass,' Josh had said to most of the suggestions, rolling his eyes. 'Will you ever stop thinking your life is an episode of *Sex and the City*, Lennie?'

'No,' she'd answered with a grin. 'Besides, it's better than thinking it's an episode of *Law and Order* — which used to scare the shit out of me when I was a kid, by the way. Ruby just found a dead body, people. We need to lighten things up a little here.'

'Says the woman who started a *Death Club*,' Josh had snorted, and I thought, in that moment, that I might be a little bit in love with all of them. The way the Death Club members teased each other, the way they all listened intently as Ruby told them about finding my body, even Lennie, who had heard the story just days before. They never once looked away from Ruby's earnestness, never dismissed her feelings when she admitted she would give anything to know more about me, and I liked that so much. I liked the way they didn't judge her or tell her to get over it, not even Sue, who seemed more serious than the other two. It made me think of those friends I'd imagined for myself, the people I was supposed to meet, and I was glad for Ruby, at least. To get to tell her stories, make her plans.

Something else, too. They know things, Ruby's new friends. Maybe not as much as Noah does, but a lot, about New York, and death, and dead girls. Josh, especially. When Ruby said she struggled to understand how no one had come forward to identify me — 'Surely *somebody* misses her?' — and Lennie wondered about how anyone could remain anonymous in this age of social media, Josh informed them that more than half a million people go missing across the country every year, with many disappearances initially unreported.

'If someone is estranged from their family,' Josh continued, 'if they don't have many close ties, or it's simply assumed they're off somewhere doing their thing, it might take a while for someone to raise the alarm. It's unusual to have a contemporary Jane Doe case, for sure. But not impossible.

'You're just lucky she's white,' he added, as they were packing up to leave the restaurant. 'With that whole "Missing White Woman" thing, your Jane is getting a lot more media attention than most, Ruby. Someone is bound to make the connection soon enough.'

Given the look on his face, Ruby wasn't sure if Josh meant this to be of comfort to her; she is reminded of his words now (perhaps I gave her a nudge), and she opens her laptop, types in the phrase he'd put air quotes around. The first search result is for something called 'Missing White Woman Syndrome', followed by dozens of links referencing variations of this term. Ruby takes a deep breath and dives in.

Here's what we learn: a disproportionate amount of media attention is given to incidents of violent crime involving middle- to upper-class white girls. Turns out, when something bad happens to young women, race and so-called class play a part in how, or even *if*, our stories get told. As she trawls through research papers and political blogs and protest pieces, a bleak reality is laid out for Ruby: it's likely *this* Jane is receiving media attention, including the growing interest of national news outlets, because she is young, pretty — and white. As if that combination is the best proxy for vulnerability and innocence. As if skin colour might determine how sorry we should feel for someone, and how much justice they deserve.

Ruby's stomach churns as she comprehends the

significance of this insidious bias; she should have known that even death would have its hierarchies and prejudices.

As she reads into the night, Ruby also thinks about her own complicity here, confronts it, as she recalls those high-profile crimes that have made the front pages not just across America, but back in Australia too. In every case that has seeped into her consciousness — enough for her to remember a name, a face, a story — the victim is a young white woman.

How had she not noticed that only some people are deemed worthy of having their stories told? There must be so many biographies buried in the ground, she realises, so many unspoken names. All because an arbitrary line gets drawn between the right kind of victim, and the wrong kind. And that 'wrong' kind of victim becomes invisible.

Something Ruby Jones starts doing from this night on: she goes looking for the dead. She searches out names and faces, she reads obituaries and crime reports and historical accounts, and the names engraved on statues and park benches. New deaths, old deaths, she does her best not to discriminate, as she stops over the name of every deceased person she encounters, takes the time to speak their names out loud.

The dead, she soon sees, are everywhere. Lost to cancer and school shootings. Police brutality. Domestic violence and drownings. Kidnappings and war, and hearts with too many holes. She finds lists and lists of ways to die and lists of names to say out loud; for the rest of her life she will pay attention. She will let the departed know they matter, especially those whose lives might otherwise be passed over. She will

179

say their names, sound out the syllables of their existence whenever she can.

She has no name to sound out loud for me.

I'm Alice, I whisper to her many times. *Alice Lee*. But she can't hear me over the car horns and the sirens and the doors slamming. I'm lost in the buzz of her phone and the sound of the shower running, the hiss of the coffee pot downstairs, and the pad of her feet against the ground. My voice is quieter still when she is laughing or crying or gasping against the memory of Ash's mouth, or when the slate eyes of a man she has just met flash behind her own, inexplicably replacing Ash's face when she comes.

The thing is. When the dead speak back, we are seldom loud enough to be heard over the clamour of all that living going on.

★   ★   ★

Two weeks pass by, and no one has come to claim me. They've made their posters, held their press conferences, asked for anyone who knows *anything* to come forward. They've attempted to put flesh around my bones, but all the while, that flesh falls further and further away. And still, no one comes for me. Still, they call me Jane. To be clear, I don't think I am a Jane at all. Jane seems like someone older, someone refined, with a real job and an apartment in her own name. Just like the one Noah lives in. Except, without the dogs, and maybe with big white flowers in vases all over the place, and maybe without a piano sat in the middle of the living room. I don't think Jane plays the piano. She does the *New York Times* crossword, and practises mindfulness and any freckles on her nose were lasered off just before her thirty-fifth birthday, and though she never admits it, she's had Botox injections every six weeks for the last two years. That's Jane. She's successful and polite, and she fits right into the corners of her name. And it isn't my name.

It isn't my name.

I want my name back. This name that was mine from the beginning. That's what I want them to use when they talk about me. I want the news stories to say Alice Lee was a girl who lived in New York City, and she was just starting to fit into the corners of her own name, her own life. Alice Lee was eighteen years old, and she had long blonde hair her lover used to wrap around his fingers, forcing her neck back so he could bear down on her skin with his teeth. Alice Lee loved that, and she loved taking photographs with the camera she stole, and she was starting to love Noah and his quiet kindness, and she loved the silver glitter of the Chrysler Building, no matter how many times she gazed up at its spire.

Alice Lee was someone who missed her best friend Tammy, and once, when she was six, a man pulled up in front of her house and tried to get her into his blue car, beckoning from the driver's seat, saying he had a special secret to share. Alice Lee was the girl who froze for a full minute before she ran inside, and she was the girl who never told anyone about that minute and that man in the blue car.

This was Alice Lee. She never broke any bones and her teeth were straight and strong, and her mother died, and so did she. Not the same way, but not so differently, either. She liked fish tacos and fairy lights and hated the taste of liquorice. She hadn't read nearly enough books, and she was busy falling in love with the world, when she was yanked right out of it.

Smile. Is that what he said to her, just before? Or during? There were sounds he made she couldn't hear, wouldn't hear, but she'd made him angry, hadn't she? By not answering his questions. She froze instead, just like that day when the strange man in his blue car tried to tell her a secret. She knew not to go towards him, could smell the danger between them, but for a full minute, she forgot how to move. And this time, Alice Lee remembered too late.

I will go to Hart Island. If no one claims me, my body will join a million others on that speck of land in Long Island Sound. A pretty-sounding name for a mass of dirt, endlessly churned, bones buried on top of bones. Three-persons deep, they say. When they remember that those bones belong to people.

They might loan my body out to a university first, before they take me to the island. I wouldn't mind this so much, I like the idea that some parts of my body might help fix other bodies, other warm, kinetic beings in need of repair. I have no further use for this mass of calcium and marrow, for the hair and fingernails and those blue, blue eyes. I don't get to coil my muscles; I don't get to taste something before it reaches my mouth or come so intensely that I'm flying. I don't suppose it really matters what they do to my body now.

There used to be an asylum on Hart Island. There was an asylum here, too, next to the mortuary. The dead and the damaged, side by side, out of sight. When a famous person dies, a princess or a politician, say, the public gets to see it. Their funeral is kind of like a celebration. There are flowers and candles and

182

photographs, and songs that tell you something about who the person was before they died. The ones left behind stand up and share their memories, they take the life that was lived, and they put a frame around it. So that people don't forget. I will not get flowers and candles and songs. If I am buried on Hart Island, no one will even know my favourite song. It's 'Try a Little Tenderness', by the way. Otis Redding. The first time my mother played me that record, I cried. I loved his soulful voice so much; it seemed he was singing to me, about me. I listened to the song so often that, eventually, I could hear Otis singing it in my head, no need for my mom's old stereo. *Them young girls, they do get wearied.* Not something to play at a funeral, I suppose. But at least I would be there. Present at my own mourning. If they take me to Hart Island, it's all gone. My favourite song, and my favourite word (sarsaparilla), and my first ever crush (Michael from Mrs O'Connor's class, fourth grade). People mourn the future that is lost when someone dies. But what about the past? What about all that is bound up in a person, and all the things that disappear when they die?

And what if you've even lost your name? What then? You will be placed in a plain pine coffin, and an inmate from Rikers will dig your grave and lower you down. Bones upon bones, names unknown, buried with the lost and the forgotten. An asylum for the dead.

I would like to be remembered better than this. Josh says we are lucky. That people will pay closer attention to a girl like me. But what if they never find out who I really am? Even worse — what if they stop caring about me once they *do* know?

What if it turns out I'm the wrong kind of victim, too?

Don't go there. Don't do that.

Skirt's too short, street's too dark.

Why couldn't you — who did you — how did you — ?

When you go around asking for trouble like that. What exactly did you think would happen!

Look at all the things they tell us. Listen to the words ringing in our ears as the bodies stack up. As another young woman is added to the pile of limbs and hearts and hopes and dreams, and all the things she'll never do. Because of all the things she *didn't* do.

Or all the things she did.

That's the part they seldom make clear. When they decide who gets to be the right kind of dead girl.

If they think of us at all.

15

The day before her first official Death Club meeting, Ruby spends her afternoon down at the morgue on 1st Avenue. She lingers in the small lobby, silently watching people in uniforms swing through the double doors on the other side of the room, heading, she assumes, to the bowels of the building, where the real work happens. Imagining coolers and plastic-wrapped bodies and the rows of carved-up remains down there, frozen under her feet. Ruminating on ribs cracked open, on organs scooped out, the recordings of last meals and the weight of hearts, and in the case of the Jane and John Does, the blank spaces where their names should be. Thinking, of course, about me.

Standing awkwardly in this room, Ruby is nearly as close to me as she was that Tuesday morning exactly two weeks ago, when mere metres separated us. A longing to see me again has brought her down here, crazy as she thinks this might make her. Sometimes, she even finds herself thinking she would go back to that morning down by the river if she could. It feels sacred to her now, that time we had together before those officers arrived, though she would not think to name it as such. Sacred is my word for it, when she still worries that I have become an obsession. Something she needs to resolve.

I know better.

Here at the morgue, Ruby wonders whether other people are getting closer to solving the mystery for her. Has Detective O'Byrne pored through enough files, looked over enough photographs and searched enough databases to have something click over in his mind, start spiralling towards my identity? And will that inevitably lead the detective to the man who did this? Ruby thinks about this more than she'd like to these days, too. Thinks about *him*. The fact that my murderer is out there somewhere, knowing what he did. Getting away with it and going about his life, which seems to Ruby so horribly, grossly unfair.

Feeling conspicuous in the small, sparsely decorated lobby, she focuses her attention on the Latin motto written across the wall behind the front desk. Mouthing the ancient words, getting lost in their rhythms, she doesn't realise she's speaking out loud again, until the impassive man behind the desk looks up, asks if there is anything that he can help her with.

Ruby's cheeks colour.

I *don't think you can help me*, she wants to answer, looking past him to the double doors, swinging. *Not unless you know the girl down there.*

There are people in this building who know my body as intimately as a lover might. They know of the tiny mole in the arch of my left foot. The faint scar on my left elbow from a childhood scab that got infected. They know my pubic area was waxed a few weeks before my death. Underarms and legs shaved, perhaps the day before. They know I am not a virgin, that my eyes are blue, and one or two of the male pathologists stop, as they examine my body, to think how pretty I must have been, without half of my face smashed in. Privately, they agree that the forensic artist's sketches haven't quite captured the fullness of my lips or the honey of my hair.

Some men get obsessed with the dead as much as

186

the living.

And it's not just these men, the ones who are required to look at me, either. Through Ruby's ever-increasing time spent online, she has been introduced to a thriving underground network of amateur detectives who frequent forums and websites dedicated to their passion: solving murder mysteries. Anonymous people, strangers to me and to each other, these true crime enthusiasts spend much of their waking hours tapping out theories on everything from decades-old murders to brand new cases like mine, their hunches and *what ifs* glowing out from computer screens across the globe.

The first time Ruby found a discussion thread specifically focused on my murder investigation, she almost couldn't believe it. But she is used to it now, because, with my identity still a mystery, the case has generated a lot of interest online. Initially, the less generous speculations about me made her mad, but she's gotten used to that, too. There are people who insist I'm this druggie chick they used to know, and others who swear I'm a prostitute they met somewhere, sometime, but thankfully, most of the forum members she encounters are circumspect when discussing the possibilities and probabilities of my life.

I am not an unusual case to this true crime crowd, not by any means. But I am shiny and new, a fresh face on the list of lost and founds they pore over, all the Janes and Johns, and the people who got to keep their names when they met their mysterious, nefarious ends.

Some men get obsessed with the dead as much as the living.

To be fair, many people see their fascination with

us as a kind of public service. An extra set of consolations, and more importantly, an extra set of eyes on the prize. These are the men and women who dedicate themselves to solving cold cases, who learn the names of the official investigators assigned to these cases, and don't hesitate to share their theories with both the police and each other. These self-taught criminologists share concerns about under-resourced police departments and clues potentially missed; they are a small army advancing through the nation of the dead. Points are scored if they can pair a recently discovered Jane or John with a known missing person. A game of Snap is played out via the keyboard, even if the cards rarely seem to match.

I am now part of the game, flipped over, examined. *Riverside Jane.* The more famous amongst us, the ones who get whole message boards for themselves, are all given nicknames like this. Main Street Jane, and Pit Stop John. Clearwater Jane, Suitcase Jane, Laneway Jane, Bus Station Jane, Barrel Jane, Sunoco Jane, Rolling Stone Jane (the last, because of the T-shirt she was wearing when they found her severed torso). *Does anyone else think that Walmart Jane could be NamUs case number* — and so begins a flurry of conversation and keyboard clicks, led by these anonymous, earnest matchmakers.

Ruby might have only recently discovered this world, but she has quickly learned its ways. She knows, for example, that I don't yet have my statistics listed over on the NamUs website, the official National Missing and Unidentified Persons System these self-appointed sleuths pull much of their information from. When she finds information about me on an unofficial site, when she reads: 'Riverside Jane: Unknown female

188

found 15 April 2014 — White/Caucasian — Cause of Death: Strangulation', she understands there is so much more to come. If my case remains unsolved, I will eventually get a NamUs profile of my own. It will contain an inventory of my remains (all parts recovered), and the condition of those remains will be outlined in polite terms (no decomposition or putrefaction for this Jane). There will be details about my height and weight and estimated age, along with an itemised list of the clothing I was wearing when my body was recovered. I will be allocated a searchable case number; I will become a series of check boxes and data entries, as the known facts of my case are divided up and classified.

A Dewy Decimal System for the dead, Ruby thought, when she first visited the NamUs site. She sat cross-legged on her bed, sipping at her vodka, as she clicked through this seemingly endless catalogue of the dead and the missing. She soon found herself unable to swallow, the alcohol coating her tongue and burning the roof of her mouth. Though Josh had suggested as much, the volume of cases on the NamUs site floored her. There were so many people missing, and so many people with numbers where their names should be.

Snap!

No one has come close to finding a match for Riverside Jane.

Ruby has frequented those true crime forums enough times now that she too sometimes calls me *Riverside Jane*. She cannot know how much I despise it; I do not wish to be tethered in this way to the place it happened. It. The thing they all want to know more about.

Central to this game, perhaps even more important than what *it* was, is *whodunit*. I am coming to understand that for many, my identity only has meaning in so far as it might help identify him. *Him*. The everyman behind each mystery, each sad, bad Jane Doe story. Never mind her after that: as soon as they know his name, he'll be the one they talk about. He'll be the one they want to know, the one who takes over the narrative.

They make movies about these men. Examine them from every angle. He becomes the central figure in the story, and the more damage he's caused, the better.

If and when he's caught, people will no doubt marvel at how he nearly got away with his crime, feel something akin to admiration for what this so-called ordinary guy almost pulled off. How did that nice man next door fool so many people? *I never suspected a thing!* Isn't this what the neighbours always say, a little awe creeping in?

You won't find Detective O'Byrne on any of those discussion threads. But here is something he is certain of: he will do it again. The nice man who murdered me. Have you ever taken years to step up to the edge of something you were wary of, and as soon as you jumped, it was like all the fear slackened, dissolved on impact? So that when you landed, you couldn't remember, not for the life of you, what you had been so frightened of before? That's how men like him explain it to O'Byrne. When they know their time is up.

It was surprisingly easy to kill her. They all say that. As if they might have done it earlier, had they only known. That's why so many of them go back for more. You can only relive the first one so long, before you start forgetting what it was like to take a life.

My murderer remembers. He walked past this very building today, in fact, pausing outside the lobby where Ruby now stands, her cheeks bright red, as the man behind the desk repeats his question.

'Is there something I can help you with, ma'am?'

Embarrassed, Ruby shakes her head, mutters a thank you, and bolts from the lobby before further questions can be asked. As she leaves, her footsteps echo over my remains, but I manage to keep pace with her as she makes her way back uptown.

I thought about following him, too. When he came by. But I only got as far as the edge of him before I pulled back.

I will try harder next time.

See, Ruby didn't recognise that Latin motto. Unable to translate the words, she had no idea it was a promise. But I know what it says, there on the wall above my dead body:

Let Conversation Cease, Let Laughter Flee. This is the Place Where Death Delights to Help the Living.

I do want to help the living. But I'm not yet ready to see where he goes.

★ ★ ★

They come for us all over this world.

Sometimes, if enough time has passed between one girl and the next, a city will be shocked awake when it happens. People will take to the streets with their signs and their anger, a crowd surge of protest and grief as they send a message across the town: *We don't want to be unsafe here.* The police will tell women to be vigilant, to avoid certain places, they'll tell men to make sure their loved ones get home safe from any place — because nowhere feels safe in those days and weeks after a dead girl is found. Women will push back hard against this, say, *Tell men not to rape and murder us! Have stronger sentencing for violent crimes! We should not be the ones changing our behaviour here!*

It might even seem that things will get better.

But after a while, the city will go back to its rhythms, it will once again become a place where women walk alone at night, and talk to strangers on the street, and only avoid *certain* places. That girl, the one they marched for, won't be forgotten, but her murder will stop being a fresh wound, eventually. It will settle on the city like a small, ugly scar.

Then, when it happens again, the city will be tired. No one will march this time, or shout in the streets; their anger will be jaded, quiet. Flowers will be laid, and candles lit, but the death of another bright young girl will come more like a reminder from now on, an alarm clock ringing.

The city was already weary when her body was found.

Time and again they will come with their flowers and candles. From Mexico City to Madrid to Melbourne and Manila, these cities will be bone tired as they watch the flowers wilt and the candles burn down.

Here lies the pain of another woman, another community, the flowers and the candles say.

There is silence for a time.

And then the alarm sounds out again.

16

When he was there on the ground dying, death did not feel like he thought it would. In fact, it didn't feel like anything at all. Time-stamps across his movements that night show two and a half hours passed between him leaving the restaurant to the west of Central Park, and his bloody, confused stumble into a bodega on the other side, where the terrified clerk used Josh's own phone to call an ambulance. He remembers the sharp pain of coming to in the park, the disorientation of tree roots and rocks and dirt at eye level, and the outline of a bicycle wheel, strangely twisted. He remembers how the pain came flooding in as he looked at that circle of spokes, a dam opening, nerves gushing. Soon, his arms were burning, and his legs were bright red flames. He could taste blood, see it, and though he couldn't make his arms reach up, he knew there was something wrong with his head, something exposed and broken. Before that — there had been nothing. Up to two hours of black, as he lay on a dirt path and his upturned bicycle wheel stopped spinning and lights went out in apartments on both sides of the park. Phones were turned to silent, laptops were clicked shut; neighbours and his wife on East 97th rolled over to face their bedroom walls. All that time, he was gone.

As Josh recounts the story of his bike accident for Ruby, a muscle in his jaw twitches, betraying his impassive tone. She has been listening intently, can almost see the dirt and the tree roots and the upside-down, spinning wheel. What she cannot see, the way I can, is the man he was in the minutes, seconds, before the accident, how much lighter he was than the man telling his story now. Physically, yes, but something else too. Josh's heaviness comes from the way his body let him down after the fall, the way it refused to hold him up. With a fractured C3 vertebrae — he places Ruby's hand against the back of his neck, helps her fingers feel the grooves — he was kept in a brace for six weeks, had to be fed like a baby, have his ass wiped by a roster of nurses, remember how to walk on his own. It does something to your sense of location within your body, spending all those days and nights lying on your back, staring at the pockmarked ceiling of a hospital room. It changes you, when you find yourself so utterly reliant on strangers to take care of your most basic needs.

He had, until the accident, somewhat thought he was invincible.

(You'd be surprised at how many people think this way.)

They are holding their first official Death Club meeting as a foursome at Gramercy Tavern — 'Farm to table is very New York!' Lennie declared when choosing the restaurant — where Ruby has found she needs to query many of the ingredients on the menu.

'They don't have nice restaurants in Melbourne?' Sue had commented when Ruby asked to be reminded what arugula was. Ruby soon learns this seemingly taciturn woman is an avid solo traveller, considers Melbourne to be one of her favourite culinary cities, and was merely teasing her. Never sure how to respond to ribbing (she has often wondered if there isn't a touch of casual cruelty in it), Ruby was grateful when Lennie suddenly tapped on her glass with a fork, making a show of calling the meeting to order.

Death Club, it turns out, is surprisingly easy to navigate. Once you get past the awkwardness of hellos, where to sit, what seasonal salad to order. Though Lennie was the official host, their newest member was granted the opening question of the night.

'Any question about death you want to ask, it's yours, Ruby.'

Nervous as she was, she immediately knew what she wanted to discuss.

Do you think people know when they die? As it happens. Are they aware?

(What she's really asking: do those of us who die so violently get spared the knowing of it? This is something she can't stop thinking about.)

As soon as Ruby set down her question, something changed in the others, an immediate orientation towards her. Josh responded first, admitting his own experiences had made him wonder about this very thing. Did he die that night in the park, when his bike hit a tree root, and his neck broke as he hit the ground? Or did he *nearly* die, which isn't the same thing at all. When he thinks back, he can only remember the nothingness of those hours he lay broken and bloody in the dirt. There was no light to walk towards, no grandfather telling him it wasn't his time. No tunnels or feelings of peace, just a silent, black expanse he felt tethered to. A dark place to which he often, inadvertently, returns.

'The thing is, once you start losing blood supply to the brain,' he is saying now, 'whether through shock, which is what happened to me, or strangulation' — he looks straight at Ruby when he says this — 'everything short circuits pretty quickly. Our most human characteristics are the first to go, apparently. Sense of self, awareness of time. Memory centres, language. Essentially, you reduce, getting more and more primal as things shut down. In that way, I'd say we might know when we're in the process of dying. But by the time we get to death itself, we don't know that we were ever alive.'

'Although studies have shown,' Sue picks up the thread, 'that some people experience a surge of brain activity at the point of death. The complete opposite of an unconscious state. There was a moment, in the car with Lisa, where she came to, opened her eyes, looked straight at me. It was like she came back, like she was completely fine. And then, in a second, she was gone.'

'You never told me that part,' Lennie says softly, reaching over and squeezing Sue's hand.

'About what happened before they got me out of the car? No, I suppose I haven't. I don't, as you might imagine, like going over the specifics. At any rate,' Sue dabs at her eyes with the corner of a napkin, 'I don't want to get too fanciful about it. An unexpected burst of brain activity right before death seems to be quite common. A last human flare sent out into the world, if you will.'

Ruby soon understands that emotions move like water when Death Club gets going; sometimes there is a steady stream of words and ideas, sometimes a touched nerve blocks the flow. Even then, with a little pressure, something true and honest cracks through. Sue's soft smile for Lennie now, Josh's sheepish grin when the latter suggests the story of his accident seems to have gotten a little more dramatic tonight. Then, it's like everyone is propelled by the same questions and anxieties, the same need to move past their current limitations. Ruby has never participated in a conversation that feels so raw and honest. Her friends back home are great, they're funny and kind and smart, but they mostly talk about work and weekends. They plan parties, and group holidays to Thailand, and when they meet on someone's couch, or in the dark corner of a city bar, they talk about everyday, ordinary things. Sometimes they argue about each other's political leanings, or attend a march for this, against that. But for the most part, her Australian friends have an unspoken agreement to glide across the surface of things. None more so than Ash.

'We don't have to talk about *everything*,' he once said.

As if the little she said was too much.

Ever since her seemingly unfounded panic the morning after the vigil, Ruby has been careful with Ash. While they still text most days, the majority of their messages have become generic, polite in the way of people who are busy thinking more about what they don't say than what they do. After holding back so much from Ash — from everyone back home — it is exhilarating for Ruby to find herself in the middle of such rich, meaningful conversation, something she would have never thought possible with people she barely knows. Though, to be sure, this evening has given Ruby a chance to get to know her table-mates better, to catch pieces of them in the light, in a way she wasn't afforded at brunch. For instance, she quickly comes to understand that Sue, with her cropped white hair and jutting cheekbones, projects a quiet, enviable confidence, whether choosing a wine, or setting down an opinion. She has travelled the world on her own, doesn't find Ruby's current isolation odd at all, and is only concerned for what she suggests might be a tendency towards aimlessness in her new acquaintance.

'Don't confuse liking your own company with doing nothing,' she advises, when Ruby admits she is neither working nor studying while in New York. 'You're a designer by trade, yes? Well, in this day and age, there's no excuse for not working from your own bed, if you have to.'

Ruby cannot imagine offering such unsolicited advice to someone she's just met, yet she finds herself grateful for Sue's polite scolding, considers laying out her whole list of problems, just to see what the older woman might say (*It's Death Club, not Confession*, she has to remind herself more than once when it comes to Sue).

Josh, on the other hand, throws out statements like grenades. Sweeps up the damage himself if he sees he has gone too far. 'Sorry,' he says more than once as the night progresses, not sounding sorry at all. 'That didn't come out the way I meant it to.'

'I write like I speak, but I don't speak like I write,' he will explain later. 'Which is how I get myself in trouble sometimes.'

In addition to having firm opinions on almost everything, Josh is, Ruby can consciously acknowledge this now, undeniably handsome. He was born in Minnesota; *Midwestern* is the term Lennie would use for his physique, possessed as he is of thick limbs and a wide chest, his body calling to mind farms and machines, and long summers spent outdoors. To Ruby, who sees every man in relation to Ash, Josh is solid, sturdy, a rock compared to Ash's cool, narrow river. *Out of shape,* Josh would say, if he knew of her assessment. Knowing, as Ruby does not, that before the accident he was thirty pounds lighter, easily buttoning himself into fancy suits or sliding into the beds of beautiful women, one of whom he married. He has not made peace with this new, heavier body, mourns the impression he used to make when he walked into a room, the way his wife would light up just to look at him. Ruby could have thrown herself across the table at Josh for all he would notice a woman checking him out these days: who wants to be appreciated for all you would change about yourself? After his wife left, he packed up what was left of desire, hid it away in the black. Content, he thinks, to leave it there.

(He doesn't say any of this out loud, of course.)

Amongst the group it is clear that Lennie is the warmth, the home fire. I see bright oranges and golds spark from her fingers, settle on the shoulders of her friends when she talks, relaxing muscles, loosening bones. She has always had this gift, a kind of radiance soaked in by the people around her, from those doting waiters Ruby noticed their first supper after the PTSD meet-up, to Sue and Josh now, any tensions they brought to the table sliding off them as the evening progresses. Ruby cannot see the glow, but she too feels it; despite the intensity of Death Club's conversations, she soon feels relaxed for the first time in a very long while.

I, on the other hand, cannot relax. On the contrary. I feel a growing sense of anticipation. Waiting as the group comes up against the single question that I want them to ask tonight, watching as they back away from it every time.

What happens *after* you die?

I could tell them, over this table cluttered with wine glasses and brightly coloured, half-eaten food, that you are indeed aware when it happens. I could explain that the black Josh can remember from the accident is simply where it begins. Death. It doesn't happen all at once. We are not a switch flicked, a power source turned off. You are still right there at the start, as the pain intensifies, a string plucked over and over, pulled so tight that you flame under the skin, and it's only after that — I don't know if it's choice or necessity at this point — you begin to leave your body. You retreat from the agony and the fire, and when you find yourself in the black, you know, instinctively, that you need to pass through it. The black is your waiting room, a brief pause in the night of your existence, before you stumble forward, searching for walls, a door, to get out. By then, nothing they can do to your body hurts you. Not in the sense of nerve and sinew and bone.

But you are definitely aware that you're dead. It's what happens next that I still don't understand.

Josh came back. I did too, somehow. I know there are others, somewhere in this new distance made of space and time, who do not come back, people who quickly move on.

More and more, I can sense their departure, like the click of a shut door, but I don't know where they go, these dead who do not live here any more.

What happens if you don't follow them? What happens after you die, if you're *still* aware? Josh had to learn how to walk again, after spending time in the black. Does that mean I can learn to speak and touch and be heard again, too? Do I get to send out that last human flare, to show Ruby I'm still here?

The way I see it, Death Club holds the answers.

The truth will reveal itself, soon enough. As long as these four questioning minds, these four sets of past experiences, future hopes and current complications, keep pressing their noses up against death, keep trying to break through the glass.

With Ruby there in the middle.

And me, their fifth member, waiting on the other side.

> Best Death Club ever!!! Josh has never talked so much about the accident. And Sue — OMG she loved you! Her turn to host next, will send you the details asap. Thank you. Mwah xoxox.

Lennie's text comes through early the next morning. Ruby, half asleep, smiles as she reads the message.

Ask if the dead can talk to us too, I whisper in her ear. But she has already gone back to sleep, my words sounding like the soft metal clang of the Venetian blinds against her open window.

★ ★ ★

Sue chooses Patsy's as the next Death Club destination, an Italian restaurant on West 56th where Frank Sinatra used to dine at his favourite table back in the day.

'Lisa's favourite movie was *On the Town* with Sinatra and Gene Kelly,' Sue explains when they first sit down, 'and she used to beg to eat here whenever we came into the city. It might not be one of Lennie's overpriced, over-hyped tourist traps. But there's a little bit of New York's history here — and a little bit of mine.'

It is a week since they met at Gramercy Tavern. In

that time, with some help from me, the four members of Death Club have thought about each other, gone to sleep with fragments of each other's stories and felt a peculiar longing for each other's company, in ways they never would have expected. And though no one is quite sure how it happened, it is Ruby the three original members keep coming back to most of all. So that by the end of the week, Sue can't stop thinking about how close Ruby is to the age her daughter Lisa would be now if she had lived, rolls the thought around and around until it is shiny, a pearl between her fingertips. Her daughter in New York. Her daughter eating at fancy restaurants and drinking fine wine. Her daughter — but her imaginings are cut off every time, because she does not yet know enough about Ruby, does not know enough about who her own daughter may have become. With so many gaps, Sue finds herself endlessly ruminating, looking for hints, for clues. What does a woman in her mid-thirties make of life these days? Ruby seems to have sprung, fully formed, from Lennie's forehead, but she must have left a whole life behind. Lovers, family, friends. A career back home in Australia. What movies does she like, what books does she love? What ideas does she have about men?

(If she had lived, who might Lisa have become?)

It took me a little longer to capture Josh's attention, or rather, to figure out how to direct it. He was not interested in why Ruby came to New York. Did not ponder her living arrangements or how she filled her days, or what she left behind in Australia. Over brunch, he had completely missed the slant of her cheekbones and the map of her mouth, remained unfazed by the smallness of her hands, the way her fingers wrapped around whatever glass she was holding, or her habit of pulling at her earlobe when she was deep in thought. None of this interested him, none of this came home with him when they parted, which wasn't exactly unusual for Josh, because not much at all about the opposite sex interested him these days. Lennie and Sue were different, he made time for Death Club because he liked the way their minds worked, the things they didn't shy away from. And because his agent agreed he might get a book out of it someday. Which is how I figured it out in the end. The hook and the reel.

Me.

Riverside Jane.

He had heard about me, of course. But after meeting Ruby, he started paying more attention to the details. And that's when he began to notice the *jogger* reference in every blog post or news article he read. *The body was found by a jogger. A jogger made the unfortunate discovery, just after 6 a.m. Jogger encounters dead body in Riverside Park.* How many times had he read a variation of this sentence and not stopped to think about this ubiquitous jogger, present in so many tales of woe? How, as a writer, had he not considered what finding a dead body must be like, especially if the discovery made the headlines, led to a massive investigation like this one. How odd that Lennie's new project, this Australian woman she'd insisted he meet, should turn out to be one such jogger. *The* jogger, in fact. Out of this spark of fascination, a small fire for Ruby was started, a wondering, and that is where I came in, tending those flames until they licked at his dreams.

It's getting easier. How to do it. Because after that

last Death Club conversation, I let myself remember something Noah said, one of those things I never understood at the time.

'You have a rich inner world, Alice. Populated with people and places that suit your liking.'

What he meant was this: we all exist in our own little worlds, our own private universes. We don't have to see a person in the flesh to think about them; it's enough that they're there in our heads, which is where we do most of our looking, anyway. It doesn't therefore matter if I'm aware. What matters is that the original members of Death Club can now see Ruby, even when they close their eyes. I just need to show them what's already there.

There are, of course, limitations. I can't, for example, make Josh think about Ruby while he's brushing his teeth or talking on the phone, but I can help turn his head when he passes the proliferation of Australian coffee houses near his workplace, or encourage him to pause over an Aussie Rules football game when he's flicking through sports channels late at night. Songs on the radio make it even easier. AC/DC. INXS. He hums along to his favourite bands from Down Under, and his mind wanders to Ruby on its own from there. My work is basically done.

Lennie, by contrast, doesn't take much work at all. That's mostly because she falls in love with people on the spot. Not romantic love, exactly, but something similar, a kind of euphoric curiosity that propels her to unravel the mysteries of a person, get to know who they really are. She had been right about Ruby's acute loneliness, the night she watched her from across the room at the group therapy session. And right, too, that loneliness, like any kind of suffering, cloaks a person, hides their endearing quirks and funny stories and good intentions. There's always someone super interesting under that cloak, Lennie is sure of it, and she's determined to help Ruby shed her layers. Knowing, without any help from me, that something happened *before* Ruby found a dead body, that her tangible grief owes itself to more than the death of an unnamed girl.

Essentially, they have positioned themselves perfectly. Taken their individual stories and found a way to place Ruby at the centre of them, a new glue to hold Death Club together. This is exactly what I wanted, a bind to ensure they keep meeting, keep talking, keep asking and answering their questions, so that, eventually, those questions lead back to me. The *real* me, not Riverside Jane, interesting as she might be, but the girl who was going to live more than seventy-nine years. Until a man took all those years away.

Is our death fated? Do we have a predestined, inescapable end, or is it all just arbitrary?

This is the question they ask tonight at Patsy's, as pasta is twirled around forks, the red sauce from Lennie's Bolognese staining the crisp white tablecloth between them.

How I might ask it: was he always going to kill me?

Sue, the first at the table to speak, is emphatic.

'I've always thought that fate is simply a construct designed to help us make sense of things after they've happened. It's how we survive the random after-effects of living.'

'My parents have God for that,' Lennie says. '"The lot is cast into the lap, but its every decision is from the Lord" isn't that the saying? Either way, they seem pretty sure he's the one calling the shots.'

'I prefer to put my faith in the Moirai,' Josh responds, flashing white teeth in a sardonic grin. 'Three old women weaving our fate, spinning, measuring, cutting. Life hanging by a thread. Much more evocative than some old guy who is or isn't his own son pulling the strings.'

Lennie returns Josh's grin.

'Alas, a lifetime of Catholic education makes it hard for me to shake that old guy off completely. Still, I can't say for sure what I think about the idea of having a specific kind of death sitting out there, waiting for me. It's not the most comforting notion.'

'Maybe it could be,' Ruby offers. 'Maybe if we knew when we were going to die, and how' — but she stops, as the memory of my battered body comes back to her, clear as a picture. 'Never mind, I don't know where I was going with that. Imagine if Jane had known, that morning . . .'

'Did he, then?' Lennie asks, biting her lip, as if unsure of asking her own question. 'The guy who murdered Jane. Do you think he set out that morning to kill her?'

(Waves crash. Water drums in my ears. I know I could help answer this one, if I really wanted to. I am there, in his universe, too.)

'From what I've read, it seems more like a crime of opportunity,' Josh answers, as Ruby goes pale. 'A case of wrong place, wrong time for the poor kid. Some asshole saw a chance to play God, and he took it. Not so much destiny as delusions of grandeur, then. Let's just hope — or pray, Lennie — that he made enough mistakes for the police to catch up with him, eventually. Although something like 40 per cent of murders go unsolved, so — '

206

'I used to pray a lot when I was little,' Lennie interrupts, catching Ruby's alarmed look and changing tack. 'I truly believed I could wind all the world's terrible things back on themselves, stop them from happening. Maybe that means I do indeed believe in destiny. Or the idea you can control your fate, if you ask the right way.'

Sue nods at this, the small diamonds at her ears sparkling.

'I prayed for a while, after the accident. I prayed for us to go back to that night we were headed to the movies, so that I could be in the driver's seat instead, be the one to absorb the impact of the crash. I used to lie in bed and try to bend time, fold it back on itself. I prayed, I bargained, I pleaded. And sometimes, when I finally managed to fall asleep, it would happen. The whole night would play out differently. It would snow so much that the roads closed, or we would find out the 8 p.m. show was sold out, or Lisa would ask me to drive, and I would slide into the driver's seat, and that man looking down, changing his CD, would hit me, take me, not her.'

She pauses, before continuing.

'Those prayers changed nothing, naturally.'

'What do you think your life would be like now, if it had snowed, or the movie was sold out?' Lennie asks softly, and I know they are done talking about me tonight.

'If Lisa had lived? I think' — Sue looks to the ceiling, takes a deep breath — 'I think I would still be living in that nice, big house in Connecticut, and she would live here in New York, and my unhappy marriage to her father would have lasted, and I would be living a relatively unremarkable, albeit privileged life. Summers on Martha's Vineyard, instead of visiting Auckland and Paris and Marrakesh. Ladies' Book Club instead of Death Club. That's how it would have played out for a woman like me.

'But ultimately, I don't know what Lisa's life would have been like' — Sue looks at Ruby now — 'because, at seventeen, she went too soon for me to really get to know her, or what I would have been like as her mother as she grew into a woman.'

For the first time, I understand it's not only the dead who have lives they don't get to live out. The people left behind have as many versions of themselves unexplored, as many possible paths that close off. Some versions are better, and some, no doubt, are worse. There is a Sue outside of Lisa's death. A woman Sue understands she will never get to be, because of a night when it didn't snow, and a movie was not sold out, and a man looked down to change his CD, and entire worlds were lost and begun again before he had a chance to look up and take note of where he was headed.

No one lives just *one* life. We start and finish our worlds many times over. And no matter how long or short a time we are here, I'm beginning to realise we all want more than we get.

As the Death Club members continue talking into the night, I leave them be, and return to where we started. A question I had not thought to consider at the time.

If my death was indeed fated — was it my fate or his, in the end?

★ ★ ★

If I had lived.

If I had reached for Mr Jackson the last morning we were together, stopped my mouth against his, kept the words down. If I had let the fact of my impending birthday slide down his warm skin, dissolve into nothing as important as our bodies and the snow outside and the heaviness of him, wrapping over and around me like a sheet. If we had made love that last day of me being seventeen, and if the next day I had decided birthdays weren't important to anyone but your own self, and asked him to paint me instead, so I could have something of my new, adult self to keep — would I have lived?

Would I have added years in this way, silently slipping into a life with Mr Jackson where I was twenty, thirty, forty years old, waking up next to him before another birthday and thinking: *I have made it another year closer to 79.1!* Would we have emerged after that first winter as a real couple, and made a real life together, one that included a wedding, and children, and a house in another town where he could teach art and I could —

Here, like Sue when she imagines Lisa, I don't know how to see the world that might have grown up around us. Would I have gone to college? Stayed home with the beautiful babies we made? Helped Mr Jackson sell his art and remained his muse, even when I passed my own mother's age and kept going, getting older and older, with him immortalising every new line on my body?

No lines, I don't want lines. He said this before our very first afternoon together. Would he still have loved me when my body turned into a well-read map?

If I had lived.

If I had not said anything about my birthday. If I had not gotten on a bus to New York City. If I had not knocked on Noah's door. If I had not — but it's foolish to think about these things now. I did not live. Because a certain man had pretended to be someone else for too long, and when he put his hands on me that last morning of my life, it was the truest he had ever been, and if I had not — not — not, it would still be nothing compared to the force of this one man's revelation.

17

Intimacy grows exponentially.

Doors unlock, people might pass through them slowly at first, assess their surroundings. But soon enough, windows are thrown open, furniture is dusted off, space is made, and seats are taken. From a slow, careful start, a rapid acceleration occurs. I once had this kind of intimacy with Noah, with Tammy. With Mr Jackson, too. Where suddenly, someone you never knew in the world becomes all you know of the world.

'I have made new friends,' Ruby tells Cassie. 'It only took me seven weeks.'

(And *one murder*, she silently adds.)

Her sister is relieved. She has been worried about Ruby's new obsession with death and murder, does not have what she calls *the macabre gene*, and though she feels bad for what her sister experienced, Cassie's solution would certainly not include spending hours dwelling on all the terrible things that can happen to women. Making new friends seems like a step in a healthier direction, and Cassie is glad for the opportunity to say yes and actually mean it, the next time their mother asks her whether she *really* thinks Ruby is doing okay over there in New York City.

An expert in omission, Ruby has not mentioned the specifics of these new friends she has made, or Cassie might pause before answering in the affirmative. Death Club would not, as Lennie might say, be her sister's cup of tea, and Ruby doesn't want anything tainting something that suddenly feels so essential.

Besides, she reasons, the very existence of Death Club is proof that some conversations are best reserved for the people who understand you. For those who know that proximity to death fundamentally changes you.

Distancing yourself from death changes you too, I could add, thinking of my old friends, what they've become.

But I don't want to give Ruby any ideas on that one.

★ ★ ★

Here are some things that happen in the week before the next Death Club meeting:

Ruby sees that her local cinema is holding a Gene Kelly retrospective and *On the Town* is included in the programme. Shyly, Ruby asks Sue if she'd like to be her date for the Wednesday night session, and she could almost cry when the answer is yes. After the movie — a light, bright love letter to New York — the pair have a drink in the bar next door to the movie house and talk about Lisa. Sue tells Ruby her daughter was an aspiring actress, spending her summers at theatre camp, winning the lead in every musical since her sophomore year. She was just months off graduating, with plans to attend a performing arts college in upstate New York, when that driver lost concentration and ran a stop sign. Lisa, driving carefully as was her nature, took the full force of the other vehicle.

'She would be your age now, just over,' Sue admits this night, and Ruby sees how some grief is fossilized, hardened into stone. This mother will never stop missing her daughter, both as the girl she knew, and the woman she can never meet.

212

'It helps to think we might have stayed close,' Sue says. 'If you and I can find common ground, become friends — perhaps my daughter would still have wanted me around at this age, too.'

'She absolutely would have,' Ruby says, and means it. They clink their glasses together, and I notice the shimmer of a gossamer thread gently winding around their pinkie fingers, expanding between them as they pull away.

On another night, Ruby and Lennie go to a roof-top bar. There is a swimming pool lapping up to the edges of the patio, and people in expensive-looking clothing stand around in clusters, looking like shiny fruits on a vine. Every so often, one or another drops away, makes for the bathroom or bar to order another round of expensive-looking drinks, their heads turning this way and that, clearly wanting to see and be seen.

'I brought you here for the view,' Lennie said when they arrived, and Ruby knew she meant the single men in those clusters, as much as the glittering of Manhattan at dusk. They stood in a corner sipping at their Martinis, and talked about many things, but Ruby found she could not form Ash's name, could not frame the reasons why she barely noticed these men, brushing by in their navy suits and pink-check shirts. The friendship felt too new, too unfolding, to risk Lennie's potential judgement. And something else, too. She was so used to keeping her relationship with Ash a secret, it almost felt a betrayal to speak about him now. At this time, when she was exposing so much of herself, in the way new friends do, Ash was the one thing she could hold back.

(Which works just fine when all is going well. But

what do you do when they break your heart?).

They left the bar around 8 p.m., when the line to buy another drink got too long, moving on for mac 'n' cheese at a half-empty diner a world away from New York's rooftops. As they ate, the conversation returned to men and relationships. Lennie was laughing at Ruby's recent, disastrous foray into online dating — 'God, dick pics are the worst!' — when she suddenly stopped and waved her fork at Ruby.

'What about Josh, then?'

'What — what about him?' Ruby felt her cheeks go hot.

'You said before that you don't really notice guys these days. But Josh is a little hard to miss, don't you think?'

'He's handsome, sure,' Ruby admitted, and in doing so unwittingly cemented this observation into fact, so that she will feel an odd sense of anticipation the next time she sees him, a nervous flutter at the heft of him. It might be nice, she reasoned over her bowl of pasta, to have someone else to think about from time to time. Which is how her own locked doors started to inch open, slowly but surely. Sometimes it really is as simple as saying a thing out loud, turning it into your newest truth.

(What? You thought desire was more complicated than that?)

What Ruby doesn't know: Lennie met Josh that very afternoon for coffee. He told her that he'd been spending time researching the Riverside Jane case, had even tried to call in a few journalistic favours from his mates at the precinct, but so far — nothing.

'It's like this girl never existed, Lennie,' he said. 'Or it suits certain people to have it seem that way.'

(When I think about the continued silence of those who *do* know the details of my existence, Josh comes as close to the truth as anyone has so far.)

As they continued talking about me, Lennie noticed how often Josh brought the conversation back to Ruby.

'She's a bit of a mystery herself, isn't she,' Lennie couldn't help saying when Ruby's name came up yet again, and Josh's shrug was too casual, too considered, to indicate anything other than agreement.

'Kind of exotic too,' she added slyly. 'With that accent and her big, brown eyes, and the way she came here on her own, just jumped right into the unknown.'

'Not sure what her eyes have to do with that,' Josh had retorted, but he was grinning, and Lennie realised she'd never seen that particular look on his face before. Something almost bashful. It was enough for her to get her arrows ready, draw back her bow. For nothing is more intoxicating to a fixer than bringing two people together. This one would take some creativity, she knew; both her targets were openly wary of romance. But she had no doubt there was potential in this match, and that afternoon Lennie determined she would do all she could to bring Ruby and Josh together, as if this had been the plan all along.

It could easily have been her life's work, by the way, playing matchmaker to the damaged like this. If she hadn't accidentally bound herself to the dead, instead.

In this week of small and significant moments, a week where those posters with the approximation of my face tatter on poles, and my real name stays locked inside people's mouths, Noah walks past the precinct on West 82nd Street four separate times. DNA from the crime scene once again comes back: *No Match*. Neither victim nor perpetrator are anywhere to be found in any local or national databases; question marks remain where both of our names should be written.

That is to say — as the days since my murder pass, certain people reveal themselves, layer by layer. And others keep holding their secrets tight.

⋆ ⋆ ⋆

Ruby and Josh show up to the next Death Club meeting, Ruby's third official meeting in as many weeks, at the exact same time. Walking through the doors of Grand Central Oyster Bar, Josh sees Ruby's eyes widen as she takes in the amber-lit, terracotta tiles arched over their heads. He had forgotten how iconic the ceiling of this cavernous room is, and Ruby's reaction makes him feel something akin to pride.

'It's a city where you should always look up,' he says, liking the way Ruby turns to look at him now. When their hostess seats them, the young woman smiles at the pair, the way strangers look at lovers, conspiratorial and approving, so that all three momentarily confuse the occasion. When the other Death Club members arrive, when it becomes clear this is not in fact a date, the hostess finds herself oddly disappointed. Love makes her job easier, diverts the steady stream of workers and tourists arriving each night, their undercurrents of tiredness and resentments buzzing about them. It would have been nice to be in the presence of romance on this spring night.

(She is not the only one who thinks so.)

Seated across the red-check table from each other, with Lennie and Sue still on their way, Ruby and Josh find conversation easier than either would have thought. Soon, Josh is telling Ruby an animated tale about the famous celestial ceiling of the Grand Central Terminal above them, a funny story I already knew, thanks to Noah. How back in 1913, on the day the terminal opened, an amateur astronomer passing through the new building stopped and noticed the blue and gold zodiac mural hung high above everyone's heads had been painted in reverse, so that east was west, and west was east. Meaning the constellations were not at all where they should be. It is a New York blunder Josh loves; it amuses him to think about the grandeur of that opening day, and the moment one anonymous, practical man looked up and burst the gilded bubble.

'I never knew that!' Ruby laughs, admitting she wouldn't know her Orion from her Pegasus. 'So, you're saying the sky is back to front up there?'

'Either that, or the mural is meant to represent the heavens when viewed from the outside, in,' Josh answers. 'The jury is still out on whether the reversal of those stars was deliberate, or a rather ironic mistake for a building dedicated to navigation.'

They are both laughing now, mimicking the consternation of those in charge of festivities on that 1913 opening day. I prefer to think of the lone astronomer just off the train, thumb and forefinger to his chin, scanning the skies, and I see Noah's face in this moment, and Franklin too, watching from the doorway, almost as if they're waiting for me. The scene is blurry, as if I'm looking through tears, but the waves don't come this time. I'm trying to understand what that means, when Lennie and Sue arrive, causing those other faces to shimmer and disappear.

We each take a seat at the table.

It soon becomes clear this will not be a regular Death

Club meeting tonight. With Josh and Ruby still laughing, Lennie asks to be let in on the joke, and soon Josh is repeating the tale of the starry ceiling above them. From this beginning, the stories traded across Cape May Salts and Martinis and crème caramels remain light, buoyant, and for the most part, I do not mind. Something about seeing Noah and Franklin like that has slipped me into a mood deeper than sorrow, and I cannot begrudge these friends wanting a night to themselves. It feels inevitable even, as I watch Lennie grimace over a raw oyster, and listen to Josh conjuring another story about New York's quirks and mistakes, while Sue explains the difference between lobster and crayfish to Ruby, biting into her first Maine lobster roll. Nobody says they are not going to talk about life and death tonight, yet they all agree to this armistice. I see this understanding pass quietly between them, and I find myself moving back from the table, letting their conversations fade.

To watch them from a distance is to see arms touching, hands grazing. Broad smiles and secret glances. Glasses clinked together, forks dropped with a clatter. Butter dripping onto the tablecloth and napkins pressed against mouths. Red wine and whiskey ordered, and small, full sighs. I see how they have travelled a great distance together this past week, like the passengers teeming in and out of the terminal above us. If intimacy is exponential, it is opportunistic too, taking advantage of nights like this to assert itself, lock everyone in place.

I am fascinated by the shift, yet that deeper-than-sorrow feeling persists. Because I know I do not belong at this table. I cannot join the living as they trade their stories, cannot share any part of my day, my past or

218

my now, the way they do. They are discovering each other, moving forward together, while I remain the dead girl, Jane. Riverside, Doe. A month after my murder, without any fresh revelations to stoke public interest, I am a news story already growing old.

Because the people who do know my stories have stayed silent. Friends — and a lover, too — whose fingers might twitch towards their phones whenever the Riverside murder is mentioned, but they never, ever make the call. Just as the members of Death Club can set me to the side tonight, the people who know me, love me, have been doing this for weeks now. Ever since, each on their own, they thought, *What if that's my Alice?* And then quickly pushed me away.

When you see it all from the outside, you realise how little of anything is where it is supposed to be. People's love gets muddled up, too. Reversed. East is west and west is east. Sometimes the reordering is unnoticeable. And sometimes, when you look up, there is a vast, empty space where the stars used to be.

★ ★ ★

Life is getting better for Ruby Jones. She has, as she told her sister, made friends. New York glitters in their presence, and this is more than she could have hoped for. Some evenings, like this last one, she might even say that she is happy.

At last.

But there is still a dead girl. An unnamed dead girl who shows up in her dreams, asking to be known. There is still that bloodied face, beseeching Ruby when she closes her eyes. This is not something she can ignore.

Ruby knows how to be sad. She knows what to do with her sorrow. But what about happiness? What about joy creeping up on despair, disorienting it with laughter and light. What do you do with that contradiction? In other words: how do you hold your pain close and let it go at the very same time.

★ ★ ★

It is Tammy who finally makes the call.

Of everyone, she has been the least able to keep me from niggling at her thoughts, though it took time for her to acknowledge things were not quite right. Unlike Mr Jackson, Tammy did not subscribe to any of the national papers; my friend seldom paid attention to the news in general, so for a while there, she had no idea about the murder over in New York. She really was too busy monitoring her father's sobriety and keeping Rye out of trouble, both men increasingly using her strength and even temper as their leaning post. Days were full, and nights made up for the days, until she'd let a few weeks, and then a few more go by without checking in with me. Back then, she still thought I was with Mr Jackson, remembered me practically hanging up on her when he came through the door, and if she's honest, this last phone call had bothered her a little. The way I had seemed so consumed by him. It wasn't enough to make her angry at me, but it was enough to stop her from messaging on my birthday (though she would say she simply forgot), and enough to keep her attention focused elsewhere.

She'll reach out if she needs me, she told herself, and that's it, isn't it.

That's how a person slips out of your life so easily.

220

Sometimes forgetting is simply waiting too long.

Time ticked on until one day, as she scrolled through an online fashion magazine, Tammy came across a story about a recent spate of unsolved murders across the country — IS THERE A SERIAL KILLER ON THE LOOSE? — and there was my face. Or a face enough like mine, so that if she closed her eyes and laid the sketch from the article on top of her memories, she could recognise the eyes, and the nose, and my mouth (though she thought at the time: *Alice would never look so prissy*). Still, she tried to argue the worry away. This was some random girl in New York, and Alice was back in town with Mr Jackson, still fawning over him, no doubt. The niggle was enough, however, for Tammy to call my cell phone. A month ago, she'd missed a call from me; there had been no further contact since then. When she tried my number after seeing that sketch, it went straight to voicemail.

Hi, you've reached Alice Lee. But you probably already know that. Leave a message and I'll get back to you as soon as I can!

She thought, then and there, about going to the cops. But what would she say? *Oh, hey. That picture of a dead girl looks a lot like my best friend. Where does she live? Um ... I guess I don't know these days. Maybe New York City? She was always talking about moving there.* Besides, what if the cops came over? There were a lot of things her dad, not to mention her boyfriend and his brothers, would want to keep hidden from someone in uniform.

It was easier to believe that some friendships simply run their course.

But last week, as the temperature got higher, and

the grey sky pushed down on the lake, Tammy drove back to town. Told Rye she wanted to collect some cash from her mother. Pulling into the gas station on the edge of town, she saw Mr Jackson standing at one of the pumps, looking at his phone. She rolled down her window.

'Hey, Mr Jac — *Jamie*. How's Alice doing?'

Later, in the telling of it, she'll swear he jumped at the sound of my name. 'You should have seen the guilty look on his face,' she'll say. 'The way he said *I don't know what you're talking about!* and got out of there as fast as he could.' But the truth is, it was fear she saw and recognised. She was the one to drive home as fast as she could.

Walking into her old bedroom, she went straight to her collection of silly portraits we'd taken together over the years. And looking at those laughing, oblivious faces, she knew. That Alice Lee would always get back to her. She would never disappear for good.

Not if she had any choice in the matter.

'Mom!' Tammy went and lay down in bed with her mother and brought up the story about my murder on her phone. 'Mom, I think something bad happened to Alice.'

Tammy told her mother everything she knew.

The truth, at that moment, began to unfurl.

I am on my way to being found.

So is he.

18

This is what I was wearing the morning I was murdered. Grey sweatpants, fluffy on the inside, with frayed ends and an elastic waist, so I could wear them comfortably low on my hips. Powder blue Victoria's Secret briefs, cotton, with a little heart and pink VS on the front. The kind of underwear you buy in a set of five for twenty dollars. Everyday underwear. A black bra under a purple T-shirt. A purple parka, light and downy like a quilt. Purple jacket, purple T-shirt. Blue cotton briefs, a plain black bra, and an old pair of sweats. And near-new sneakers, dirt-caked from climbing down onto the rocks, and the struggle. They found me in the bra and the T-shirt. Catalogued me in the bra and the T-shirt. Made an assessment of my social class, my occupation and my intentions that morning, based on my hair and my orange nails, and these few items of clothing he left behind.

The missing clothes are in a backpack, stored in a private locker. In the basement gym of a building downtown. People, hundreds of them, walk past this locker every day. Some have even read about me, followed the Riverside Jane case. One or two went to the vigil that night. Wondering who could do such a thing to a young girl. Looking askance at men on the subway whenever they travelled uptown, walking past that downtown locker twice, five, ten times, a day. Sweats, blue underwear, a pair of sneakers, and a jacket, the blood stains I left behind more like rust these days. And a camera, a vintage Leica. Film and

Summar lens missing. An object stolen twice in just a few weeks, now wrapped in plastic inside a basement locker, code: 0415.

Every riddle has an answer. No matter how long it takes to solve, the answer was created at the exact same time as the question. This is what Detective O'Byrne thinks, as he sounds out my real name for the very first time, starts putting the small facts of my life together, with the help of Tammy's stories, and the results of Gloria D's DNA test ('*I thought she was with Tammy*,' my former guardian cries, over and over. As if this explains her carelessness).

'Alice Lee,' O'Byrne says, thinking about all the people who let me down. 'Who did this to you, kid?'

I thought my name would be enough. That my identity was the riddle they were all trying to solve. But for O'Byrne, it is just the beginning. My name was only ever a clue. For him, the real puzzle is what happened down there by the river.

At least it's me the detective directs his next question to. As if I have a say in the matter:

'How do we find the bastard, Alice? What is it we're missing?'

★ ★ ★

Unlike O'Byrne, Ruby generally tries not to think about him. Has stopped jumping at loud noises, makes an effort to smile back when men say hello as she shops for snacks at the grocery store or purchases another bottle of vodka over on Broadway. She doesn't want to be the one looking askance at strangers, not in a city where she only needs the fingers of one hand to count the people she actually knows. But he hovers

224

at the edge of her thoughts, all the same. Casts his shadow, slips around the corners of her consciousness, so that she always seems to catch the back of him, disappearing.

She tries not to think too much about him. But, deep down, Ruby knows she is as tied to my murderer as she is to me. That something is unfinished between them. And sometimes, she wonders what would happen if she followed him around those corners. If she came face to face with the man whose terrible crime she discovered.

I'll admit, now that O'Byrne has put the idea in my head, this is something I have wondered, too.

★ ★ ★

Josh is the first member of Death Club to say my name.

Alice Lee.

Tongue against teeth, he sounds out the syllables, tries to draw me out from the scant details he has managed to uncover before they hit the news. My life makes for a small list on this day I am officially identified: small town girl from the Midwest, parentless, no known occupation or address in New York. Nothing yet to help determine motive, nothing to suggest what I was doing in the park alone that morning. But there is a name, and a beginning. This is something. Riverside Jane is in fact Alice Lee.

Alice.

Josh looks at the photograph that will soon be shared with the public. Sees a beautiful young girl with blue-sky eyes and a freckle-dotted nose. Tries and fails to reconcile this with what happened to me.

It seems impossible — but then, it's always unfathomable, isn't it. What we don't know of the future when a happy picture is taken.

Josh got the tip from a friend at the *Daily News*. A woman he slept with once or twice after 9/11, when the whole city was shaking.

'They've identified that girl you're so interested in,' she told him on the phone. 'Some kid from Wisconsin. I'll text you the photo they've sent out. Feel free to thank me over dinner some time.'

But it's Ruby he asks to dinner that night. Fumbles with how to contextualize the question, and ultimately settles for this: *I have something to tell you about Jane.* He doesn't want her to think it's a date, yet when she walks into the small Italian restaurant near Lincoln Center, heads to where he is sitting at the bar, he holds out his phone towards her as if it is a bunch of flowers.

My smiling face fills the screen.

'It's Jane?'

Gripping the bar stool offered to her, Ruby looks at me, the real me, for the very first time. She has imagined this moment for weeks now. The relief of discovering my identity. It doesn't feel like she thought it would. The pain, suddenly, has become unbearable.

Jane.

Alice.

Ruby, my name is Alice Lee.

When she says my name out loud for the first time and starts to cry, I want to reach out, tell her I've been here all this time. But I cannot make the world move in my direction, not even this tiny corner of it. Were that possible, I would tilt her right into my aching arms.

226

* * *

Knees slanting, coming closer.

They are at another bar now, one of those secret, behind the wall and up the stairs places that never stays secret for long. They share a small couch set behind velvet curtains, the only seating available at this hour, and when they sat down Ruby had a flash of that young couple she saw in the dive bar on the day she found my body. How the girl had her leg draped over the boy, and how pristine their love seemed, glistening in its newness, when she had felt so very tired and afraid. Is it possible she wants that glistening for herself now?

They have talked about me all night long. Passed that photograph of me between them. Imagining a life, sculpting ideas around the few things they know, so that by the third Manhattan — my drink! — they have crafted a dozen versions of me. The memory of cherries in my mouth, I whisper outlandish suggestions to help them along. *Girlfriend of a mobster! Heiress on the run!* They can't hear me over the clink of ice cubes, the jazz playing in the background. But I play sculptor just the same. And when Ruby tells Josh she wishes she'd had a chance to meet me, to know who I *really* was, I wish back just as hard.

Over dinner, Josh admitted he had been investigating the Riverside murder, telling Ruby about the network of friends and industry contacts he's talked to about me, so that she imagines a map of people across the city, lines connecting pulsing dots all over town. He tells Ruby his interest is clinical, that it's a fantastic mystery to be solved, but I know the truth. This is his way to her. Ruby Jones. One of the few people to make him feel buoyant again.

I see what happens when he looks at her now. After that night at Oyster Bar, I can see the bright blue light that starts just below his ear. How it curves under his jaw, travels down his neck, and out into his chest, shooting off in all directions. He thinks there is darkness where desire used to be, but he has been looking in the wrong places. His longing resides somewhere deeper, a vivid blue far below his dark thoughts. *It's supposed to feel like this*, I want to tell him. It's supposed to shake you out of that inertia you're hiding behind. I want to take my index finger and run it from his ear, down his neck and onto his chest. There, I'd need both hands, I'd need all my fingers, spread like arteries, or an explosion. And every place I touched — here, here, here — I'd say: *There she is*. There is the way she tilts her head when she's listening to you, there is the constant glisten of her eyes when something moves her. There is the curve of flesh under her cotton shirt, and the way she self-consciously pulls at the fabric, unaware that she pulls you in, too.

If the living could see all that light, the city maps drawn under the skin, they'd be awestruck. Looking at Ruby and Josh right now, they'd see how nervousness and anticipation might seem the same on the surface, but they're so very different at the source. Nervousness is rushing water, river mouths, but anticipation is something far more delicate, little bubbles that go pop, one bright burst after another, until the body is a glass of champagne, a million golden beads of air, rising.

It's beautiful. To see how much joy the body can hold.

'My friends back home would not understand me

any more,' Ruby is saying now, those little beads forming. They are talking about Death Club specifically, and their mutual fascination with death and dying more generally.

'I'm not even sure they'd like me these days. I might be too . . . problematic.'

'I wasn't the easiest guy to be around after the accident, either,' Josh admits. 'Not for anyone who knew me before.'

'Your ex-wife, you mean?' Ruby asks, her eyebrows raised.

Across the table, Josh pulls a face.

'Let's just say she didn't cope so well with the new me. Or I stopped dealing so well with the same old her. Either way, it got messy pretty quick.'

'They say divorce is a kind of death,' Ruby says tentatively, reaching out to touch Josh's hand across the table. 'That must have been tough, when your world was already upside down.' Josh opens his mouth as if to say something, and then shakes his head. 'Yeah,' he finally responds. 'It wasn't great. But that's all in the past. For both of us.' There is nothing Ruby can add for now; she removes her hand and steers the conversation back to safer ground.

'I still don't understand how nobody missed Alice all this time. Why did it take so long for someone to notice she was missing?'

'My guess is that the people who knew her best had things to hide,' Josh answers. 'Most people do. Or maybe she just knew really shitty people.'

And just like that, they're back to the game. Imagining my life. Playing with it. Only this time it makes me mad. Because once again, Josh has come so close to getting it right.

There are people who chose to push me away. To stop — or never even try — looking for me. Because they wanted to distance themselves from me. Even after it was clear something bad had happened.

But that's going to be harder now, isn't it. With my name on everyone's lips.

★ ★ ★

The night is nearly over. It is the kind of date I should have liked to have had, one day. Manhattans and jazz, and all that electricity under the skin. I decide to play a little game of my own. On behalf of everything I've lost.

Knees, a nudge, more forceful this time. I take my anger at all the people who let me down and reshape it.

As Ruby runs her forefinger along the rim of her cocktail glass, pulls at her earlobe, Josh doesn't move, can't move his leg away from hers. Was that some kind of otherness he felt just now? A push from someone unseen?

(It makes sense that the guy who died and came back is the first to really feel it.)

I want to sit myself down in front of them. Show her the nerves that flicker wherever they touch. Shift her fingers from glass to his lips, say, *Here, this place, is home*, and I think if I whispered this to Josh just now, he might actually hear me. I try my hardest, but the words come out as a saxophone solo, filling the room.

This is your night. I say it louder this time, and the curtains rustle. *Let go!* I shout, and the candle between them flickers. My voice is music and flame and velvet, now that I know how to hear it. I am everything that

230

touches lightly, everything that lingers. Less and less like limbs and hair and teeth and bone. More like air and sensation and the spark that shoots a river of blue all through a man's body.

This new sensation feels like power. The ability to make the world move in my direction, after all. It is an extraordinary feeling. Formidable. After being tossed about for so long.

I know exactly where to take it.

★ ★ ★

The man who killed me sits at home, just a block or two from the river. Candles flickering, night air whistling. He takes a long drag of his cigarette, watches his breath turn into a spiral of smoke. He thinks of how powerful he was in that moment, down by the river, and his conceit causes me to create a crack in the sky, thunder that shakes him in his chair.

My sudden, glorious anger fills the room. This man should be the one thinking about limbs and teeth and hair and bone.

Because — the wind hisses, the candle flickers — all that I used to be, all that he took from a girl named Alice Lee, will soon come knocking at his door.

★ ★ ★

The next day. Ruby cannot stop thinking about Josh. The man who gave her the gift of a name for her dead girl. They'd talked well into the night and it was 2.30 a.m. when he hailed her a cab, a light rain falling. Saying goodbye, Josh leaned in and kissed Ruby's damp cheek, and he stayed close as she turned her mouth

231

towards his. A slide into their first kiss, something soft and careful and quick, but still, she held her hand to her mouth the whole way home in the cab, a little giggle rising out of her, so that the driver laughed too, said it was nice to see someone having such a good time of things.

It *was* a good night. But what happens the next day? Had they unintentionally crossed a line, buoyed by alcohol and the rain and their strange circumstances, and would there be an inevitable retreat from each other when the sun came up? This is not supposed to be so confusing, Ruby thinks, not at thirty-six years old. Josh texted to make sure she got home — a good sign. He hasn't messaged this morning. Not such a good sign. The kiss brought back butterflies — not just a good sign, but something of a miracle, given how long those wings have remained flightless under her skin. She has no idea if Josh felt their flutter. Definitely a bad sign. She is done with not knowing how a man feels about her. She has to be.

Scar tissue is never as supple as that which it replaces. Like I've said before, you don't arrive in another city and actually become a brand-new person. It comes with you, the habits, the circular thoughts, the fears; all that baggage comes along for the ride. Last night with Josh, right before they kissed, Ruby felt the pavement tilt beneath her. It lasted a second at most, but it was enough to feel the world was opening up, shifting at last. She had thrown her arms out wide and spun around, face turned up to the rain. A gesture she'd seen in a hundred movies, in a hundred moments like this, and Josh had laughed, grabbed her arm to keep her steady, but really, in that moment she wanted to stay dizzy.

(We both had revelations last night.)

There have been no grand gestures today, however. Just another innocuous message from Ash — *Hey, you up?* — she has thus far ignored. She doesn't want to tell him about the name she cannot stop saying out loud (and she *can't* tell him about Josh, though I wish she would).

If you could see Josh and Ruby from their separate corners as they wait.

People hold their longing in different places. For Josh, yearning lives in his fingertips, so that when it all gets too much, he rubs his thumb and forefinger together to alleviate the pulsing ache, or spans his hands wide, cracks his knuckles and moves his fingers about. Whether reaching for women or words, Josh's hands give away his desire. For Ruby, longing resides deep within her arms, it comes as a bone-dense feeling she tries to shake off, a discomfort to squeeze out. Neither of them has ever really learned how to sit with this kind of intensity, allow it. To feel desire is to pursue it or to run from it, nothing in between.

Ruby doesn't know Josh has been waving his fingers about, reaching for her, all day.

His message comes through while she is sitting, arms tightly crossed, on a stoop near her local laundromat, waiting for the dry cycle to finish.

The buzz of her phone makes her jump, though she has been listening for it all day.

> Ruby. Thank you for last night. I had a wonderful time, although the ending was a little unexpected. I feel like there's something I should have told you when it came up, so I wanted to clear the air. I'm still married. Separated. But technically married. If

you're free tonight, maybe we could talk about it in person?

Ruby drops her phone; it lands on the pavement with a clatter.

Not even I saw that one coming.

19

Here's what happens when they know who you are. It changes. *Everything* changes. They begin to dig into your life. Because 'Dead Girl' needs an even bigger hook to keep people interested. The fact of her loss could never be enough, so they pick through the past, sift through the bones, the reporters and news editors who don't get this kind of treat nearly enough, the shock and tragedy of pretty, dead girls.

I have made some things easy for these storytellers. No mother (suicide!), no father (who is he?), and there is enough small-town history for people to snack on. Enough colourful people who went to school with me to keep the theories about the cause of my demise coming. But most leads are a disappointment, a dead end, no matter how deep the digging goes. Good student. No record. No serious boyfriend, as far as people could tell. Not a single scandal of my own, until —

★ ★ ★

Mr Jackson sits in his studio, waiting for the knock. Charcoal fingers twisting, a package of photographs face down in a locked box, hidden in the closet. Knowing he can't throw the pictures away, perpetually contemplating burial or burning, but never quite able to bring himself to destroy them. He hasn't looked at a single picture of me, not since the day I left. When he came home and found the house empty.

Cooled down, mind cleared, he went from room to room, searching for me. Intending to apologise. To say that it didn't matter now. That we could finally go out into the world together. Discovering the money and his mother's Leica gone. His terrible words from earlier in the day, echoing. Assuming I had gone up to the lake with Tammy. And knowing we would never get back what we had.

He sat on the bed and cried when he realised what he'd lost. Just like he sobbed again on a day, some two months later, when my name lit up every television and computer screen across town. *Local girl, Alice Lee. Brutally murdered in New York City.* No longer able to pretend I had simply stopped calling, no longer able to hide the truth from himself, he finally let himself imagine a stranger pawing at my skin, saw him breaking me open and leaving me there on the rocks. For somebody else to find.

Mr Jackson. Not the only person to wade into the muck of my life, but the only one to know the softness of my skin, the tender flesh, the way I dissolved like snow.

He is certain he will never look at those pictures again. Never revisit the honesty, the beauty he has inadvertently preserved. But he knows too, they are a ticking bomb, a catalogue of his mistakes. Just like he knows, inevitably, the knock will come.

Still, when they show up at his door in their dark blue uniforms, with their notebooks out and guns tucked, he is unprepared. Sits on that small, sheet-covered couch, shaking. *Just a few questions. Not a suspect. Might be able to help with the investigation. If we could just —*

And the female detective. Her eyes taking in the

books on their crates, the paintings, the coil of his body.

'What was she doing here with you, anyway?'

The lies come easy. She was a troubled young woman. She had nowhere else to go. She needed a place to sleep, some shelter for a few weeks. She'd been a good student; he'd showed her some care. Maybe she'd spun a story or two to her friend Tammy, tried to make it seem more exciting. 'This kind of thing can happen with teenage girls, right?' They should know that Tammy herself was a bit of trouble, and no matter what she might have said, he never touched Alice. She was just a poor kid he was trying to help out of a tight spot. He simply wanted to help her on her way.

It cannot be his fault he never imagined where she'd end up.

★ ★ ★

Ruby starts running again. Josh's message, just as she was feeling her way towards him, has set her spinning. For the first time, she considers what she should have said to Ash all those years ago, when he told her he was engaged. Sees a different version of herself, where she went home alone after that first drink with him, bemoaning timing and missed opportunities, another *almost* in her life. What if she had been that woman instead? One strong enough to walk away, no matter how intense the pull? It does not necessarily feel good to ignore Josh's texts, to shut him out, but she knows this temporary discomfort is nothing compared to the pain ahead if she falls for another man who can't decide. Besides, he'd lied to her, hadn't he? When she said divorce was a kind of death. That's when he should have told her the truth. That's when he should have said he was technically still married, because omission is a lie too; she knows that well enough.

She is angry at Josh for being dishonest, when she thought she had found someone who valued the truth. This makes her upset with Lennie and Sue, too. She is certain they knew he was still married, and certain they should have told her, when Sue had readily shared the facts of her own divorce, and Lennie talked about romance all the time. How is it possible that Josh's *wife* never came up in conversation, not once? In quieter moments, Ruby knows she is being unreasonable, that separation is not the same as marriage. But it's not exactly an ending either, so she lets herself feel the sting of betrayal, decides she wants nothing to do with any of them right now. It's not only Josh's messages that she leaves unanswered as the week goes by.

When Ruby is adrift, I am adrift. In the days after finding out about Josh, we return to wandering the streets of this city, neither coming nor going anywhere. She considers moving home to Melbourne. I don't even know where home is any more. Just when I think I have it figured out, the game changes all over again. I thought that once I had my name back, once those waves stopped crashing around me, I'd know what to do. Maybe even find out where those other girls go.

But here I am, still unseen. *Who Killed Alice Lee?* is not really a question about me, is it? But it's the only one people seem to ask now.

At any rate, without Death Club as our compass, we seem to have ended up back where we started. A lonely woman and a lonely dead girl together in New

York. Ruby Jones and Alice Lee. Stuck in our tug of war between the living and the dead.

★ ★ ★

She never goes back to the river. Has avoided the park since the morning of my murder. Won't even walk along Riverside Drive, there above the Hudson, the promise of summer drawing people from their expensive houses, thawing them out, so that the streets and the fields and the running tracks are never empty these days, at least not until the sun goes down. Ruby has returned to the rocks a thousand times in her head, has pored over photographs of the crime scene, so that it exists as a map in her head, but anytime her feet turn towards the park, something in her rebels, pushes her back. She wishes she could talk to Lennie and Sue about it. Or better yet, Josh, who once told her that he'd had to force himself to return to the scene of his bike accident, how it had taken him weeks to build up the nerve. And how, when he finally got there, he soon discovered he couldn't recognise a thing. He sat down in what might have been the wrong place entirely, his blood soaked into the soil around some other tree, and realised how inconsequential his accident had been in the grand scheme of things.

'It's not as if the place remembers you,' he had said to Ruby, shaking his head.

If they were still talking to one another, Josh could have walked down to the river with her, he could have held her hand and assured her that — but here, Ruby stops her train of thought. Josh is not the man she thought he was. They had an interlude and now it's over, and she simply needs to be more careful with her judgement from now on. Stop giving her heart away so fast.

(Why do people, the good ones, always seem to blame themselves when someone deceives them? Seems to me, when that happens, the bad guys get away with more than just their obvious crimes.)

Perhaps it is her current isolation, so soon after she thought she'd found her people. Maybe it's a way to evict Josh from her head, to think about something else today. Or perhaps it was merely a matter of time, an inevitability. Whatever it is, on this Tuesday in late May, six weeks to the day after my murder, Ruby finds herself back in Riverside Park, the grounds humming with people now, runners and cyclists and skaters rolling past signs on metal poles that flap ads for the twilight movies and sunrise yoga classes starting soon.

(I would have loved this place in summer.)

On this sunny day, as Ruby cuts through the upper levels of the park and heads down to the waterfront, her recollections of that earlier, stormy morning feel more like a movie than a memory. Dank tunnels and dead ends have been replaced by dappled trees, families strolling, dogs on leashes. Following the river, the running trail is more like a freeway today, people moving fast and slow, back and forth. It seems impossible to Ruby that she had once been down here all alone. Her head moves left and right, taking in every benign marker she passes. Nothing looks familiar n the sunlight; it is like she has never been here before.

It's not as if the place remembers you.

The morning Ruby found me, the park had pressed down on her, closed her in. Now it all looks blink-bright. Water sloping towards New Jersey on her right, sports fields and banks of stairs on her left. The park is wide open and sprawling, postcard perfect. It's not until Ruby comes to the exact place, not until she bends over and puts her hands on the metal railing, just like she did that morning six weeks ago, that her body protests. Reminding her, in a rush of adrenaline and heart constriction, that there is no movie in her mind. Instantly, looking down at the water, she is back inside the reality of what happened here. The sky cracks and cars swoosh overhead, rain soaks through her, pools in her eyes, and there is a girl face down at the water's edge, not getting up, not turning over when Ruby shouts at her. She remembers the body being picked up, carried out from under the path, remembers bright red, and the pale of naked legs. Sirens flashing, the bright colours behind her eyes, silver foil wrapped around shaking shoulders. Men with gloves on, searching. Somewhere amongst these mental images, Josh suddenly appears, and Ash too, as confusing and disorienting to her senses as it is to remember finding the body of Alice Lee.

Ruby is trying to breathe through these jumbled memories when a man comes up beside her and offers a friendly smile.

'Nice spot down here, isn't it,' he says, so tall and broad shouldered that for a second, he blocks the sun.

'I ... .' Ruby blinks at the vastness of him. He is wearing neat shorts and a polo top, and he smells of something woody, expensive. His eyes are bright blue, sparkling, and if this spot isn't nice at all, if it is the place Ruby found the body of Alice Lee, this man is at least something clean, fresh, separate from the horror. It might be nice to forget for a moment, she thinks, almost desperately. To ignore what she knows about this place.

Ruby turns away from the river to face him, turns away from Josh, from Ash. From me.

(I should have known she'd do that, eventually.)

'It is pretty special, yes,' she says to the blue-eyed man.

'Whoa! What is that accent?' he shoots back, coming closer.

Ruby tries to widen her smile.

'I'm Australian. I guess I haven't picked up the New Yorker accent yet.'

And so, it begins. He asks her how long she's been in the city, tells her he lives in the neighbourhood. Asks if she likes this part of town. As they talk, Ruby can tell the man is well looked after, from his tanned skin and bright eyes, to the inconspicuous designer labels stitched everywhere from his shirt to his shoes. Those straight American teeth. Dressed in her worn-through running gear, she does not miss how he glances at her body between sentences, assessing her, too.

'I'm not bothering you, am I?' he asks at one point in their conversation.

'No, not at all,' she says, and almost believes it. 'It's nice to have someone to talk to.'

'Would you like to join me for coffee, then?' he asks. 'I've always thought about visiting Australia, and I'd love to ask you some questions about it.'

If Ruby feels a heart-patter of wariness, it gets lost in that desire to forget where she is, what she knows.

'Sure. That would be nice,' she responds, and before Ruby has time to think better of it, she is following the man to the crowded patio of a small cafe, taking the seat he holds out for her. His name is Tom. He tells Ruby he works in finance — 'Yes, down on

242

Wall Street!' — and his style of conversation is breezy, brash, so that she only has to nod at his commentary or answer his questions directly, rather than come up with something new or interesting to say. As Tom chatters away in this fashion, Ruby finds her thoughts drifting to Death Club, missing the way her new friends listened as well as they talked. There is so much she could tell them, especially after coming back to the park today. It is a week since she learned about Josh. At first, they sent messages about the next meet-up, which she didn't reply to. Then individual ones, to her. And now, the unanswered messages have stopped coming, and Ruby is unsure how to reach across this newly created divide. Something, she fears, has been irretrievably lost in the distance Josh's revelation has opened up between them.

She is sipping at her latte, trying to put Death Club out of her head once and for all, when Tom puts down his coffee cup and looks out across the water, appears to weigh something up before he speaks.

'You know, Ruby. A girl was murdered here in the park. Just a few weeks ago, back in April.'

Ruby feels her cheeks grow hot.

'I did know that, yeah.'

Tom is still staring into the distance, his eyes squinting against the sun.

'Such a terrible thing to happen. And it's usually so safe around here. I only bring it up because you said you're here in New York on your own.'

He turns, looks into her eyes.

'As a woman on her own, you need to be careful, Ruby.'

(They want you to be grateful. When they show off their care in this way. Ruby understands this, and

243

she bristles at this man's concern, no matter how well intended she thinks it might be.)

'I'm careful enough, Tom,' she says, her smile stopping half-mast. 'Most women are, actually. I can only assume Alice was trying to be careful, too.'

'I wouldn't say being alone in a city park in the dark is careful,' Tom responds, an arch in his voice, as if Ruby has offended him, but then he sighs, shakes his head. 'Sorry. What could I know about such things? About what it's like to be a woman. It's just — I have sisters, nieces. And I feel sick thinking of anything like this happening to them. At any rate' — Tom shakes his head again, as if reshuffling his thoughts — 'what a terrible conversation to have on such a nice day. Tell me more about why you decided to come here. Like I said, I've always wanted to go to Australia. I think Sydney first, then . . .'

And he's back to his sunny-side-up conversation, just like that.

For Ruby, however, the spell has been broken. He knows about the murder. There's no way he wouldn't, when it's still all over the news. She had thought, hoped, she could escape it, even for an hour, but what did she expect, coming down to the river like this. She scolds herself for her optimism, even as she feels that sense of prickling unease return. Tom, so light and breezy just moments before, now settles on her skin as an irritation. How can he be so blithe, so unaffected by the things going on around him, she wonders? He has not even noticed the change in her mood.

Ruby knows she is being unfair. Understands she shouldn't resent this cheerful man's lack of complications, but the absence of her Death Club friends feels even more stark, as he launches into another glib

244

story, this one about the time he met Mel Gibson at a bar downtown.

'Top bloke,' Tom is saying, mimicking an Australian accent poorly, and Ruby forces a smile, but all she can think of is excusing herself, getting away from this failed attempt at normality as soon as she can. Back home in Melbourne, they used to say there could be four seasons in a day, temperatures dropping rapidly, sunshine giving way to hail with no warning. She thinks now that she has become the weather.

Her reprieve comes when Tom's phone, face down on the table, buzzes.

'I might have to get that,' he says.

'Please go ahead,' Ruby nods. 'I need to get going myself, anyway.'

Tom looks disappointed but makes no effort to stop her when she pushes her chair back, stands up.

'I think,' she says, 'I lost track of time.'

'Well I'm very glad you did,' Tom replies, before waving away the cash she attempts to put down on the table.

'Absolutely not, Ruby. A gentleman always pays. Though perhaps next time we meet in the park, you'll let me buy you a real drink.'

The suggestion is playful, implicit. He wants to see her again. Ruby feels something pull tight in her chest. The weight, she will think later, of being wanted by the wrong man. For now, she smiles her practised smile and takes Tom's hand, offered to her across the table.

Strong, warm fingers wrap around hers, squeeze tight.

'Until we meet again.' Tom presses down on her hand one last time before letting go. 'And I meant what I said before. Be careful, Ruby. It's not as safe out there as it might seem.'

He looks back at her once after they part, turns and offers an exaggerated wave, before taking a set of stairs two at a time, up out of the park, and away. Instead of following him, heading home, Ruby finds herself walking back down to the water, following the winding path until she comes to that little curve of beach again, water slapping up against the rocks.

Lowering her head against the metal rail, Ruby struggles not to cry.

A girl was murdered here in the park. Just a few weeks ago.

I know because I found her.

This is what Ruby could have, should have, said. She should have told Tom the truth about this nice spot down by the river.

But where on earth do you go from there?

She isn't the only one who has been avoiding the scene of the crime until now. The push-pull for Ruby all these weeks, the coming to the edge of things and then backing away, was me. I kept my hands on her chest, pushed back hard whenever the river called. Because I know how it calls him, too. I see the trail of blood he follows, can hear the rush of it in his ears. He's careful, of course. Has every reason to be in the park any time he returns to the rocks, no different from any other man on the West Side. This is his backyard, after all. A place he knows.

I'd say I come here almost every day, is how he'd answer, if anybody ever asked.

The truth is, I wasn't just keeping Ruby from him. When he comes here, when he stands and looks out over the water, I can feel his pleasure, the swell of it in his chest, the fizzing in his fingertips. He bites into the pain he caused, feasts on it as if stripping meat from a bone, tasting those last terrifying moments of my life over and over. It used to overwhelm me.

But I can see him better now, this man. I no longer back away from the world he has created. I'm staying close, as I wait for another chance to bear down, push through. My anger burned bright and fast, that night my name was spoken out loud. It was a brief, beautiful flame. But I'll get that second chance, I know it.

To make him feel the weight of my remains.

★ ★ ★

Something Josh left out of the story, when he told Ruby about returning to the scene of his accident. Looking for the tree root that upended his bike, searching for some memory of his pain, and finding nothing was as he remembered it. It wasn't until he had given up his search, accepted the impartiality of sticks and stones and dirt, that he saw it, gleaming beneath a nest of rotting leaves. The face of his watch, cracked in a hundred places, hands bent and stopped, one on top of the other. As his body hit the ground, the impact must have dislodged it from his wrist, sent the small disc flying. Picking up this remnant, examining the damage, Josh felt a strange kind of relief. He had been looking for proof. Something to validate how totally his world had been rearranged — and there it was. Cupped, now, in the palm of his hand. Passed over in the weeks after his accident, missed by anyone who wouldn't understand its significance.

The truth doesn't always announce itself loudly, see. Sometimes it is small enough to fit in the palm of your hand.

If you know what you are looking for.

★ ★ ★

Sometimes, when Ruby is down at the river, I come sit with Lennie at the mortuary, watching as she tends to her dead. Most of her charges have long since left their bodies behind, but occasionally I can see someone hovering, carefully patting Lennie's arm, or touching their lips to her forehead as she works. I see the fine hairs on her arm stand up, feel the prickling of her scalp when this happens, and then the person is gone. Her dead girls briefly show up other places too, following her to restaurants, or standing close by as she scans the racks at her favourite vintage clothing store. I only ever catch glimpses, flickers, but I now know that what Lennie thinks of as her terminal clumsiness, the trips and knocking of glasses, is really just the women who love her accidentally coming too close.

Back at the mortuary, I've also been there in the private viewing rooms, watching family and friends sit with their loved one's body. I've looked on as each grieving person brings their love and memory and pain into the room, seen the way it all mixes together, before flowing out in a stream of colours. To see this grief up close is to look at light passing through a prism, like a rainbow, but so much brighter. It is the most glorious thing, this arc of remembrance, as if the beginning and end of a person was only ever light.

The living cannot see this, of course. They get busy with whatever it is that picks them up off the floor. Soon enough, grief is replaced by other emotions.

Anger, despair, disbelief, resignation; all the tools it takes to survive. But that first mix of colours, that fusion of grief, lights up the room. It illuminates the dead, and it reminds us we will not be forgotten; we get to leave our light behind.

Watching these private, poignant moments unfold, I understand something else, too. It matters *who* remembers you. The people who knew me remain distant from one another, they each carry around their own, unshared memories of Alice Lee, as if I was many things, or nothing, depending on who you asked. Ruby has tried to bring all of these pieces together, bring me into focus, but she can only get so far with their resistance, and a dead girl as her guide.

Maybe this is why I'm still in that tug of war between the living and the dead. Because I am no less broken into pieces than when Ruby found me, down there on the rocks.

★ ★ ★

They are learning *some* things. Piecing together the story of a girl called Alice Lee as best they can. But there are still so many gaps. What would they say about me, if I filled in some of those gaps for them?

She once posed for pornographic pictures.
She had an affair with her high school teacher.
She let the old man she lived with buy her things.

Or this. She couldn't sleep after calling Mr Jackson one last time, got up at 5 a.m. and stumbled out into the heaviest, most beautiful rain she had ever seen. Zipped up her purple parka, her camera tucked under the jacket, pressed up against her chest. Thinking about portfolios and school submission, and how life was a lot like this storm, washing away the bad things, and some of the good things too, but that was okay, because there were so many good things to come. And then some man, some man with his series of bad days and disappointing mornings approached her as she tried to take pictures of the storm, and he was angry when she wouldn't look up, wouldn't engage with him. He watched her set up those photographs of the river and the rain and felt all those bad days swell up in him like a balloon, until he released the pressure through his fists, through fingers coming down hard on this young woman's body. Puncturing her as if she were the one who needed deflating. He was angry that she did not smile. Angry at her dismissal. When his cigarette went out, when he asked if she had a light, and she shook her head no, he said she was being rude, and it wasn't only the sky cracked through when he bore down on her with his righteous indignation.

Such self-preservation all these years, only to find herself unbound by a man who was angry at the light going out.

So, he took hers instead.

Shook her, fists on flesh, struggling, elbows pushing. The split second where she stood a chance, and then she was down, hitting rocks and earth. And he towered over her, enjoyed how large this made him feel, as he smashed that camera lens down on her forehead, over and over. Immediately disgusted by the mess of her face, he wrapped his hands around her skinny, wet throat. Discovered he could destroy the entire city that was this young woman, everything she had been and would be. The rubble of a life, and he was the bomb, exploding. It felt — as he unzipped his jeans, turned her head away so he did not have to look at the unseemliness before him — like he was the most powerful man in the world. That everything was his for the taking.

He never did get that light for his half-smoked cigarette. Had to wait until he got home, rummaging around the all-sorts bowl, looking for matches, careful and quiet. The storm intensifying, a girl's bloody underwear stuffed in his pocket, the rest of her belongings gathered like gifts.

She should have been nicer to him. He was only asking for a light. It certainly seemed to him, later that morning, as he listened to the rain and the sirens blaring, his fingers quivering towards them, that the calming pleasure of a cigarette might have slowed things down a little. Had she smiled, tried harder, he may even have given her the chance to say yes to his advances.

(This is the world he has created. I'm ready to tell you a little more now. Stay with me as we take that closer look. But don't you believe a single thing he says about me.)

20

Noah watches as people in uniform fan out through his apartment, considers the elegance of their movements, their certainty of purpose. The way each member of the investigative unit deftly lifts and dusts and kneels. Alone and all together, a single question in pursuit of an answer. To Noah, observing from his armchair, it looks like a complex, beautiful ballet. Franklin sits mournfully at his feet, unsure of these busy strangers who don't smile at him, nor his human. All of them overlooking the young girl in the room, watching from her seat at the piano.

Noah went to the police as soon as they released my name. Said he might have details they'd be interested in. Offered up his apartment — 'No warrant necessary' — and consented to the blood tests and swabs, dismissing any offer of coffee or condolence. He was there for one thing, and one thing only. To help them find the man who hurt Alice Lee.

Noah still doesn't like to think of me as dead.

When I disappeared the very same day they found a young girl's body in Riverside Park, he refused to think that anything could, or had, happened to me. That first day, he turned away from the sirens and the stories, cancelled all of his dog-sitting appointments, and sat in the living room with Franklin, waiting for me to come home. They sat there together as the hours passed, watching the rain smash against the windows, and they were still there the next morning, this man and his dog, listening for the front door.

252

When the days passed and that door never clicked open, something in Noah closed down. It was easier for him to believe I had become restless and moved on, than to live with the possibility that those things in the news, those terrible things, had happened to his Baby Joan. For the first time in his life, he chose to look away from the facts, something I never would have imagined. Not from Noah, who taught me about dust and stars. Not from the person who always knew how things worked. When he turned away like that, I mistook what it meant; I thought he shut me out because he didn't care. He wasn't the first one to leave me, after all.

Now I see he cared so much that he knew the truth would break him.

He should have gone to the police earlier. Should have accepted what he already knew, deep in his bones, to be true. But know this of my Noah, please. He was not thinking of his own safety when he stayed away. He was only ever thinking of me.

Perhaps I should have understood this earlier, too. That he was never going to be like the other men in my life. That I was right to believe in the kindness of strangers. My lack of faith helped keep us apart after I died — but I'm here with him now. Watching as those investigators examine my stack of IOUs, taking the Post-it notes down from the refrigerator door, reading them one by one, all the little promises I left behind. A single blue note flutters to the ground, and a young officer bends to retrieve it. *Girl Things*, it says, a badly drawn smiley face in place of the full stop. *$9.87. Recurring.* Noah cannot read the note from where he is sitting, but he can see the officer pause, look up at the ceiling, the small piece of paper pressed to his chest. Noah already knows what each of these IOUs says, has memorised every good intention I left behind, and he feels a sudden, fist-tight clench where he knows his heart to be. *Recurring.* The writer of that note thought she had months and years ahead of her. She had plans.

'Baby Joan,' Noah says softly, reaching for the note. Funny, sweet, uncouth Alice, in love with New York like the city was a person, and completely ignorant of her poetry.

'Is this middle C, Noah?'

He hears me ask this, that last night we had together. Clanging down on the piano key as he nodded from this same armchair, muttered something about how noisy I had become, and I had wrinkled my nose at him, laughed, thumping down on as many keys as my fingers could touch.

'Please stop!'

And now there is a rasping, wheezing sound filling the apartment, sliding down the walls. The lifting and dusting and kneeling ceases, everyone stops what they are doing, orients towards the noise emanating from the armchair in the living room. It is the sound of a man unaccustomed to weeping, as great, wracking gasps shake through his body for the first time in his life. Franklin whines, pushes his nose against Noah's leg, knowing something has gone very wrong here. Wondering why I am not moving from my seat at the piano, why I'm not coming over to comfort them both. The dog turns from Noah and looks right at me, his chocolate eyes pleading. I push down on middle C, as hard as I can, and he barks.

Good boy, Franklin. Good boy, I whisper, but I cannot be heard over the sound of Noah's sobs. The investigators gather around him, their well-practised dance interrupted by the rawness of this grief. Everything I owe this man sits, sealed, in plastic bags on the kitchen table behind them. The brief story of my life in this apartment, this city, and the simple promise of that word.

Recurring.

How to let them know this was the safest I had ever been.

★ ★ ★

Ruby messages her old colleagues, the ones who said they'd love to see her when she'd settled in. Both text back within minutes. *I'm free two weeks from Thursday*, says one. *Let me see if I can reschedule my spin class next Sunday*, says the other, and Ruby puts the phone down, embarrassed.

This is how you die alone, she thinks.

You're not alone, I want to say.

But I don't think a dead girl will make her feel any better today.

★ ★ ★

I suppose, living with Mr Jackson in secret for a month, I got used to going unnoticed by everyone else. Or perhaps it was all those years with my mother, moving from place to place. Shimmying through the cracks of another town, another coming or going, sliding into new schools or friendship groups so as not to be questioned when I arrived, nor to be missed when I left. Thinking about it, I guess I had already perfected the art of invisibility, and Mr Jackson merely understood how easy it would be to keep me hidden away.

255

The problem is, once you get used to going unnoticed, you think no one else can see you either, like a dog with his head under the couch who doesn't understand his tail is still in plain view (Gambit, Mr Whitcomb's ancient terrier, does this any time he accidentally pees on the floor). Head down like that, you forget there are those who spend their lives looking for girls who feel unseen. There are men actively hunting such women, they can spot them from a mile away, and they know just what to do when they find them.

You forget. Or maybe it's something Ruby never even knew.

That some men are constantly vigilant. Watching for the girls no one else will think to look for when they're gone.

★　★　★

She returns to the park every day now. Without Death Club as her guide, Ruby continues to feel lost, alienated. It doesn't help that the true crime forums already have another mystery to fixate on, a girl named Beth who was found decapitated in Arizona — *Clang!* goes the alarm — and the national media has turned its attention to the poor girl, too. The daughter of a city councilman, Beth has already given up her secrets (some of them at least) better than I did.

What will it take, Ruby wonders, to finally feel like she knows enough about me?

When she comes down to the river these days, she still takes the time to say my name out loud. Once or twice she even thinks she sees Tom approaching, that broad man with his broad smile, and she can't quite tell if she's relieved or disappointed when it never turns out to be him. The return of loneliness will do that to you. Get you all turned about. Make you forget what you know about men and desire.

What she forgets, down by the river, lost in her thoughts, is this:

If someone really wants you, they will always find a way.

21

'We've got to stop bumping into each other like this.'

Ruby is down at the river, the place she has returned to, day after day this week, as May gives way to June. Sometimes people stop beside her, look out across the water like she does, some even smile and say hello, but for the most part, she has been left alone. The place of my murder is now a kind of chapel, a refuge for the loneliest woman in New York City. That's what she considers herself to be these days, embarrassed at her self-pity, but comfortable with it, too. As if she has finally given herself permission to feel the hurt that propelled her to New York in the first place.

Last night, Ash asked if she would send him a photo. *Something to keep me up*, he said in his message, and she knew exactly what he meant by that. This felt more familiar than their recent *How are you* and *Guess what I did today* texts, but as she held her phone camera at this angle and that, she couldn't shake the performance of it, the way it made her feel like an actor in her own life. Not tonight, she said eventually, and for the first time ever, before turning out the lights. As soon as the sun came up again, she took herself back down to the river, as far away from Ash as any place that ever existed.

It's as close to me as she can get.

When Tom shows up in the park today, he places his hands next to hers on that metal rail, his voice so close to her ear that it makes her jump.

She turns to face him, steadies herself.

'Tom — hi!'

Perhaps, in the mess of her life, Ruby is happy to see him again, after all.

'I was hoping I might find you here,' Tom confirms, with his broad, confident smile. 'I've been thinking about you, Aussie.'

'Oh.'

Ruby flushes at his directness, at the space he immediately takes up, standing so close to her, acting for all the world like he has been invited to do so.

'Well, I don't meet a beautiful Aussie woman every day, do I,' he adds with a wink.

He is definitely flirting with her this time around, and Ruby is tempted to rally, but she finds herself unable to speak. It feels too light, in this place of heaviness, to flirt back. There is also Ash to consider. And Josh, the memory of his kiss and his betrayal still smarting.

Oh, go away! she says to these other men in her life, the ones who crowd her thoughts and don't show up when she needs them. Their absence prompts her to say something — anything! — to this man who clearly likes her, a man now looking at her so intently. She is about to respond to his overture when a gull squawks above them, and a runner, breathing hard, thuds past on the pathway, almost brushing up against her.

'Hey, watch it!' Tom yells towards the man's retreating back, putting his hand on Ruby's arm to pull her close. 'A whole park and that idiot has to run right up on us. Fuck you! *Fuck! You!*'

Swearing loudly at the runner, Tom's fingers squeeze around Ruby's forearm, turn white against her skin. It is only a brief pressure before he lets go, but the sensation lingers. Even as Tom runs that hand through his hair, shakes his head, Ruby can feel each finger coming down, the compression of her flesh. She watches as the runner moves further away, becomes less distinct, taking Tom's sudden display of anger with him. Such a small moment, surely more imagined than real, given how finely tuned to danger she is these days. There is no reason for her heart to start thudding like this. She cannot let her paranoia ruin every moment, every encounter, she tries to tell herself. Not when Tom is only trying to look out for her.

Isn't he?

Ruby tries to relax. People lose their temper every day. Tom was probably just trying to impress her, play the hero, based on what he said about being careful the other day. She has just forgotten what it is for a man to treat her nicely.

For his part, Tom does not seem to have noticed the shift in her demeanour after he touched her so forcefully, the way she leaned out from his closeness, rubbed her fingers at the spot where his had landed. Instead, the offending runner off in the distance now, Tom is smiling again, his face turned towards the sun.

'Another beautiful day,' he says, eyes closed. 'Such a relief after all that rain.'

Rain coming down like a sheet. Her breath a ghost. Yellow reeds undulating on the water. Ruby physically shakes these intrusive memories away.

'It certainly does change things,' she says, turning her own face skyward, so they are standing the same way now, side by side, pulling the sun towards their skin.

After a time, Tom puts his hand on her back.

'I'll admit I was surprised to find you back in this

part of the park, Ruby. After I told you what happened here.'

She could make a joke. She could tell Tom she came back to this particular spot because that's where they first met. Finally play the game he seems to be wanting her to play. Ruby decides, instead, to tell him the truth.

'I found the body, Tom. I found Alice Lee.'

'What?' Tom looks startled, then confused. 'What do you mean?'

'Sorry. I know it's so weird, right. I mean, I'm the jogger who found her body. That's me.' Tom's mouth falls open for a second, and then a strange look crosses his face. His features seem to sharpen as he stares at Ruby, his expression suddenly eager.

'What did she look like?'

'Huh?'

Ruby blinks at Tom's strange question, the barely concealed hunger of it.

'Alice Lee. What did she look like? When you found her.'

Ruby shakes her head at Tom and backs away, moving into the middle of the path. Away from the metal rails and the water and the way he is looking at her. This is not the response she had expected at all. It is too close to his overreaction when that runner brushed past them, too far from his ready smile and mindless chatter. She feels, suddenly, as if she has made a mistake. No matter the width of his smile.

She would remember, if she wasn't so shocked, that she's felt this way with him before. This, if nothing else, should give her permission to shut the conversation down, but before she can respond, Tom is reaching for her arm again.

261

'Forgive me, Ruby. That is such a clumsy question. What I meant to say is, are you all right? I heard she was in quite the state when they — when you — found her.'

How many times does politeness keep us rooted to the spot? We stand on the brink, making a choice whether to tip over into trust or disgust, and we remember all our training, the lifetime of it. The doctrine of *nice*, the fear of hurting someone's feelings. In this moment, Ruby wants to back away from Tom's prurient interest, wants to ask this pushy man to leave her alone for good — but she doesn't know how. Like so many of us, she has never learnt the right words, and so she smiles small, accepts his apology, lets his hand continue to rest on her arm.

'Come,' he says now. 'Have that wine with me.' He checks his watch. 'It's after eleven. And I'd say you very much deserve a drink, after everything you've been through.'

When Ruby nods, acquiesces, she feels as if someone is trying to move her head in a different direction. It is an odd sensation, but as she once again sits down across from Tom at the crowded cafe, her companion ordering two glasses of Pinot Grigio — 'Trust me, you'll enjoy this drop' — the feeling persists. As if her every move is met with a force pushing her the other way.

You're being ridiculous, she silently scolds herself. *Over-cautious. Hypervigilant, as that PTSD doctor from Boston might say. This is what happens when you don't trust anybody, least of all yourself. Sitting here with a perfectly nice man, you think everything is a dire warning.*

And that's no way to live in the world, unless you want to be alone for ever.

With this thought, Ruby shakes her resistance off,

visibly, though Tom misses her shiver. She concentrates on things that are tangible, real. The warm metal of the cafe table under her fingers, the smooth plastic of the cup Tom passes to her, the acidic wine she sips, then takes in a gulp. Slowly, purposefully, she comes back to herself.

'It's good, isn't it,' Tom says, tilting his own drink at her, and when she says yes, she almost means it. From here, he makes it easy. Tells her stories, orders more wine any time her cup gets close to empty. Compliments her accent and eyes and bravery for coming to New York on her own, and gets up from his chair when she excuses herself to go to the bathroom a few too many wines in. When she returns to their table, there is another wine waiting and a cheese platter has been set down on the table between them.

'I'm clearly finding ways to keep you here longer,' he says as she sits back down.

It is her fourth, maybe fifth drink, and Ruby's limbs are now feeling loose. The tension coiled at her neck is gone. She considers this might be the New York she would have come to know earlier, had she not gone for a run that fateful morning. An uncomplicated New York, where she can drink wine on a weekday afternoon, sun-basking in the attention of a handsome stranger. This is the New York of romantic comedies and sitcoms on TV: wounded woman meets confident guy, puts up her guard, but he wears it down. A single lens on their responsibility-free lives, while people in the background go to work and do normal, everyday things to keep the city running. Extras making the movie look like real life.

Ruby bites down on the plastic edge of her cup, thinking about that lens. She is, she acknowledges, now quite drunk.

'That's an interesting face you made just now,' Tom says. 'What were you thinking about, if you don't mind me asking?'

'Movies,' Ruby admits, too far gone to be self-conscious. 'How life in New York seems like a movie. Or is a movie, and I just don't know it.'

'Interesting. So, what kind of movie would this be then?' Tom reaches over the table and covers her hand with his. 'Comedy? Mystery? Romance?'

Ruby stares at his hand over hers, takes in the yellowed nicotine stain of his index finger, and for the first time, the pale circle at the base of his ring finger. She pulls her hand away.

Tom flexes his fingers towards her, sees what she saw. Bringing his opposite thumb and forefinger to the shadow wedding band, he rubs at the skin and sighs.

'Divorced,' he says, not looking at her. 'Only took my ring off over the winter. I guess these things leave a mark.'

When he looks up, his blue eyes are wet.

'But I won't depress you with the script for that particular drama.'

Ruby is unsure how to respond. Allowing herself a brief moment of imagining herself underneath this man, the beckoning of those blue eyes pulling her in. Just as quickly, the image morphs into tangled limbs, clumsy touches, awkward goodbyes. All the leftovers of sex without desire, and she silently berates herself for even considering this an option. The dangers of loneliness, she thinks, offering Tom what she hopes is a stop-sign smile.

'I'm sorry to hear that, Tom. Break-ups are never fun.'

'You experienced your own drama recently, from the sound of it,' he responds. 'Finding that murdered girl, Alice Lee. That must have been terrifying for you.

'Sorry!' he quickly adds. 'It's clear you don't like talking about it. I've just never sat opposite someone who found a dead body. In my own neighbourhood, too.

'And to think,' he continues, not sounding sorry at all, 'they might never find out who did it. It's enough to keep you up at night. What people can get away with, especially after what they say he did to her.'

Ruby thinks of Josh, of his statistics and suppositions, the way she could talk to him all night about the murder, and how he was always so respectful of Alice, and she suddenly resents this man before her. Refuses to offer Alice Lee up to Tom the way he seems to want her to. She realises, with a second jolt, that the wine, the cheese, the compliments, they were just a way to get them back to this. To another man fascinated with dead girls for all the wrong reasons. The realisation sobers her up instantly.

'I probably should get going,' Ruby says quickly, her discomfort refusing to leave her alone this time. 'It's getting late, and I have to be somewhere.'

'You keep running away on me,' Tom says, frowning as she stands up from the table. 'Can I at least have your number and take you out for a proper meal next time?'

'I . . . ' Ruby does not know how to respond. Feeling, suddenly, that she has been backed into a corner and has been the one, foolishly, to put herself there. She is trying to come up with a response that won't embarrass either of them when Tom stands up too, comes to her side of the table. Before she has time to register what is happening, he reaches out, pulls her towards him. She thinks he is offering a farewell hug, but instead his hands go to her face, and his sour-wine lips push down hard against hers.

'Sorry, I couldn't resist,' Tom says when he pulls away from the kiss. 'I have been wanting to do that all afternoon.'

Ruby feels as if she is going to burst into tears.

'I really have to go,' she says, trying to hide the quiver in her voice. 'Thank you for . . . for the wine, Tom.'

(We placate, we soothe. Anything to get ourselves out of there.)

If he senses defeat, Tom's smile doesn't falter.

'I'll give you some time to change your mind on that date, Ruby' — it is only now that his smile turns to a slight frown — 'and until then, be careful around here. Like I said to you before, it's not the safest place for a woman on her own. Shake your head at me all you like. But what on earth were you doing in the park that morning? When you found the dead girl? She was out here, taking her pictures. But you have no excuse, when there are a thousand other places to go for a run.'

'I misjudged the weather,' Ruby responds after a time, no other answer possible. 'And I guess I thought you could never really be alone in New York City.'

'Indeed.' Tom's eyes flick to the other diners at the cafe, and then back to her. 'Just promise me you'll be more careful from now on.'

'Thank you, Tom. I appreciate your concern,' she manages to reply, before they finally, mercifully, part ways.

Ruby retreats along the river, knowing, without

looking back, that Tom's eyes stay on her as she goes. She has a fleeting thought, not unlike the one she had the day of her police interview, when she passed the young man at the front desk of her apartment building and felt him watching her, that Tom might know where she lives, might follow her all the way up to her room if he could. This makes her so uneasy that she breaks into a run and does not stop until she is streets away from the park, streets away from him, those tears she has been holding back now spilling over.

What was it she had thought when she first sat down with him today?

This is what happens when you don't trust anybody, least of all yourself.

Is it possible, she wonders, her chest heaving, and her legs shaking, that she has gone the wrong way, yet again? It is a thought she decides to follow no further, as she turns and heads for home.

★   ★   ★

The night of Ruby's accidental date with Tom, a message comes through from Lennie:

> Josh finally told me what happened. He's a dumb ass, but it's not entirely what you think. Text me back. I miss you xoxo

Another text comes in from Sue:

> I've left you a dozen messages, Ruby. Call me back, please.

And from Josh, not long after:

> I know you're mad at me. I would really like the
> chance to explain things. In the meantime, I
> found something you might be interested in . . .

He sends her Noah's address. Reduces the map of
New York to one pulsing dot.

It's as if I have been waiting for this all along.

★ ★ ★

When Ruby shows up at Noah's door, he is not entirely
surprised. He had been expecting something like this.
That someone with a connection to me would eventually seek him out. Still, to meet the woman who
found my body is its own shock; he assumed it would
be someone from my past. As he shakes Ruby's hand,
invites her in, he resolves to never ask her anything
but the barest details about that morning. It is the one
thing he won't ever want to know.

He offers Ruby tea, coffee, whiskey, and she is
tempted to go for the latter, though it is only 9 a.m.
Noah sees the gleam in her eye, and decides, immediately, that he likes this Australian woman; anyone
unfazed by the idea of liquor at this hour is okay by
him. Franklin also gives his seal of approval, nosing at
Ruby's hand when she sits down, asking for a scratch.
He looks for me still, the old mutt, and he finds me
sometimes, too. But this morning I remain at a careful distance, anxious for this meeting to go well. For
Ruby, yes. But for Noah too, who is just as lonely as
she is. My New York bookends, the man who let me
stay with him, and the woman who stayed with me.

They talk a little about themselves, and then Ruby takes a deep breath, asks the question she has carried around since that morning by the river.

'What was Alice like, Noah?' He stares at Ruby for the longest time, knowing how important his answer will be. When he finally speaks, his voice has an uncharacteristic tremble.

'Alice was rough around the edges. Uneducated, yet the smartest young woman I've known. She absorbed information like a sponge, and then she dripped what she learned all over the floor. She was beautiful, yes, but far too quick for loveliness. There was nothing lovely about her. She was raw and unfinished, and though it turns out no one had ever really let her be a child, she still behaved like one at times. Being around her was amusing and exasperating, and occasionally, illuminating. She was very easy to love.'

(I was? I have never before considered this.)

He tells Ruby so many stories, all the things he paid attention to. He talks about my mother, and my birthdays. About my growing love of photography, and how I treasured an old Leica. He's now certain I stole that camera from that 'no-good teacher', the man I had told him about, but only just (I should have known Noah would comprehend what really went on between Mr Jackson and me). He says I loved the Chrysler Building with a passion, that I often sounded like an unpolished Joan Didion when I described New York, and that when he first saw me, I looked for all the world like the homeless waif I was. He even cries a little when he talks about the last time he saw me, how I was annoying him before bed, clunking around on the piano, restless in a way he wishes he had noticed. Wishing he had kept me up late, pushed harder to

269

uncover my secrets.

'If I had known . . . '

Noah trails off and Ruby, thick with everything she has been told today, reaches for his hand. When he doesn't pull back, she squeezes her fingers around his.

'How could anyone know,' she says softly, and when she asks him if it would be okay for her to visit again sometime soon, he says yes.

★ ★ ★

It isn't until much later that afternoon, as Ruby sits on her bed, thinking about everything Noah told her, that something Tom said yesterday comes back to her.

She was out here, taking her pictures.

Ruby sits up, pushes her fingertips together, brings her hands to her mouth. Noah said something about a Leica, didn't he? Amongst all those other startling, beautiful stories. She concentrates hard, hears Noah saying Alice loved her old camera and had planned to enrol in a photography school, so she could keep taking pictures of her beloved New York. Was this common knowledge, something already out there? In all the articles and forums and news bulletins she has scoured since the murder, Ruby can't recall coming across anything about a camera. Turning off the TV, she opens her laptop, googles my name for the thousandth time. She finds no mention of a camera or photography or *pictures* in any of the news stories. Next, Ruby returns to her favourite sleuthing websites, scans post after post for discussions around why Alice Lee was out there by herself that morning in Riverside Park. Perhaps Tom has been here on these forums, too. Indulging his fascination with the dead girl from his neighbourhood, and that's where he picked up such a specific piece of information. Clicking through the scores of entries, Ruby encounters the usual theories — prostitution, sleeping rough, online dating gone wrong — but once again, no mention of anything to do with Alice Lee taking pictures in the park.

A girl was murdered here.

Ruby's heart begins to hammer.

She tries to pull other sentences to the surface. Thinks hard about Tom's questioning of her, sees a flash of him snapping when that jogger came too close. It's nothing, it has to be nothing. That kiss clearly unsettled her, and she's been spending too much time on those damn forums, finding tenuous connections, potential matches — *Snap!* — where there are none. It's just because she's lonely again. Trying to fill up the absence of Death Club any way she can.

Still. A thought comes creeping in, persists. What if it's no accident that she and Tom crossed paths again this week? If Ruby had gone back to that rocky beach a week ago, or a week before that, would she have found this man already there, looking out over the water, just as she herself had done the morning of my murder? What if Tom had been there well before she came along, and she was simply the one to discover the damage he'd left behind?

What if. What if. What if.

What if Tom was always there, in that *nice spot* by the river, waiting to see what happened next.

★   ★   ★

271

She won't ever think of her foot cracking down on something round and black, the shattering of the plastic lens cap I lost when I was making my way down to the river, with the Leica tucked under my jacket to protect it from the rain. In my haste, I never even noticed when the cap dislodged and fell to the ground.

With so much that has happened since that morning, Ruby has long forgotten her prayer to the god of lost things. Which means she'll never realise I accidentally told her about the camera, right from the beginning.

No matter.

She has a bigger realisation waiting for her. She really is almost there.

22

When Ruby is buzzed up to Sue's apartment, Lennie is already seated in the kitchen chopping vegetables, sharp metal perilously close to her fingertips each time she brings down the blade.

'Don't disappear on us again,' Sue had gently scolded when she opened the door, but Lennie is less subtle when Ruby walks into the room.

'Where the fuck did you go, Ruby?'

'I'm sorry,' Ruby says, feeling her eyes start to water. 'I had some things to figure out on my own.'

The two women had responded to her SOS text within minutes; before she knew it, she was on her way to their Brooklyn apartment building for the first time, comfort and a home-cooked meal beckoning.

> Something weird has happened. I need to talk to you both.

That was the message Ruby had sent, after going over Tom's comments again and again. Feeling as if she might go crazy in her small room, she had reached out with her heart in her throat. To find Sue and Lennie still open to her was a relief, cool air rushing into a stifling room.

Taking a seat next to Lennie now, Ruby watches as Sue silently adjusts Lennie's grip on the knife handle before returning to her own chopping and dicing. The casual intimacy of this gesture is maternal, beautiful, though neither of her friends seems to give it a second thought. Ruby stares into the wine glass Sue had ready and waiting for her when she walked into the room. Thinking that perhaps the best friendships are like this. Quiet and certain. She wonders at how long it's taken for her to contemplate this notion. That being seen and known is better for you than being someone's enduring mystery.

I don't understand you sometimes! Ruby would need more fingers and toes to count the many times Ash has directed this sentiment at her.

She opens her mouth, wonders where to start with her story about Tom, when Lennie turns to face her.

'So. Josh. You talked to him yet?'

It is almost a relief to push Tom to the back of her mind, even for a minute, and focus on something she might actually have the words for.

'There is something I never told you about why I came to New York,' Ruby says nervously, as Sue stops her chopping and dicing. Lennie is already demonstrably holding her breath.

'I left because I was having an affair. With a guy — Ash — who's getting married later this year. I've been the other woman for so long, and it's horrible to wait for a person to choose you, and when Josh said he was still married, I saw all of that starting over again . . .'

The rest comes out in a rush, the heartache and embarrassment and loneliness that followed her from Melbourne to New York, and before she can stop herself, Ruby is crying, causing Lennie to jump up from her chair, wrap her in a fierce hug.

'It all makes sense now,' Lennie says, her own voice cracking. 'I knew something was up with you! I just wish you'd told us sooner.'

'Agreed,' Sue adds, massaging her fingers through her cropped hair, a gesture Ruby now recognises as an attempt to gather her thoughts before speaking.

'I'm very glad you told us, Ruby. And you'll get no judgement from me on how or who you choose to love.

'As for Josh,' she continues, 'you should know it's not the same situation. He's been separated for a while now. I tell him all the time to hurry up with the divorce papers, but he's such a procrastinator when it comes to his personal life. We had hoped' — Sue looks at Lennie, who nods emphatically — that you might be a catalyst for him to finally get moving in a new direction. You're basically all he talks about.'

Ruby blinks at this information, tries to absorb it. There have been so many revelations coming at her these past two days, she can hardly keep up. It hasn't even been that long since she found out my name and now —

Alice Lee pops into her head with a startling clarity and Ruby stops, remembers why she came here tonight. She takes a long swig of wine, shakes Josh off for the time being.

'Thank you for that. *I think*. But . . . there was something else I wanted to talk to you both about, actually. Something happened yesterday.'

Taking it slow, Ruby tells Lennie and Sue about meeting Tom. About how he showed up at the exact place she found my body, and how charming he was at first, before he kept trying to turn the conversation back to the murder, even when she made it clear she didn't want to talk about it.

As Ruby goes over their encounters, she thinks of Detective O'Byrne, and the last time she had tried to explain what happened down by the river. How he'd said it can take time to remember details 'better', especially the important ones. She is conscious of getting the details she *does* remember about Tom in the right order, wants to give her friends the clearest explanation she can. Still, she pauses over Tom's comment about 'pictures'. Struggles to describe that particular detail, and all that came after it. The unwanted kiss, and Josh's message. Meeting Noah. The gift of his stories about Alice. She knows that each beat of the story is bursting with significance, but what if she's reading the signs all wrong? When was the last time she knew something to be completely true?

Ruby suddenly sees Josh holding out his phone like a bunch of flowers, my smiling face filling the screen.

Taking a deep breath, she carries on, finally able to admit just how uncomfortable Tom made her feel, the way he kept pushing himself on her, and onto me too.

'There's something this guy seems to know that he shouldn't,' she adds, arriving now at the place she started, coming up the stairs to Sue's apartment tonight, her confusion held out in front of her, and her fear too, that her friends might shut the door in her face. She feels exhausted to have come this far, and from the looks on Lennie and Sue's faces, they are right there with her.

'Oh my God, Ruby. Do you really think . . . '

But for once, Lennie is lost for words and she trails off, looking to Sue for help. The older woman is silent, thoughtful, as she refills each of their wine glasses almost to the rim. If Ruby didn't know better, she'd swear Sue's hand is shaking.

'That man, whoever he was, had no right to make

you feel that way, Ruby.'

Sue is indeed trembling, though not from fear. From rage.

'And Alice, that poor, poor girl. She was basically the same age as my Lisa. What happened to her makes me so mad. The entitlement of these fucking men who destroy lives, just because they can.'

'I've never, ever heard you swear — ' Lennie starts, then stops. 'You're right. It makes me fucking mad, too. And scared.'

Wine slops over Lennie's glass, she watches it spill onto the table, before she turns back to Ruby, her dark eyes wide.

'Do you really think he could have done it? This Tom guy.'

Still, Ruby doesn't know for sure. How could she. Reading true crime threads and wandering around the internet with her imaginary magnifying glass could never prepare her for this. Not even seeing the machinery of a murder investigation up close, those forensic investigators, Jennings, her clumsy interview with O'Byrne, could give her the tools she needs to determine Tom's motives down at the river yesterday, or any of the days before. How do you crawl into the mind of a murderer, and would it look any different from that of any other man, when you got down to it?

'For all I know,' Ruby answers slowly, 'Tom is a great guy. Just a little forward. And a bit weird about Alice. That's not enough to make him a murderer.'

'No, it isn't,' Sue responds. 'And so what I'd like to ask you is this. Something we don't ask ourselves enough. Do you trust your instinct, Ruby?'

The question feels as large as the room, and all three

women pause to consider it. Thinking about the nights they've crossed the road to avoid a parked car with its lights still on or pretended to make a phone call when someone walks too close behind them. Remembering the times they have shifted seats on public transport, or said *no, thank you*, to that offer of a drink. Self-preservation as a replacement for instinct, because being right would be the real danger here.

Ruby feels her body arch towards this sudden real-isation, a shudder that almost lifts her from the floor.

'I'm afraid to be right,' she says, holding out her arms to examine the tiny hairs standing up from her skin. 'Because — can you imagine what that would mean?'

Something Josh had said to her that night at the secret bar comes back to her now. When they finally knew my name.

'They're not always monsters, Ruby. Sometimes they're normal guys, who turn out to be capable of terrible things.'

It is a truth so small she almost missed it. So did I. But there it is. Half-hidden by the rocks and the dirt. Just waiting to be found.

★　★　★

You mustn't blame me for what happens next. Though I suppose some of you saw it coming. And maybe it is my fault. The way it all plays out. But I would never purposefully put Ruby in danger, please know that. I would have shown her this last, important detail in a different way if I could.

★　★　★

She can't sleep. Lennie and Sue thought she should go to the police straight away.

'In the morning, maybe,' she'd said before she went home, thinking, hoping, the midnight hours might help her find the words she would need to make that call. Knowing Detective O'Byrne would need something more concrete than her instinct, her discomfort. But the words don't come. Instead, her head is filled with half-finished conversations. Weeks, months, years of them, and Tom's voice is the loudest now. Something — *everything* — is wrong with their interactions, this seems obvious now. Why did he . . . and why would he . . . and what was he . . . Ruby kicks off the bed covers in frustration. What is it that she's missing here?

Tom knows something about Alice.

That's what she returns to, time and again. The impossibility of it, and yet.

She was out here, taking her pictures.

It doesn't make sense that he knows this. She is the one who found the body, she is the one who has spent night after night following breadcrumbs all over the city, piecing it all together. How can Tom be in possession of such an important detail that she herself did not know?

Fuck it.

This feels just like that other morning. The room too small, her thoughts too big. To Ruby, it almost feels like a dream as she gets up in the dark, puts on her running shoes. When she exits her apartment, makes her way towards Riverside Park, the streets are just as empty as that other morning. It's not raining today, that is something different. But the stillness, the silence, her frustration, feel exactly the same.

Checking her watch, Ruby calculates the sun will be up in half an hour. The sky is already changing colour, lifting up off her nose, and this emboldens her, lengthens her strides as she enters the park.

I can feel the adrenaline coursing through her now, the way it propels her towards the river, and I want to yell Stop! Find a way to turn her around. I would open up the sky, pour torrents of rain if I could. Crack the earth open, bring down the trees. But she keeps running, she can't see me or hear me, and she cannot see what is waiting for her, down on those rocks. I speed between the river and the track she makes through the park, desperate to keep her away. There are other runners, cyclists, dotted around the park this early morning, and I try to rearrange them, move them into her path, but nothing works. Gusts of wind, branches bending; my panic is the lightest touch, and Ruby is moving too fast to feel it.

And then, mercifully, she stops. The sky is still dark, the river darker, and she stands, suspended high above the place where it happened. Knowing there are steps just ahead of her that will take her down to the water. She wonders: is this what Alice felt? Heading down to the river that morning? An inexplicable pull towards the water, a wilful ignorance of her own safety, because she had something she wanted, needed, to do.

What on earth were you doing in the park that morning?

Ruby takes the steps carefully, quietly. When she reaches the middle level of the park, she finally sees what I have been trying so desperately to keep her from: Tom Martin below her, standing on the rocks, shifting something from hand to trembling hand. He has come here every morning this week, always before the sun comes up. Planting his feet on either side of where he found me, closing his eyes. I've come here every morning, too. Observing his growing desire for Ruby, the mud brown of it, and wanting to scream. I whispered the words in his ear, that very first meeting. Willed him to speak them out loud.

A girl was murdered here.

I set that gull squawking, soured the wine. Put my hand over his lips when he kissed her, so she felt the brittle of my bones instead of his warm flesh. But it wasn't enough to stop this.

It wasn't enough to keep her away from him.

And now I can feel Ruby shaking. Instinctively, she has backed up the steps, creating enough distance to allow her to run if Tom suddenly turns away from the river, sees her standing there watching him. He would have to scramble up over the rocks, climb over that metal rail, there might be enough time for her to escape if he sees her. Ruby makes these calculations in a split second. But her safety is far from assured, she knows this.

Fight. Flight. Freeze. What do we choose in these moments? Ruby is both rooted to the spot and ready to run. And something else too, the thing that scares me most. A white-hot rage is boiling within her, flames replacing blood. She imagines barrelling down the stairs, engulfing this man. *How dare you!* she wants to scream. How dare you! There is no question now. She knows. The man who kissed her two days ago is the man who raped and murdered Alice Lee.

What was the last thing she said to him?

Thank you, Tom. I appreciate your concern.

What neither of us said, what none of us say: *You took up all the space. I didn't know how to say no and you never waited for my yes. I need you to leave me alone now.* We swallow the words and the warning bells, so that we take on the doubt, dismiss what we know to be true. We demur, placate. Say just enough and smile just enough and let them touch us just enough, hoping the moment will pass.

When he climbed down onto the rocks, when he came up beside me in the splattering rain and said, 'Nice spot, isn't it,' I wasn't so much afraid as alert. Attuned to his interest in me and aware, immediately, that I would now be responsible for managing that interest. Knowing I would have to be careful with how I responded to his advances, that my reaction would determine whether he made to lodge himself next to me — or encourage him to turn and leave me alone, the only thing I wanted him to do. Here's what I was thinking, just before he materialised out of the haze of rain. I was thinking about how freedom and safety are the same thing, really. It was just after five thirty in the morning and the air was vibrating and whistling around me. I had removed my parka, was using it as a kind of umbrella for the Leica, and my arms were bare, exposed. The smack of raindrops and the icy air on my skin was exhilarating. I was wide awake, watching the buildings on the other side of the Hudson wake up too, light after light coming on, flashes against the dark sky. Thinking about freedom and safety, how unfettered I had become. The thread pulling me back to Mr Jackson finally loose, if not quite severed entirely.

When my ex-lover had answered the phone earlier that morning, clearly foggy from sleep, I remained silent at first, listening to him say 'Hello?' over and over, until finally, I heard him exhale against my name.

'Alice?' He sounded weary. 'Is that you?'

'I'm sorry for taking your mom's camera,' I said in response, and I heard another sigh, before Mr Jackson asked me where I was calling from.

Glancing about my bedroom in Noah's apartment, I observed my new life. Brochures for the photography school on the dresser, a blank set of Post-it notes waiting for my pen. A book on common dog behaviours. Purple runners at the base of my bed, toes pointing towards the door. Outside, I heard a train-rumble of thunder, and through a peek of curtain I could see the hazy orange and blues of the stormy, pre-dawn sky.

'Home,' I answered, knowing this to be as true as anything I had ever said.

I waited seconds, minutes for Mr Jackson to ask me if I was okay. I waited for him to press into my absence this past month, probe it, but instead he stayed silent. And I knew right there and then that he did not want to know where I was.

'I have to go,' I said finally. 'I just wanted you to know I'm alive.'

His continued silence was a wave of truth, waiting to break all over me.

I hung up the call.

It was that stifling silence that pushed me out the door, into the early-morning storm. I needed space, needed to stretch out after finally seeing how small he had tried to make me. All that time with Mr Jackson, I was only ever someone to control. He never gave me room to make mistakes, to discover who I was for myself. He needed me to behave in a way that suited him, and even more, in a way that preserved his idea of me. For a while, that had been enough love for me.

Not now.

Freedom then, would be escaping this containment, once and for all. And that's when my heart slowed, and the world expanded. Stepping into the park, unafraid. Propelled towards the water, my new, giddy freedom a hand at my back. Passing the wood-chipped dog runs where I would bring the puppies on the next fine day, and the empty sports fields turned to mud that would teem with people in the summer. Turning my face to the rain, then away from it just as quickly, as water stung my cheeks. Feeling the crisp preparation in the air, before lightning once again zagged across the sky and thunder echoed in its wake. Knowing I was as wild as this storm, as full of potential. To capture this would be to give that photography school my self-portrait. Show them the artist I intended to be.

And then the stranger was climbing down over the rocks, coming towards me. Staring at my bare arms, pointing his extinguished cigarette at me, asking if I had a light. It must have been the way I shook my head slightly, or how I turned my attention back to the Leica. My last clear thought, staring through that small viewfinder, was how much lightning bolts reminded me of blood vessels. Veins branching out across the sky.

And then it was him, not the lightning, that split me in two.

Though she'll never trust these memories after, when she looks down at him now, Ruby sees everything Tom Martin did to me that morning, catches the blinding red of it, flashing across his body. I'm not even sure how it happens. The way she can suddenly view the world from my perspective. There I am, climbing down onto the rocks to get closer to the water, liking the way it reflects the lightning, mirrors the sky.

There I am, peering through my viewfinder, framing the world, thinking it is mine for the taking. And there I am, startled, when I sense someone is behind me on the pathway, his eyes a gleam in the dark. Ruby can see every grotesque, electric pulse of him as he approaches me, and more than that — to my absolute horror — she can suddenly feel everything I felt that morning.

As if what happened to me is happening to her, too.

'Hello there,' he says, and I think at first that I am going to be okay. He looks normal, this man, in his neat shirt and regular shoes. An insomniac like me, I presume, or a storm chaser, someone more comfortable out in the rain than tucked up in bed. *No need to be scared*, I tell myself, but I am, all the same, when he climbs over the railing too, takes his time to come up beside me.

'Got a light?' he asks, holding out his half-smoked cigarette, and this time I catch it. The way his voice is far too measured, careful. As if he is barely restraining himself.

'No,' I say, squaring my shoulders. Hoping this makes me look stronger than I am. *Never let them see that you're afraid* — I read that once, and I do my best to fool him, standing there with my camera between us. I've had near misses before, felt danger as a pulse in my throat, and for a while there, as he tries to make conversation about the weather, my camera, what it is I'm doing out here all alone, I think this is going to be one of those times. I keep my answers short, polite, buying myself minutes until the sun comes up. But then he tells me I'm beautiful, says 'Do you like to *fuck*', and I know, deep in my bones, that this is not going to be a near miss. When he commands me to smile, when he comes at me with all his smug determination, I acquiesce. Thinking, one last time, that I know what to do here. That I can survive this, if I just play it his way.

Like I said. It surprised me. At the end. The way I had no chance. How swiftly it happened when Tom Martin ended my life.

Ruby sees, *feels* everything that happened to me, and then she turns and runs, nausea rising in her, replacing her fear. So that when she reaches the safety of the upper levels of the park, she doubles over and heaves, vomiting up everything she has witnessed.

There was just enough time, before she fled, for her to hear a splash, the unmistakable sound of something being thrown into the river.

It is a detail she will remember better this time.

★ ★ ★

I think she's hurt. I don't know if I should go to her. Should I go to her . . . Tell me what I need to do.

For weeks Ruby has worried that she let me down. Though she never said it to herself, or out loud, she wondered if she could have done something — anything — differently that morning. If she hadn't got lost or slipped on the rail, or if she'd paid more attention to her surroundings in those minutes before, when she was more worried about the rain. Was there some moment she missed, some way she could have changed things?

All this time, Ruby has been searching for absolution. For a way to say sorry for arriving too late, for not being able to get to the girl, or to whoever came before her, in time. Her obsession with the murder, with me, was her apology.

'Truly, you did everything right, Ruby.'

That's what Officer Jennings said after she found me. Today, when she picks up her phone with shaking hands and dials the number on the card Detective O'Byrne gave her that terrible morning, weeks and a lifetime ago, Ruby finally believes it.

Noah was right. New York really is made for second chances.

23

It begins. They get his DNA from a cigarette butt flicked onto the rocks, right where he left me that morning. It matches the traces of his identity found all over my body. Before he left that crass genetic fingerprint behind, investigators watched as Tom Martin kept returning, over and over, to the crime scene. When Ruby made the call, when she reported Tom's comment about 'pictures' and what she'd seen and heard down by the water, she hadn't known *Camera Lens* was fourth on Detective O'Byrne's list of blunt force weapons, underneath the word *Torch*, but above *Wrench* and *Hammer*. Circled in red pen over and over, after Noah asked if they'd found the Leica — the only thing, along with the purple sneakers and jacket, my benefactor could say for sure was missing from my room. Camera lens. A weapon of opportunity. This fitted Detective O'Byrne's profile of the man they were looking for. An anger-retaliatory type, someone impulsive with his rage. The excessive force used, the way the body was left face down, subjugated. Every offender leaves a series of clues about himself, and Detective O'Byrne had known the motivation of the man who killed Alice Lee from the moment he saw the placement of the young girl's body on the rocks.

Ruby's call was metal up his spine, bringing him to his feet. It wasn't enough to bring Tom in, but O'Byrne was a patient man. The detective immediately had his team of undercover officers position themselves down at the river each day, a small parade of inconspicuous investigators jogging, stretching, sitting in the sun, eyes flicking when the tall, blonde man returned again and again to the river. Watching as he leant over the railings, stared out across the water. At the same time, detectives canvassed every camera store, every pawn shop in the vicinity. Showing an image of Tom Martin, asking, 'Have you seen *this* man? Have you seen this man?' over and over, looking for the proof they needed in a manner so direct that people stuttered over their *No's*, wondering what would happen to the poor store owner or cashier who might say yes. One or two guessed this was all to do with the dead girl, the pretty one in the news, though they never said my name out loud, reluctant to find themselves caught up in something they had absolutely nothing to do with. Not this time around.

That same week, at O'Byrne's request, they searched the river. Calculated shifting tides and weather patterns, and the days since Ruby saw Tom down on the rocks and heard him throw something into the water. The current gives up its secrets eventually. Messages in bottles show up on foreign shores a hundred years after being tossed into the sea. The Hudson River connects to the Atlantic Ocean, shares the same roiling water, feels the same pull of the moon. And so, they find it one night, in the brackish muck. Offered up by the tides, handed over. A Summar 50mm screw mount lens. Nickel-plated steel. Specks of my blood like rust in the grooves of the aperture ring. Turns out the past sticks to whatever it touches. You cannot simply wash it away.

Detective O'Byrne is quiet, thoughtful, as they inch closer to the unequivocal proof they need. He is certain they will not find the camera itself; this is a man who would like to preserve his souvenirs. Which leads O'Byrne to the matter of the photographs. *Pictures*, as Tom called them. That slip up of his was deliberate in its way. Men like this eventually give themselves away, they betray their own secrets, because they so desperately want to stay at the centre of things. Narcissism makes a person careless, no matter how clever they might be. If Tom held onto the camera, had it hidden somewhere, the undeveloped film must have been calling to him. Not knowing what was on that roll, especially when the body remained unidentified so long, would have a man like that burning up. Those *pictures*, whatever they might reveal, would be the ultimate proof of his achievement. Only he would know who the girl was. He could own every part of her now.

By O'Byrne's calculation, Tom Martin would have been less likely to get the film developed once his victim was publicly identified, once that Jane Doe sketch was replaced with real-life images of Alice Lee. Impulsivity has its limits, so they'd be looking for activity soon after the crime, and somewhere outside the city. These men might be careless, but in O'Byrne's experience, they were seldom openly stupid.

It was the twelfth film-processing lab they checked. A boutique store specialising in analogue photography, just two hours' drive from Manhattan. Well-promoted online, easy enough to find via a Google search. When they showed the lab owner a picture of Tom, she bit her lip and said, Yeah, I think I remember him. He was here, maybe a month ago. From out of state, he said. Most people like him mail their film to us, and we send back a CD, but he said he wanted prints. He never came back, actually. I have those prints here, somewhere. And the negatives, too, of course. Some of them didn't turn out so well . . . '

I left behind my version of the city. I took pictures of the strained wire bridges and the Chrysler Building, and people streaming out of the subway. I snapped Lady Liberty from the deck of the Staten Island Ferry, and the reflective rise of One World Trade Center. The disorientation of Times Square, and the statue of my namesake in Central Park, little kids hanging off her like decorations. I was in every one of these places and I captured every moment, and now they exist as proof I was here. Detective O'Byrne thumbs through each photograph, scans every black and white image, and it is the second to last shot that feels like a punch. Heavy rain. Rocks. A swollen river. The lights of New Jersey hazy on the other side of the water. And then the last picture I snapped. Lightning reflected in the flowing river, and because I was still learning, the hint of my purple sneaker in the bottom left of the frame. Here in his hands, he is holding my last moments. He is seeing what I saw, right before a man came out of the rain, and got angry enough to put his hands to my throat. To rip the camera from me and smash it down on my skull. Angry enough to thrust into my dying body, scraping my back against the rocks, heaving over me and pouring into me, and I was not there any more, I was already outside of myself, but it was still my body as he fell, grunting, over what was left of me. Hot breath and stickiness on cold skin. The wretched sound of him tucking himself back in, zipping himself up. The sound that said he was finished. Done with me.

O'Byrne was right. Tom couldn't resist the mystery. Found the memory of what he'd done was not enough to keep him satisfied. So, he carefully removed

291

the film, found a photo lab he thought would be far enough away from the river. He had always intended to come back for the prints, but then they found out my name. And my face was everywhere again. My real face this time, the one he had looked away from as he killed me. Realising how stupid he was, how caught up he'd been, Tom never went back to collect those pictures.

But he could not stop returning to the river. At first, he was careful to avoid the scene at unusual times, at five a.m. and midnight when he felt the strongest pull; he made sure he only ever went down there when he could blend in and remain inconspicuous. When Ruby finally came along, he *was* there, waiting. And from the moment he saw her leaning over the rails, her eyes closed, muscles flickering, Tom was certain she was aware of what had happened there. He assumed, a strange pride swelling in his chest, this woman was caught up in the drama of the dead girl. He had seen others like this at the vigil, that night of candles and outrage. So many skittish women, foolishly thinking their fear was anger, or that it made any difference in the end. He had bowed his head that night, standing next to his wife, and she had squeezed his hand when she saw a tear wind down his cheek. She thought he was crying for the girl, but he was crying at the beauty of it all, for the magnificence of this grand tragedy he had orchestrated. How could it not fail to move him, after he had felt unseen, unheard, for so long?

When he approached Ruby and asked her to join him for a coffee, Tom never thought to imagine she was the one who found the body. This incredible news, when she finally told him, was like electricity, a body

292

heat reminiscent of that first moment he struck me. It felt like fate, the way the Australian was delivered to him so easily. Finally, he would have the chance to talk with someone who knew. Someone who was there. After so many weeks, it was beginning to feel like a dream. Talking about it would make it blessedly real again, but she kept refusing, swatting him away, and it was taking all of his energy not to explode. Sitting across the table from him that second time, drinking wine he paid for, eating food he ordered just for her, Ruby was so pious and polite, he had a visceral yearning to strike her, to watch her fall. To fall over her, himself.

It was too bad the weather had not gone his way that day.

It was an accident, that verbal slip when he said goodbye to her. He was too caught up in the idea of Ruby out there alone that morning, thinking about how easy it would be to drag her over to the construction site further along the river — metal and dirt for this one, not rocks and water — and he just wasn't paying attention to his words. Still, the Australian hadn't reacted at the time, there was nothing in her face to say she had picked up on his mistake, and he never expected the truth of his words to be followed. The breadcrumbs of those *pictures*, taken all over this city.

His second mistake, leaving that cigarette butt behind, offering up his DNA when they couldn't yet take it from him, occurs the same day Detective O'Byrne holds my pictures in his hands. Something carelessly discarded, something found. I like to think it all happens at the exact same time.

★　★　★

He never expected the knock at the door. The same kind of knock made for Mr Jackson. Only this time, when Tom Martin answers, there are men who stand at attention on the other side of the door. His wife comes into the hallway as they clasp handcuffs around his wrists.

'Tommy?' At first it is confusion. '*Tommy!*' Then fear. She lunges towards her husband, but the officers block her way.

'Ma'am,' they say, holding her back. 'I'm sorry, ma'am.'

So polite in these last moments, before they take apart her whole existence, before they deliver a revelation that leaves her gasping on the floor. Her husband arrested for the rape and murder of Alice Lee. She held his hand tight at the vigil. Gently laughed off his concerns about being careful these days, when that man could be anywhere.

That man could be anywhere.

There will never be enough days to scrub clean the lies Tom Martin has poured all over this woman's body. Each revelation that will come — the hard-core, underage pornography on his computer, the fake profiles he's posted on dating sites, the bags of amphetamines hidden in his closet, an ex-girlfriend who said he had stalked her when she left him. And soon enough, the details of how he smashed an eighteen-year-old girl's head with the lens of her camera, squeezed her throat with his nicotine-stained fingers, and continued his assault of her body as she lay dying on the banks of the Hudson River. How he scooped up her underwear and shoes and jacket and unscrewed the bloody lens from the camera, all the while standing over the battered body of a teenage girl. Though no one else will understand the specificity of her horror, this is the part that will come to haunt his wife the most. The calmness with which her husband must have packed up the evidence of a young life. The calculation of what to keep and what to leave behind.

Nothing will ever again be true for this woman. It is never just one life these men destroy.

★　★　★

Now it's time for his story to be told. For the papers to sift through his life, figure out why he did what he did. But it doesn't really matter, does it? You already know enough about him. I don't want to tell his story. I don't even want to say his name any more. I don't see why he is the one who should be pieced together, remembered.

I am Alice Lee. And this is *my* story.

★　★　★

They got him.
They got him.
At first, Ruby is stunned. To live with a question for so long — it takes time for the answer to feel right, to make sense. She stares at that man's face in the news, goes over her time with him, and it feels as though something is crawling all over her skin, burrowing in. Not the dull, staring-at-walls sadness of finding my body, but a burn, an itch that infects her.

I do my best to take my memories back, those awful things she could suddenly see and feel, but somewhere, in the haze of her fever, she refuses to look away from what she saw. In the end, I simply sit with her. Whispering other stories, sweet and soft ones, so Ruby might have more than one truth to remember when the fever breaks.

The female members of Death Club comfort as they can. Sue delivers food, pies and cakes and muffins, things that are warm and fresh. When Ruby cannot get herself out of bed, Lennie brings flowers, makes sure her windows are kept open. Side by side, they read the onslaught of news stories, confront those terrible truths together, and on the first, fitful nights after the arrest, Lennie stays to help Ruby fall asleep. She calls Cassie when Ruby, sitting next to her, cannot find the words, and provides assurances of safety and care to worried family and friends back home: 'She's had a shock, yes, but she's been brilliant. Really, Cassie, your sister solved a freakin' crime. I think she may even get a medal.'

Later, when her fever subsides, Ruby makes three phone calls. First, a conversation with Cassie and her mother to reassure them she really is okay, all things considered. By now, news that the Riverside murder has been solved has crossed the Pacific, made its way into Australian papers and magazines; Ruby is the invisible thread throughout, the unnamed beginning and end of things. Few readers will ever know how she tied this story together, but that's the way she wants it to be.

'The story,' she says, 'always belonged to Alice.'

After talking with her family — ending the call with a promise to avoid dead bodies from now on — Ruby calls Noah. She guesses, correctly, that he will be tentative about these new developments, will want to know the specifics of how she came to identify the man who killed his friend, but will not want to discuss the man himself. He cannot even look at the mug shots, he tells Ruby. Unaccustomed to rage, to the incessant, vengeful desires evoked by looking at those photographs, Noah instinctively understands men like that feed on such reactions; he resolves to starve my murderer of oxygen, until he is reduced to nothing.

'You brave, brave woman,' Noah says as they close the call. 'Thank you for everything you have done for Alice.'

The last phone call Ruby makes is to Josh. He answers on the second ring, as if he has been waiting for her.

'I'm sorry,' they say at the same time. As if they have been waiting for each other. He tells her Sue's lecture was fierce, worse than his own mother's, and that Lennie was furious with him.

'You don't kiss someone without the full story,' she told him. 'You don't take away that choice!'

He asks about what happened, expressing his awe and confusion at the events he has missed in such a small amount of time.

'You can tell me anything,' he says. 'I'm here for whatever you need.'

Ruby, tired of saying the same things over, asks Josh for his own full story instead.

He tells her that his marriage disintegrated after the bike accident. In those first few months of recovery, his body began to feel like a foreign object, something illogically attached to him, and he often felt like one of those walking corpses, neither here nor there in any situation. It was like his real body had gone on ahead without him. Knowing this could not be true, feeling his pulse flicker in his wrist, and the gnawing pain of bones slowly fusing back together, he rationally understood he was still an electric current, alive. But the black kept pulling him in, the tar kept spreading, until his mind was thick with it. The sardonic writer he used to be was trapped in this viscous, and he was not the only one who wondered if he would ever write — or feel light — again.

At first, Lizzie had been supportive, staying close to his bedside in the hospital, hovering around him at home. But the longer he lived in the darkness, the more restless his wife became.

'You have situational depression,' she kept asserting, flicking through websites on her iPad, presenting little facts to her husband each night. 'It says here that situational depression is common in men who' — and off she would go, reading aloud from this magazine article or that, hunting down expert opinions on why, after leaving the hospital, Josh remained reluctant to get back to his old life, his old self. Trying to resolve why he was suddenly a blank slate, why none of the usual things impressed upon him or moved him and, why — a fact most alarming to anyone who knew how kinetic he had been before the accident — this new state of being did not seem to panic him, no matter how many long days and longer nights had passed.

It took Lizzie six months to leave him. She's been out in LA for over a year now, writing for a TV show. At first, she held out hope the old Josh would come back.

'We'll get you a shaman,' she had said, around two months after settling on the West Coast. 'They can go so much deeper than the others. Down to where you've gone.' She sent him meditational videos and links to yoga retreats in Bali. Things to bring him back to her, to the indulgent rhythms of their relationship before he decided to bike home through Central Park one night and his wheel hit a tree root, and everything got rearranged. She missed their rooftop parties, and their drug-hazed fucking, and seeing her husband's name as a byline in her favourite magazines. But eventually, her love ran out. Just a little, and then a lot, as if it had only ever come from a limited supply.

Lizzie has long since stopped talking about smudge sticks and heal-all desert plants, and now her emails and texts reference divorce papers, and selling the apartment on East 97th. He has been avoiding this next step, he tells Ruby, not because he wants to work on the marriage. Rather, he has been happy for things to stay just as they are. Afraid, he admits now, of what another change might bring.

'Things changed the wrong way.'

'I understand,' Ruby tells him. 'I really do.'

She thinks of something she learned when she was very young, growing up on the edge of a wild, open ocean. When you get caught in a rip, you have no choice but to give in, to go where the water wants to take you. The force of the rip will eventually dissipate, but only if you let it carry you far enough out to sea. Safety comes from moving with the current until you are free of it, and then, only then, can you turn and swim like hell for the shore.

Ruby knows how to navigate the natural phenomena that is a changeable ocean. Why should it be any different with a natural disaster like love, she asks Josh. No one ever ends up where they started from, but you do make it home, when the time is right. If you have kept your head while being tossed about.

Sometimes it is surrender, not struggle, that saves a life.

★ ★ ★

Ruby does not call Ash. He is the one to text her, says he heard a rumour at work suggesting she helped solve a major crime.

> Holy shit Jonesy, what an adventure! I can't wait to talk to you about it. In NYC, maybe :)

She knows he means no harm with this cavalier response, but she also wonders when Ash will ever take her seriously. Knowing the answer is implicit in the question. He does not want her to be serious. She is his escape from serious. And this is a part of their bargain she can no longer uphold. Now that the *something* she has wanted to happen has so thoroughly happened. Now that she is unsure whether she is the same woman who said yes to Ash after she knew he was engaged. That version of herself seems irreconcilable with the strong, capable Ruby who sat in front of Detective O'Byrne and detailed her encounters with the man who killed Alice Lee, offering up enough perceptive information that she will be considered, in the looking back on this crime, to be the steady hand that turned a complex murder investigation towards its conclusion.

This is not a woman Ash has ever known.

This is the woman she wants to be.

> I don't want you to come here, Ash, she eventually responds.

300

You should commit to your fiancée. You've made your choice and I don't want to keep you from it. Go get married. Time for us to let go.

Ruby stares at the ceiling for a full hour after sending this text. They say it's the truth that sets you free. But sometimes it's a lie that does it. There is no reply. Ash will not reply. She lets herself wallow one last time, aches over the images she has crafted of them together in New York. Tastes daydreams of dark bars and glittering rooftops, rolls them around on her tongue, feels the tang of her yearning for him in her mouth. Swallows. There was a life she did not get to live. It was so close, but she cannot continue to hold onto something already gone.

I loved you.

She does not send this final truth across the ocean. The words too small for this moment, this ending. Only silence is large enough to hold her sorrow tonight.

* * *

There was one other print in the pack. The very first snap, long before all those photographs of New York were taken. When that black and white film was loaded, when instructions were given by a teacher to his student.

'Here's where you look. Because this is a rangefinder, you start with two images, and this focusing lever helps you bring them closer together. It takes a little time to get the hang of it, but eventually, from those two different views, you end up with a single, clear image. See?'

301

He was so close, the camera so intimate, that I turned away, right as he snapped the picture. My hair is a silver glow across the frame, phosphorescence in the dark. And though you cannot see my face, I know that I am laughing.

This is not the kind of thing you forget.

24

Ruby takes a long walk uptown. Once, when she was running north along the river, she thought she might keep going until she reached George Washington Bridge, but the immense structure seemed to get further away the more she advanced, and it was close to dark when she turned around, began the uneven trek back to her neighbourhood in the West 90s. Today, she starts on Broadway and just keeps walking. Past blocks that look similar enough to her own, taking note of cafes she might come back to next week and consignment stores with last winter's designer jackets in the window. When she gets to the unmistakable expanse of Columbia, Ruby pushes open a metal gate and steps into the university grounds. It is familiar in the way so much of New York is familiar, the sprawling steps and imposing buildings having appeared in so many films and TV shows she has seen. She crosses the main courtyard, heading east, smiling at the small groups of students sitting alone or in clusters, wondering what they are studying today, thinking she too might like to start classes here in the fall. If she decides to stay. Exiting the university, she turns towards home, following the western boundary of Morningside Park, marvelling at the space this city makes for its people. Knowing there is still so much for her to discover about New York.

As Ruby makes her way over to Amsterdam, the Cathedral Church of St John the Divine rises up before her, impossibly ornate amongst the low-rise buildings of modern, residential New York. She has no time for God, but the church itself is so beautiful, so compelling, that curiosity leads her up the wide stairs, through the thick double doors. Inside, the cavernous cathedral echoes with sunlight, a kaleidoscopic flower beckoning her forward, and Ruby finds herself stunned at the vista. She scrambles for a five-dollar bill to put in the donation box at the entrance to the nave, and she shifts her weight to her toes, not wanting to clomp her feet against the floor. Perhaps it would be different if the church were filled with worshippers, but here, on this mid-week afternoon, she is one of only twenty or so people moving slowly amongst the thick columns and arches. She feels a serenity she had not expected, a peacefulness, despite the obvious grandeur of the church.

And she remembers to look up.

Quietly exploring the cathedral, a lump grows in Ruby's throat, expands until it feels painful to swallow. A wall of names, of dates and dashes, too many to speak out loud, makes her feel faint, and she considers sitting down, trying out a version of prayer to steady herself, but there's another woman standing here before this wall, before these names, and she is already praying, head bowed, tears streaming down her face. Ruby blinks back her own tears and moves on.

When she arrives at the Cathedral's Poets Corner, the lump in Ruby's throat finally dislodges, hot tears spilling over, causing the words etched across the stone tablets of the floor and walls to blur. She is standing before a memorial to the wordsmiths of this country, the ones who have painstakingly translated the human experience into tiny, perfect sentences.

Writers who mapped the world and its sorrows with their words.

Alone, she reads aloud quotes from those poets whose names she knows best.

There's Millay with her songs and epitaphs. Dickinson describing captivity and consciousness. Emerson and Hemingway asking only for truth, and Hughes with his soul deep as a river. Baldwin, talking about disturbing the peace.

And this.

Walt Whitman. A man, a poet, who so loved New York, and was loved by New York in return.

I stop somewhere waiting for you.

It is others who move away now, leaving the sobbing woman alone with her poets and her sorrow. Generations of writers reaching down to wrap their arms around her, gently pressing their means of survival into her bones.

★ ★ ★

She invites Josh over as soon as she gets home. Says she has something to tell him, but there are no words when he walks into that tiny studio, fills it up, and she rushes at him, pours herself over his skin before he has the chance to say hello.

When they make love this very first time, they are clumsy, careful. Learning their way around the new body before them, this new tangle of nerves. They laugh against each other's mouths and close their eyes when they should keep them open, but there is no embarrassment or hesitation in these hours of exploration. They teach each other, welcoming the lessons, and when Ruby comes against Josh's hand she feels as if she is expanding into the vast, empty corners of her body, the hollow finally filled.

I've been stopped here, waiting for you, she whispers, but he is electric now, the blue light humming all through him drowning out her admission. No matter. They will try this again and again. And they will get better at finding each other, each and every time.

★ ★ ★

Noah pays for my funeral. He does not attend the service itself, staying true to his claim that he will never visit Wisconsin. But he pays for the flowers and the casket, and the sandwiches served after. The burning of my body, too. Asking only whether they might consider doing something special with my ashes. He talks of nebulae, of bright night skies and dying stars, and nobody understands.

'Ruby,' he says. 'We will have to do something ourselves. For her.'

On the day of the funeral, media reports say the little chapel on the corner of Pearson and Flushing is packed with mourners, with people spilling out onto the gravel driveway, craning to hear the service inside. There are kids from my high school, and gawkers from out of town, and Tammy and her mother sit in the front row, next to Gloria. Mother and daughter and guardian united, enjoying their brief moment in the spotlight. They have meetings with crime show producers already booked, and last week they gave an interview for one of those weekly tabloid magazines. I don't mind. I'd like to give them something outside of this town, outside of these people. Tammy was always good to me. Perhaps this is a chance for her mother and Gloria to do better, too.

In that interview, Gloria spoke about my mother. Things I knew. The extreme violence of her childhood, the disintegrations of home and family, until she ran away at eighteen years old, and no one bothered to come find her. The way she brought me up on her own from there, wanting, Gloria said, nothing but the best for her Alice. Things, too, I did not know. How that traumatised child never really grew up, how my mother suffered from breaks in reality I must have thought were games at the time. She did, it turns out, whatever she could to ensure my safety, from dealing drugs to sleeping with cold, old men for money. Forgetting to protect herself and getting deeper and deeper into trouble with her own mind, and the law. Not even Gloria could say what caused my mom to pull the trigger that afternoon, but she did say this:

'I know that woman loved her daughter with all her heart. At least now, they can be together.'

Mr Jackson does not attend the funeral either; he is already long gone from town. House packed up and art studio closed. He won't be returning to school in the fall. Impossible now, with all those rumours buzzing about him. Most of the young girls he taught scoff at the idea of this man taking advantage of Alice Lee. *More like the other way round*, some of them say, because they like him better. Unaware of the tremble under my skin when Mr Jackson first asked me to take my clothes off, these young girls can't understand you sometimes say yes as a means of survival. Not until it's their turn to say yes, some day.

At any rate, my teacher has gone to ground. He will emerge, eventually, with his own story to tell, a wound that will draw other young women to him, call them over. There was a girl he loved, and she died, he will tell them. Rearranging the truth until he believes it. Convinced he seeks solace, not power, when he takes another seventeen-year-old girl into his arms and into his bed.

One of these girls, eventually, will share her story. This time, there will be people looking for her, and when they find her, there *will* be another knock at Mr Jackson's door. That knock won't happen for some time yet, but you can hear it well enough, can't you?

Now that we know what to listen for.

★ ★ ★

My friends go down to the river together. It is the first day of summer. A whole season has passed, and the sky is blue, bright.

Noah carries long-stemmed roses, a rainbow mix of colours. Ruby holds a small silver padlock close to her chest. They greet each other warmly and hug. Franklin has a purple scarf tied neatly around his furry neck.

There are lots of people out and about on this clear day, as Noah and Ruby weave around children and dogs and fields with baseball games in their fifth and sixth innings. Ruby is once again struck by the idea that people actually go about their lives up here. Neighbourhoods full of children and families and sports teams and pets, hours spent together in a communal backyard.

They walk past one of the dog runs. Off their leashes, a clamour of pups and old mutts rush around, chasing balls and tails and each other. Ruby stops for a moment at the fence, thinks of me, considers how she might have jogged right past me at this very spot someday. Imagines the striking, yellow-blonde girl calling back a wayward beagle or pug, diving for a designer leash, dogs circling around her. Noah sees this too, the might-have-been of this meeting, and gives Ruby a gentle nudge with his shoulder.

They keep walking towards the water.

Both Ruby and Noah grow silent as they approach the little beach. The river is calm today, the view clear across to New Jersey. To Ruby, those wooden posts poking up out of the water still look eerie, a reminder of hidden depths. But aside from these markers, she acknowledges there is nothing extraordinary about this place, nothing good or bad or mysterious. This place would have remained one small, innocuous part of a sprawling city park, were it not for an angry, entitled man, and an April morning when life stopped and started, all at the same time.

'Are you all right?' Noah asks, bright, beautiful flowers framing his face.

Ruby nods.

'I was just thinking. How this place is really nothing special.' She looks down at a discarded juice wrapper, fluttering on the rocks. 'I could have run past here a thousand times and never given it a thought.

'And yet,' she turns to Noah, her fingers pressed tight around the padlock, 'this is also the most incredible place. It's where I found Alice. I felt so guilty at the time. Like I should have done more. But what if I'd kept on running that day? What if I never stopped. Can you imagine what I would have missed?'

'Can you imagine?' Noah repeats, before taking one of his roses and tossing it into the river.

They watch as the flower bobs around, a bright

yellow star dancing across the murky water. Silently, they throw the remaining roses over the railings, one by one, bright, beautiful colours suffusing the dark surface of the Hudson. As the last of the flowers land on the water, Ruby crouches down and clips the padlock around a wire at the base of the metal railing. Feeling the click as it closes shut, tracing her index finger over the letter A engraved on its shiny surface.

On the path behind them a child shrieks, giggles, and Ruby stands up, takes a deep breath, New York City filling her lungs.

'Thank you, Alice Lee,' she says quietly, and then she turns from the rocks, from the river, and walks away.

★ ★ ★

If I had lived.

The woman sits down on the park bench next to me, tries to catch her breath. She had been running south along the river. Forgetting she would have to double back until she had gone just that little bit too far, almost as far as the Cruise Terminal. Now she's got her head between her legs, willing everything to slow down, and she might not have noticed me today, but for Franklin sticking that wet nose of his up against her lowered cheek. His welcome sign.

She jerks up at his touch, startled, but then her face softens into a smile.

'Hey there, young man,' she says, scratching behind the grinning dog's ear.

'Your dog,' she laughs, turning to me, 'is quite forward.'

'Oh, he's not mine,' I start to say, but this no longer

feels true. Instead, I smile back at her.

'Yes, Franklin is a true New Yorker. Knows what he wants.'

'Something I have yet to master,' the woman responds.

'Where are you from, then?' I ask, struck by her accent.

'Who knows, sometimes,' she answers, and we look at each other really, truly for the first time. Sky and earth, meeting.

'I'm Alice,' I say, holding out my hand.

'Ruby,' she responds, our touch a small spark.

'I just moved here a month ago,' she continues, and we soon discover we arrived on the same dusky night, on the cusp of the same rainy spring.

'I ran away,' I confess, and she tells me she came here to get away from someone. A man.

'Me, too!' I exclaim, finally playing the right kind of snap.

'You did? How old are you, Alice?' Ruby asks, her eyebrows raised.

'I'm eighteen. You?'

'I'm thirty-six. So, you're exactly half my age, then.'

'Or you're exactly double mine,' I shoot back, and I know then, in the way she laughs, that we're going to be friends. We talk on that park bench for at least an hour, Franklin at our feet, shifting his watery gaze between us. We discuss our strange new city, and the places we left behind, and we dance up to the edges of the men we came here to get away from.

'It's complicated,' she sighs.

'It sure is,' I reply. Knowing I will get to tell her the full story.

Someday.

We stay chatting so long that when a raindrop unceremoniously plops against Franklin's head, we are both surprised to see the sky has gone dark. Heavy rain, on its way yet again.

'I got stuck here in the park recently. On one of those really stormy mornings,' Ruby says, holding her palm out in front of her, feeling the air. 'I'll admit it was kinda scary, being out here alone.'

'Last Tuesday? With all the thunder and lightning?' I ask, excitedly. *Snap!* 'I was out here too, taking pictures of the storm. Maybe not my smartest idea, but the photos turned out really great! What doesn't kill you, and all that.'

'You should be careful — ' Ruby starts, and then shrugs. 'Actually, you seem like a girl who can take care of herself. And I'd love to see your pictures some time.' She looks thoughtful now. 'It's nice to know I wasn't out here alone after all, Alice.'

If I had lived. Had somebody else not decided for me that morning, we might have discovered we were looking for each other the whole time.

We might have met and shared our stories in such a different way.

★　★　★

That Ruby should be the one to find my body. This is one of the two most remarkable things. The way she stayed with me, took me home with her. Suffered the nightmares and confusions, lived with my questions, and her own. She pushed through her own wild waves and kept me afloat, there beside her, before she even knew my name.

Strangers can change your life. Isn't that the truth.

312

I changed the life of Ruby Jones — for the better, I hope. Even though there must have been times when it didn't feel like it. When she might have preferred to keep that sorrow of hers simmering, instead of having it all boil over the way it did.

And Noah. Placing that ad. Knowing someone like me would come along. Noah with his IOUs, and his small smiles, and his New York lessons, telling me all the things I wanted to know. And some of the things I didn't.

I changed his life, too. I know it. Pulled him back into the world, right before I was pulled out of it. I only wish we'd had more time together before it happened. That, and I should have known from the start. Noah never stopped waiting for me to come home.

Ruby and Noah. My bookends in New York. Think of all the risks they took when they let me in, how far they had to travel to meet me. So that when the two of them finally came together, all the little pieces of me came together, too.

Pull the world into you — and nothing seems so far away anymore.

★ ★ ★

'You need to join Death Club, Noah.' Ruby repeats the invitation offered up to her a lifetime ago. Before she knew my name. Before they knew each other. And Noah accepts the offer, because he is as lonely as she was back then, and because, sometimes, you get out of your own way. Sometimes you follow yourself home.

The other Death Club members are excited to meet Noah, and agree to this spontaneous meeting at the dive bar near Riverside. *My local*, Ruby explains, texting the address. *Come take part in our memorial for Alice. One rule only* — this she will enforce until she and Noah are ready, until the trial and resultant conviction make him impossible to avoid — *no speaking about that other man, please.*

I watch as each member of Death Club arrives. Lennie, tumbling through the door, the fine dust of every dead person she has ever worked on surrounding her, as close to a nebula as anything I've seen on earth. Sue arriving next, all that latent motherlove and concern preceding her. Then Josh, hastening to the bar, thinking of Ruby's mouth against his, the way she wraps herself around him, so that his whole body looks like fireflies as he walks towards her this warm June night.

They greet Noah as if he is a long-lost friend. Nobody minds the sticky floor and the uneven chairs and the distracted barman watching his game. These five members of Death Club — six if you count Franklin, lying at Noah's feet — are simply glad to have found each other. Dotted around the table, they look like a constellation, and I trace the pattern they make, memorise it. Knowing, as hours pass, as they glow brighter, that something is changing this night. They are talking about me in different tones, mystery and urgency has been replaced by sadness, poignancy. If I had lived . . . but I did not. I was murdered down by a river while I was going about my life, loving the sky and the rain and Noah and this newfound feeling I might get to have a happy life, after all.

(If I can make it there. And I so very nearly did.)

I think I understand. That they no longer wonder who I am. Tonight, they get to remember me, instead.

314

So, what happens next? It is Noah who poses the question, as I knew he eventually would.

Where do the dead go? Are they lost to us, or are they still there — here — with us, now?

'Can both be true?' Sue asks in response, thinking of Lisa, and those rare, beautiful times she has returned to her mother in dreams. I am not the only one, it seems, who shows up in this way. As I consider this, I catch a glimpse of Lisa herself. Somewhere not too far from here. She is willowy, beautiful, and though I cannot be sure, it looks as though she is holding out her hand.

Something is changing this night.

'Well, basic physics tells us that energy is constant,' Noah responds in that familiar, easy way of his. 'It can neither be created nor destroyed; it simply changes state, finds its expression elsewhere. Thinking about it that way, every atom of Alice has always existed. Always, in one form or another. Perhaps this means she's everywhere now, not just the one place, as we are.'

The idea that I don't have to choose. That I can leave and still be here at the same time. I feel the tension of my existence start to slacken.

I look at Ruby, salt tears tracking down her cheeks as she considers Noah's words. She has her own choice to make, I know. Whether to leave New York, or set down roots, stay. We arrived here the same night, we left the same things behind, and we have both spun past where we used to be. Perhaps, I want to say to her now, the decisions we make next won't really matter. If you remember to look up, you'll see the sky changes anyway, even when you think you're standing still.

The world keeps turning. Go or stay, Ruby — we are both *already* somewhere new.

I should not be surprised at this next part. The feeling of my mother's hands in my hair. The members of Death Club are discussing science, and heaven, and the times they are certain they have heard us — the dead — whispering to them.

'I've so often felt she was here with me, just out of sight,' Ruby says, and I feel as if I am dissolving, only this time I don't fight it. It is like falling asleep after the longest, loveliest day.

It's getting late. Drinks are scattered across the table, and the bar is now playing soul classics, at just the right volume. Sam Cooke. Al Green. Marvin. Aretha. Otis. Down by the river, water laps at a rainbow of brightly coloured roses, as gentle waves pick them up and carry them towards the open sea.

Them young girls, they do get wearied.

Josh reaches for Ruby's hand, and the sky changes yet again.

Acknowledgements

Here we are.

First and foremost, thank you to the amazing women who made this possible: my agent and ultimate HW, Cara Lee Simpson, and my publishers, Darcy Nicholson and Jane Palfreyman. You have changed my life. For good.

My gratitude to Thalia Proctor, Sophie Wilson and Christa Munns for the editorial guidance from afar, and to the team at ANA for helping Alice Lee travel the world. To her past, present, and future champions at Sphere/Little, Brown, Allen & Unwin, and beyond: thank you for being our village.

So. Much. Love to my family: my mum, who gave me the gift of stories and grand obsessions. Karena, Tanya, Shane and Jodee, who helped grow me up. My in-laws for joining the dance. And my remarkable nieces and nephews. You are my pride, and my joy.

A special shout-out to my bookend, Karena, who is always right there with me in the arena, and Keith, whose generosity in all things wine and wisdom has kept me sane.

So many dear friends and workmates have helped shape this book. Know that I am deeply grateful for your support. With extra-special thanks to: Stef Bongiovanni, Laura Bracegirdle, Karen Lovell, Claire Amelia Graham, and Vail Joy for reading this story when it was still just bones. Jessica Lewis for giving me my start. Susan Witten, who does the real work. Jacqueline Taylor for making Manhattan(s) feel like home. Simone Turkington for the magic. And my safest of havens every step of the way, Stacey Lemon, Paw Paw, Brock, Aaron Beckhouse, Lindsay 'L.K.B' Andrew, Chris Sullivan, Sonya Cole, Inez Carey, Michael 'Beth' Buttrey, Conrad Browne, and Clinton Bermingham — I could not do this (life) without you.

Kisses to Nippy and Ruby, my constants through the toughest of times.

Biggest love to my Little One and very first reader, Sophie Allan.

And lastly, to Johnny B, who taught me to go hardest in the straight. I had to learn how to find you again, Dad. Turns out you were right here at the finish line, cheering me home. I love you.

SPECIAL MESSAGE TO READERS

THE ULVERSCROFT FOUNDATION
(registered UK charity number 264873)
was established in 1972 to provide funds for research, diagnosis and treatment of eye diseases. Examples of major projects funded by the Ulverscroft Foundation are:-

- The Children's Eye Unit at Moorfelds Eye Hospital, London
- The Ulverscroft Children's Eye Unit at Great Ormond Street Hospital for Sick Children
- Funding research into eye diseases and treatment at the Department of Ophthalmology, University of Leicester
- The Ulverscroft Vision Research Group, Institute of Child Health
- Twin operating theatres at the Western Ophthalmic Hospital, London
- The Chair of Ophthalmology at the Royal Australian College of Ophthalmologists

You can help further the work of the Foundation by making a donation or leaving a legacy. Every contribution is gratefully received. If you would like to help support the Foundation or require further information, please contact:

THE ULVERSCROFT FOUNDATION
The Green, Bradgate Road, Anstey
Leicester LE7 7FU, England
Tel: (0116) 236 4325

website: www.ulverscroft-foundation.org.uk

740009856041